Switch Me Off!

Tim Roy

JoJo
Publishing

Published by JoJo Publishing – 'Making a Difference'
Yarra's Edge
2203/80 Lorimer Street
Docklands, Vic., 3008, Australia
Email: jo-media@bigpond.net.au or visit www. jojopublishing.com

First published 2008

This novel is a work of fiction. Names, characters, places and incidents are either the product of the author's imagination, or are used fictitiously. Any resemblance to actual persons, living or dead, or events is entirely coincidental.

Edited by Mr. Martin Challis and Peacock Technology & Publishing Services Pty Ltd
Cover design by Adam Laszczuk
Typeset in Adobe Caslon Pro by Michael Hanrahan Publishing Services
Printed in China by Everbest Printing Co. Ltd.

National Library of Australia
Cataloguing-in-publication data:
Roy, Tim.
    Switch Me Off.
    ISBN 9780980354737 (pbk.).
    I. Title.
A823.4

Contents

Dedicated to
Bill (William) Fennessey.
A life unfinished.

Chapter One

An empty promise

I walked into the office of Dr Tom Peterson. The June afternoon was bitter and so was I. This was my second visit to the city of Brisbane from the Whitsundays to see the shrink. My file was sitting on the unattended receptionist's desk. Inquisitive to know its contents, I commenced reading.

Patient's name: Paul Roberts

Diagnoses: Post-Traumatic Stress Disorder (PTSD)
                  Acute Delusional Disorder
                  (Persecutory type)

Veterans' Affairs accepts conditions to be service related.

Patient has recognised operational service with SAS.

There was no mention of my covert operational career, I noted to myself. The sound of a door closing startled me; I quickly replaced the file. No one entered the reception.

Instinctively, I sat down with my back to the wall to observe all angles of the room.

My mind slipped into a hyper-vigilant mode rapidly absorbing visual images of the room: carpeted floor, one door, six chairs, table in centre of floor, magazines (*Time* and *Woman's Day*). No one else was in the room; if there had been I would be observing bulges in clothing and the position of their bags.

I had to quell paranoia, another symptom of the myriad mental conditions attributed to me. It had been explained that paranoia is common for people who suffer PTSD.

I had been trying to break the hyper-vigilant habit, but I felt vulnerable when dealing with arranged appointments by the Department of Veterans' Affairs.

The words 'Acute Delusional Disorder' ran through my mind. This was just another label added to my name; my credibility further stripped; something else to cope with.

Bitterness overwhelmed me. They can train individuals and ensure they're switched on to do what they are told, with no regard for the consequences. Back in the civilian world though, they must adjust on their own; a huge oversight of the military and government.

Someone should have switched me off!

The receptionist returned to her desk and picked up my file.

'The doctor will see you now. Please follow me.'

The government spooks released me from my covert duties and promised to get me help for the mental malfunctions I was suffering, but they stuffed up. They handed me over to walk the path of Veterans' Affairs incompetence, and be exposed to how arrogant this administration is towards soldiers and operators who have to swallow a lot of pride to ask for help.

The ignorance of the bureaucrats that were posted to Veterans' Affairs kept alienating my resolve to get help. The shuffles of directives to do this and do that were ridiculous. Fuck do this and do that! It had taken them years to do this and do that and still with no commitment to my health, until now. The pain received from their denial of what I had done for my country, without question, paled, because while on the merry-go-round I discovered that SAS soldiers who suffered mentally and physically on the night of the Blackhawk disaster were being denied their entitlements too. I now knew what I needed to do.

Today would tell me of this doctor's commitment to my mental health. I hoped he had read the New South Wales Ombudsman's report that I had left with him on my first visit. He might be of some help if he could see how blatantly the truth had been disguised and that the Department of Veterans' Affairs was covering up the past to ensure veterans like me couldn't access their just entitlements. I knocked on his door. He answered, 'Please come in. I will be with you in a moment.'

I entered his office and sat in the biggest chair. The leather seat squeaked from my weight being introduced to its ample padding. The effect gave me an uncomfortable experience, equal to fingernails being dragged across a blackboard. I tried to diminish the effects that my senses were suffering. To my right a bookcase stood proudly, its antique value obvious. The presentation of softcover and hardcover books was orderly. The colours of the book spines intermixed to create a multitude of spectrums of colour and titles floating before my eyes. This is not reality, I thought, as I squeezed my eyes shut momentarily to relieve the apprehension that presented itself every time I wished for the same reality as everyone else's to be in front of my eyes. I opened my eyes. The confusion of words and colours in free space subsided as the books returned to their original location. A heavy sigh escaped my lips; I froze, still half-swallowed by the plush leather chair, refusing to allow the chair to emit any more sound.

With clenched teeth and sudden rapid breathing I feared the doctor might commit me on the spot. I turned sheepishly towards the doctor's seated position at his desk, completely convinced that he had seen the distress I suffered when I faced the antique bookcase. He hadn't. He was completely engrossed reading the ombudsman's report. He had two pages to finish. I was relieved to see that he was showing an interest in my concerns. He finally looked up and said, 'This would be a great book, better still a movie.'

I had heard it all before. Friends who had read the report would make similar comments. I moved towards his TV and video machine situated against the wall; his eyes trailed me. His comfortable demeanour allowed me to continue with my desired process.

I inserted the tape of the interview that I carried with me to share the exposé with those who asked to witness what the government didn't want to exist. Veterans' Affairs had finally succumbed and realised that as much as they wished to deny my existence and the effect I had on national security, they couldn't lie about an incident that the media had presented to the Australian public.

The opening scene showed me sitting at the table in my campervan; the journalist sat opposite. Dr Peterson stared into the television, his pen poised to write onto his pad. The journalist opened the presentation.

'Tonight on *A Current Affair*: the Tactical Response Group of New South Wales Police Force who keep on getting it wrong.

'Today we are at Mrs Roberts' house. What happened here last night is quite extraordinary. A simple household became a siege site. The Tactical Response Group raided this house with the assistance of the military police and the bomb disposal group.

'Mrs Roberts' son, an ex-SAS officer, was having an open garage sale, selling off his past to collect funds to enable him and his girlfriend to travel around Australia in their campervan.

'Mr Roberts, can you explain to me what happened last night?'

'I was awoken last night after midnight when I heard loud bangs on my mother's house front door. As I put a pair of pants on, there was a knock on the campervan door. I opened the door to see three police officers. One had a pistol pointed at me. The other two had their pistols drawn in an extremely dangerous fashion.'

'Mr Roberts, what do you mean by extremely dangerous?'

'In my training, short barrel weapons are to be considered dangerous, and people who use these weapons should be trained to understand their capacity. Last night, the officer who banged on the door had a weapon pointing at his back from a fellow officer. The officer to the rear was pointing his gun at the officer to the front.'

'If you didn't have your training, what would've happened if you had panicked?'

'Two cops would have had additional holes in them. If I ran back into the campervan they would've riddled it with gun-fire. They were that nervous. I calmed the

situation before it escalated into a lethal situation —
for them and me.'

'Did you know that the police were informed that there
were four to six ex-SAS officers hiding out at this
address with explosives and weapons?'

'No, but if they had been told that information I would
like to know where they get their intelligence from.'

'In your training, what would you have done if you had
been placed in charge of the raid?'

'Firstly, I would know the location of the target. I would
do surveillance. I would ensure that the civilians in the
vicinity had protection. The police didn't. A simple covert operation at the garage sale would have confirmed
that their intelligence was flawed.'

'The police also informed us that the army bomb disposal officer identified an anti-personnel mine in your
possession. Is this true?'

'No. That claymore mine has "inert" written on it for a
reason: it's a training item. The army officer involved
in the raid on me is totally incompetent and probably
got excited about the weight of the claymore mine. For
operational training, we glue in steel weights to ensure
we practise with an operational correct-weighted
load.'

The presentation portrayed an army corporal at the nearest army
base who explained to the journalist what the inert claymore
mine's capabilities were.

'Corporal, can you tell me about the item known as an
inert claymore mine?'

'The inert claymore mine has the word "inert" written
on the mine. The mine is only used in training.'

I blanked out and didn't realise the presentation was finished,
until Dr Peterson stopped the tape.

'The hardest patient to treat for paranoia is the one that has
reason to be paranoid!' he stated, looking at me with soft eyes.

'Well, Doc, what do you think? Am I deluded about what
they are denying?' I asked, straining to show no stress in my
voice while pointing to the ombudsman's report.

'No, I don't think you are. In fact, it's very easy to see where
the police have doctored the documents. It is clear they had
automatic weapons on the night of the raid on you and your
family,' he offered.

'What can we do from here?' I asked.

'To ensure the validity of your claims, we must demonstrate
your willingness to recover. Therefore, I want to admit you to
hospital today if possible. Is that convenient?'

My plan was going to be conducted tonight. I needed to
buy time.

'No, Doc, that is not convenient. I have to front the Veterans' Review Board tomorrow morning. Can I have two days
before I admit myself?'

He thought for a moment.

As he paused my mind raced ahead to the activities necessary to activate my plan. I had to return to my hotel room to collect my stores and equipment. I had to go for a run to guarantee
that those who were observant noticed perspiration on the body
of a diligent courier, my chosen subterfuge occupation.

The doctor broke the silence.

'Can you admit yourself tomorrow after the hearing with
the Veterans' Review Board?'

I had to do some quick thinking.

'Okay, I will admit myself tomorrow after I've met with them.'

An empty promise.

'Good, I will contact Veterans' Affairs and tell them of your decision to go into hospital under my care tomorrow. Could you please wait out in my reception until I have finalised all the necessary details with Veterans' Affairs?'

'Sure, Doc. Thanks.'

'I look forward to hearing more of your story.'

Unfortunately, Doc, I won't be there to give you the satisfaction, I thought.

'Thanks, Doc, I'll see you tomorrow.'

I shook his hand briskly.

I believed he was genuine and committed to helping me with my mental health problems; unfortunately, he wouldn't get the opportunity.

I returned to the reception room to experience another bout of hyper-vigilance: carpeted floor, one door, six chairs, table in centre of floor, magazines (*Time* and *Woman's Day*).

Nothing had changed. I had no control over these symptoms of PTSD. The rapid images started to escalate and include the memories of my preparation, such as the reconnaissance of the target, the conversation with the local cop, the organisation of the stores and equipment, and the booking of an alternative hotel room.

The images invading my brain had no chronological order. The speed of the flashes was distressing. I tried, and I kept fucking trying, to ease the information overload I was experiencing. The affliction of PTSD was debilitating. It was apparent that the plan needed to be conducted immediately.

To regain normal function of my faculties I conducted a mental check to make sure I had thoroughly covered all aspects required to ensure a successful mission.

After taking a deep breath, my mind slowed, allowing me to remember details, locations and actions. Images poured through my mind of my first visit to the Veterans' Affairs Board, where I conducted my initial reconnaissance; my purposefully abusive phone calls, determining the authorities' reaction and response time; and my conversation with Dirk, my policeman friend whose role as the chief siege negotiator for Queensland interested me, as did his willingness to impart critical information regarding the Tactical Response Unit over a few beers.

My mind calmed. I opened my eyes slowly and focused on the furniture in the reception room. My breathing had slowed and I felt relief from the pressure within my brain. I was ready to commence the mission.

'Your bed has been approved, Mr Roberts.' The receptionist broke the silence.

'Thank you.'

I smiled back at her. I was ready to get on with the job.

The Veterans' Review Board had organised a hotel for my stay in the city; however, I wouldn't be staying there. I had already placed my luggage in a different hotel. This was a purposefully designed situation that would create more time on target, as the police would be interested in locating my belongings.

Ironically, the hearing with the Veterans' Review Board was the same date as my discharge date from my covert duties. Three years to the day. Three years of torment, three years of struggling to be recognised.

Tonight I would be infiltrating the head office of Veterans' Affairs in Brisbane. It was time to get even.

Chapter Two

Infiltration

I returned to the hotel room to organise the equipment I needed: a Stanley knife to cut through the plasterboard roof; two clean rags, one that would be tied to my feet when I entered through the roof to ensure that I didn't add additional mess from the roof cavity, the other to wipe the commissioner's desk; two pairs of black overalls, non-descript, to allow the sniper team to have the least amount of information to pass to their command; gaffer tape to bind my hostages and plastic ties (these would be used as handcuffs); two lengths of BlueWater static rope; a climbing harness; two dumars (mechanical climbing devices) and two carabiners (these items would be used to secure me to the elevator cable); a Phillips head screwdriver to remove the light fitting in the foyer; a lock-picking set needed to access filing cabinets; a torch to be used in the roof cavity; two balaclavas, one to hide my identity plus a spare; an SAS-issued gasmask; a gun belt with pistol holster and magazine pouches; butcher's paper to be used to cover the hole I would cut out above the commissioner's desk; a dentist's mirror, which I would need to be able see into areas before I approached them; and a small backpack that

11

would hold all the insertion items, so I could carry them onto the target site. The last item was a replica 9 mm semi-automatic Browning pistol.

I held the replica pistol confidently, feeling the muscle states within my body, which proclaimed that if it was real, loaded and fired, the round would find its mark. The authentic weight of the weapon sensed by my hand produced a mistake that I didn't need to own. My mind uncontrollably spun to unknown destinations: I was transported back to my SAS barrack room, standing in front of a mirror; the image of myself, with sweat dripping off me, holding a Browning replica pistol firmly and slicing rapidly to the right as my body flew through the air engaging imaginary targets with double taps, dry fire.

The double tap: two rounds fired in quick succession. Easy enough to do. I was smiling, as now everything that I had learned was being displayed in my practice, the ultimate: a key-hole double tap. In a keyhole double tap, when the two rounds are fired and pierce their intended target the two holes produced are linked together, resembling an old-fashioned keyhole.

My first keyhole double tap target hung up on my wall. It was a photograph of a well-known foreign terrorist, with nine holes in it, in a circle within a diameter of ten centimetres, with one keyhole on the target.

Another location, another time: I found myself reliving what had happened on the range where the target had hung, the Close Quarter Battle Course of the SAS. I had raised my weapon and engaged my target with my last two rounds, knowing that as a professional that counting my rounds was paramount. My magazine would be empty after this, but I wouldn't need to refill my weapon, because my target was going to be assessed. Excitement washed over me, followed by confusion — excitement, because in front of me was my first keyhole effect; confusion, because I had fired ten rounds and there were only nine holes in the target.

'How did that happen?'

I must have said it loud enough for the instructor to hear me.

'You were concentrating. You look distracted, Paul.'

'I don't know where my last round went.'

'Look closely at your target, Paul.'

I studied my target for what seemed an eternity while the instructor was observing other operators' shooting stances. I strained to see where my last round had gone.

It finally dawned on me; there in front of me was the evidence that I hadn't lost the round. (A lost round would mean removal from the course as, in reality, poor shooting to that degree would kill a hostage, or worse, one of your mates.)

'It went through the same fucking hole,' I proudly proclaimed, as the instructor took my target off me with a minor smile.

'Right, this is what we do now: no more shooting, dry practice to continue in the mock-up for the aircraft target range. The reason for this directive is due to the inconceivable action that as an operator you have achieved on this target,' the instructor explained. 'You have felt it now.'

'What, shooting through the same hole?' I asked.

'No, that's not what I want, that's too slow. Now look at your target and explain to me what I mean.'

A logical question to someone who has been trained in the characteristics and dynamics of small arms fire. After once again studying my target, I answered his question.

'Jump!'

'Yes, now explain jump.'

I knew what he wanted; he wanted the correct tabulated data memorised by every operator.

'Jump, the term given to explain the action when a round leaves a barrel. Due to the gaseous explosion from the primer of the round, the gas propels the round towards the target. As the round and the gas leave the barrel of the weapon, the weapon will naturally jump up.'

This is inevitable — it's always a consideration with accurate shooting — but I was now going to the instinctive level. The keyhole effect must have happened before the 'jump' on the weapon took effect. Now the single hole in my target had an explanation. With two rounds entering the same hole, the 'jump' had occurred, but my weapon and body position had returned perfectly to their original firing position when I engaged the target with the second round. The double tap was too slow by a miniscule fraction of a second.

'Now what have you learned, Paul?'

'That if I am steady enough, accurate enough, and have the correct position, and if I'm quick enough, I can fire two rounds in quick succession. You can get the second round down range before the jump of the weapon can take effect, which will result in my target having two round holes, one on top of each other, looking like the keyhole of a doorway.'

'Now dry practice. Only you can remember which muscles are tightened and which are loose, so go and train your mind to remember your instinctive shooting position by practice, practice, and more practice.'

I dropped the weapon at my feet as I found myself still staring into the hotel room mirror. The mission, I had to focus on the mission.

My mission had two phases: the first being the infiltration of Veterans' Affairs offices; the second being the capture of the Commissioner of Veterans' Affairs and forcing payment to other ex-SAS operators who were getting dicked around by the department. I knew this action would result in the activation of the SAS Counter Terrorist Team, which I desired.

* * *

For the infiltration, I was wearing shorts, a T-shirt and a simple name tag with the word 'courier' written on it. My running shoes were the best that money could buy. I had jogged about two kilometres to create perspiration on my body.

With my small backpack on my back, I bounded up the stairs of the government building, three at a time, entering the foyer at half pace.

The security guard looked up from his desk, just as I was slowing my jog to a fast walk. I stated, 'Delivery for Veterans' Review Board.'

He looked at the clock above him; the time was seven minutes to five in the evening. He gestured with his hand to proceed and did not say a word. I breathed a sigh of relief.

The door of the first elevator to my left opened. Four people got in with me. I perused an improvised invoice, as though trying to locate my destination, remaining in the elevator until it was empty.

Then I pushed the button and rode up to the twenty-fifth floor. The door opened; no one entered. After another deep breath, I raised my arm with my palm pushing the manhole lid upwards. It moved freely.

I placed my finger on the 'close door' button and pressed the button for the second floor. I put on my climbing harness and then squeezed my body up through the manhole. I had rehearsed this move many times, achieving a consistent duration of fifteen seconds. I quickly secured my dumar climbing locking device onto the steel elevator cable. A length of BlueWater static rope now attached me to the elevator via a carabiner on my climbing harness. I felt safe and comfortable riding up and down the shaft of the elevator.

I reflected on the hours of training, fast descending on elevator cables as a method of entry into siege situations. It must have been about an hour and a half before the lift finally rested for the night. I was probably on the seventh floor; someone was working back fairly late.

I slowly raised the manhole door and lowered my dentist mirror to survey the surroundings. The elevator door was open and I could see a doctor's surgery.

'Excellent,' I said to myself.

Only someone in the reception area could see into the foyer, and fortunately there was no one at the desk.

I had to find the fire exit; I knew it wouldn't be locked. During my reconnaissance I used the fire exit from the Veterans' Affairs offices to the Veterans' Review Board office. These doors opened easily and did not have locks. Also, there were no alarm sensors in the stairwell.

With a quick twist of the wrist with the mirror in my hand, I located the fire exit doorway. I silently lowered myself into the elevator, staying low.

I used my mirror once again to ensure no one could see my exit from the elevator to the stairwell. No one was watching and all it took was one quick move. My first rush of adrenalin kicked in. Once inside the stairwell I stopped and listened for any unforeseen activity and also to control my breathing. I began to ascend the stairs.

I was outside the door to the Veterans' Affairs offices. I knew there was a sensor alarm in the foyer. This would activate once I entered. The alarm response would be indicated on the security panel on the ground floor.

I had substantial knowledge of these types of alarms: I knew that a simple moth could trigger them off so I wasn't expecting a quick response from the on-duty security officer on a floor that only housed administration offices. However, an inspection was expected and I assessed that I had between two and three minutes to complete the infiltration.

I had rehearsed my next move down to forty-five seconds. On my reconnaissance, I noticed a chair placed directly under a fluorescent light fitting within the waiting area.

I needed to remove the light fitting, which was countersunk into the roof. With this done, it would allow easy access. With a chair positioned directly under the light fitting, the height problem was eliminated.

Additionally, the concern of furniture being out of place during an inspection was not a consequence. There were two long Phillips head screws to remove, which held the light fitting in place. Once they were gone, the light fitting housing could be eased into the roof, leaving a hole big enough to crawl into.

I left the fire exit doorway, starting to count quietly, 'One thousand, two thousand, three thousand, four thousand.'

The red light on the sensor flashed. I made a mental note not to rush. I had plenty of time.

The chair was still in its convenient position. With the Phillips head screwdriver in one hand I began to remove the screws. They came out easily; I pushed the light fitting housing into the roof cavity and raised myself through the now exposed hole, pulling the cord that was attached to a rag that my boots had been standing on. I made a visual check to ensure there were no telltale signs of my entry.

In the roof, I held the light fitting in place for about fifteen seconds before I heard the lift arrive. The light-fitting removal must've taken longer than I thought, or the security officer was more diligent than expected.

My heart pounded as he checked the door locks of the offices. Then he spoke into his radio, 'Nothing to report.'

The elevator doors opened and closed and the lift descended. As I couldn't see anything, I waited for a period of ten minutes just in case the security guard was trained as well as I was — he might have been trying to trick me into believing he was gone.

Never underestimate your enemy.

Still no noise. He had gone ten minutes ago. I pulled the light fitting into the roof to free my hands. I fished around the backpack for a small torch, and turned it on, placing it between my teeth. I quickly dressed in a pair of overalls. I replaced the light fitting in its original position and, using gaffer tape, secured it to the support beam.

I rested for about an hour. My mind was racing. I knew what I had to do, but it was going to take time. The knowledge I had gained from the reconnaissance assured me the administration offices housed no alarm sensors. This would allow me to move around freely. However, I had to cut a hole in the plasterboard ceiling to be able to access the particular office I wanted.

This office was that of the Commissioner of Veterans' Affairs, but I had to find it. I looked around the roof with my torch to find the biggest area of space that didn't have framework. This would indicate where the doors were affixed. I was in an area that had a lot of framework, indicating a small collection of offices.

With the torch in my mouth, I moved to the far end of the roof. I shifted the torch to my hand so I could penetrate the darkness with wide-sweeping movements to observe my desired locality.

Of course, the Top Knob would have windows and the best view, I thought.

It took about another hour, due to the slow speed at which I was progressing, to discover the biggest area of space that didn't house doorway framework. I finally found it and moved to the middle of the roof of the office below me. Balancing on the crossbeams, I then located the light fitting and rested again.

With the Stanley knife, brought along for this purpose, I cut a small hole in the plasterboard next to the light fitting so it would be partially obscured. Only after the event, during a crime scene inspection, would the authorities detect it.

I removed the dentist mirror from my pocket and lowered it into the recently cut-out hole in the plasterboard ceiling. I had to establish three factors: the first was to locate any sensor alarms, and there were none; the second was to ensure that I had the commissioner's office.

In the reflection was a glass panel in the centre of the door, and there it was: embossed gold letters: 'COMMISSIONER'! I breathed a sigh of relief, but had one more factor to establish, which was the distance from where I was to his desk. I was coming in over the top of it. I didn't want to cut the plasterboard anywhere else because the shavings from the cut would be collected. If I misjudged the distance, shavings on the carpet would be a telltale sign that would compromise me. I established the distance that needed to be travelled. I was about halfway to my required destination, when suddenly I heard a key go into the commissioner's office door.

I tensed. The light came on. A vacuum cleaner started up.

'Fucking cleaners,' I whispered.

I had to get back to where I was when I had removed the spy-hole to re-affix the cut-out section. As soon as the cleaners saw the shavings, I was sure they would look up to investigate.

There was one more problem: I couldn't move fast because the crossbeams creaked, a factor I had established earlier in the evening. I was kicking myself for not being more professional and replacing it before I left the area.

'Don't panic, don't panic!' I repeated to myself.

I removed the backpack, feeling for the gaffer tape roll, quickly pulled a piece off and secured it to my overalls. Once this was done, I started walking slowly back along the cross-beams towards the spy-hole.

Slowly moving, I used the 'Ghost Walk' technique taught to me many years ago: the individual transfers the body weight to the front foot and, once balanced, brings the rear foot forward and continues. It's an extremely slow and arduous process. My muscles and joints cried out in pain. I wasn't as young and fit as when I was required to do this activity for a living. I was about two metres away from the spy-hole, and panic was rising; it was now or never.

It was either adrenalin or fear, I wasn't quite sure, but I was really shitting myself. I crouched, balancing on the beam with my arms at full stretch. My hands slid until my chest contacted the beam. I began to inch forward. I located the cut-out piece, pulled it back to me, reached down and slowly pulled the gaffer tape off my trouser leg.

I put the cut-out in the centre of the two-inch-wide tape, slowly sliding it along parallel to the crossbeam. The light started to diminish and with a slight jiggle, the piece fitted and I was in darkness. I froze. I was extremely pissed off with myself for this oversight, plus my bladder was crying out for release. The chemical rush I had just experienced was torturing me. The cleaners took another ten minutes to finish, and by this stage I had reached into my overalls, in a lying position, fully squeezing my dick shut.

After a short conversation, the cleaners packed up their equipment. The door shut behind them. I had to urinate quickly; the pain was building to an uncontrollable level. I couldn't piss just anywhere; the urine would seep through the plasterboard, leaving another sign that would compromise my mission.

I decided the elevator shaft wall would be the safest place to release the pain in my groin. With the cleaners still working in other offices below, I once again had to move very slowly to my destination.

My hand was still squeezing my penis shut. I determined that I had fifteen metres to travel to the lift wall. This distance seemed like a mile as my painful discomfort escalated. I experienced bloated penis. My penis shaft ballooned from the effort my cramped hand applied to its opening. Dizziness demanded release. Crouched over, I spied an empty soft-drink bottle with a nice wide opening two feet in front of me. It must've been left behind by some worker.

'Thank God for litterbugs!' I grimaced.

I picked up the bottle and placed it between my legs. I proceeded to twist the top off with my free hand. I passed the bottle through the opening of my overalls and placed my penis above the mouth of the bottle, slowly releasing the pressure of my hand that had now been squeezing my bloated penis shut for the past twenty-five minutes. I needed to temper the flow; I was worried that the cleaners below would hear me.

The whole exercise took about three minutes, the longest three minutes of my life! I was furious with myself, now sitting on a cross-section of beams, awaiting the departure of the cleaners out of the Veterans' Affairs offices.

Why hadn't I assessed that cleaners could be present?

I reflected on what I was taught during my operational years with the SAS. This was knowledge that I was to pass on to other newer members.

'It doesn't matter how many rehearsals you do, the mission will never go to plan. Be flexible, adapt and adjust.' These words of wisdom were frequently voiced.

I took comfort in those words. That was what I had done, exactly, and I wasn't compromised. I continued to rest and waited for the cleaners to depart. Finally they left, so I proceeded back to the gaffer tape that secured the cut-out piece of plasterboard. I had to ensure I was correct about the distance between the light fitting and the commissioner's table.

After a quick scan with the mirror I felt comfortable with my first assessment and continued to move on. I looked forward to getting out of the roof. I created another small hole and on inspection found there was a highly polished wooden desk directly below me. I felt a rush of relief.

I cut a square big enough to fit through and I quickly lowered myself. A rag covered my now filthy running shoes; I removed them while on the desk. My socks were equally as dirty so I removed them as well, then I rolled up the legs of my pants. The desk was filthy now, so I brushed as much dust off my overalls as I could so I wouldn't get it on the carpet.

The desk was covered in dust. I stepped off it and quickly remembered my oversight that had almost compromised the mission earlier in the evening. Do it now!

I reached into the backpack, grabbed a clean rag and wiped the desk down thoroughly. With this done, the filing cabinet was my next interest. Taking a lock-picking set from the backpack, I began to pick the lock of the wooden cabinet.

A memory came to me.

I was carrying a bag of padlocks into the Charles Gairdner Hospital, Perth. An SAS friend of mine had fallen two storeys off a training building and had broken both of his wrists.

The padlocks were his recuperation training: he would sit for hours and, in extreme pain, he would pick the locks until they were all open. As his strength returned and his coordination improved, I would bring more difficult locks for him to pick. We would sit for hours watching the cricket, picking locks together.

'Clunk!'

The familiar sound of the lock releasing itself from its locked position snapped me back to the task at hand. I smiled a wry smile and pulled the second drawer open and began looking for the section starting with the letter 'S'.

There it was: sixteen files; the names I recognised, belonging to operators who endured and survived the Blackhawk disaster. It was the sticky notes attached to them that infuriated me. The front cover that housed the files had only four letters written on it: 'XSAS' (ex-Special Air Services).

My anger rose as I read the simple comments attached to these files. One began with 'Prolong as long as possible.' Another stated, 'Requires second psych review, given labels that discredit the individual.' Another, 'Continue to send correspondence to old address'; another, 'Place under surveillance to create anxiety'; and another, 'No contact for six months.'

All of the files belonged to men that I had served with, but here was the final proof that there was a conspiracy against Special Forces operators. This confirmed what I had always suspected about the Department of Veterans' Affairs. My mind accepted that having this information, I was justified in carrying out this mission.

I placed all the files relating to the ex-members of the SAS who had claims with Veterans' Affairs into my backpack, and re-locked the filing cabinet. I climbed onto the desk and pulled myself into the hole I had made. A quick glance ensured there was no dust left on the desk. I quickly affixed the butcher's paper over the hole and secured it with gaffer tape. I then waited to complete Phase One of the operation.

I was steaming at the evidence I had, totally consolidating the truth of my conspiracy theory. My mind raced through the incidents I had experienced and suffered or those of other operators that I knew.

Well, tomorrow the Veterans' Affairs bureaucrats were about to find out what can transpire when you push the buttons of a professional killer who has yet to be deprogrammed. My thoughts began to slow. I was definitely looking forward to the conflict.

What had let me get to this desperate stage of my life? Was I deluded as the psychiatrist had assessed? Did Post-Traumatic Stress Disorder combined with an army operational mentality and my exposure to covert operations make it impossible to adjust to civilian life?

I wished I had been deluded about the tragic loss of life on the night of the Blackhawk helicopter disaster. The memory, the horrific memory that I could never extinguish, controlled me.

As the heat in the roof surrounded me and the beads of sweat on my face started to cascade, the familiar sensation, however obscure, presented itself. I looked down at my hands expecting them to be on fire — they never were. The heat and tingling sensation that gloved my digits produced fear, debilitating fear, that now indicated I would lose control and be flung back to a reality that constantly haunted me.

There is no light to my front, but I can distinguish the outline of the Blackhawks. There are four in total and they seem to be off target to the right as I look at them. The lead helicopter is making dramatic moves to get to the drop site. Blackhawk II *and* Blackhawk III *seem to be racing each other to the same drop site.*

I'm in a room which is designed to observe the outdoor training exercises so individuals can later be critiqued on better ways of conducting counter-terrorist assaults. The benefit is that the troops learn how best to stay alive and kill their targets more proficiently. The glass window in this room is always hot to touch. I'm resting on a set of crutches due to an accident early in the training day when I broke my ankle. My seat on the helicopter has been taken by a younger soldier.

'Fuck, they've collided!' I always yell.

No one is in the room with me to hear the devastation in my voice.

Night becomes day as one of the Blackhawks bursts into flames. The screams from my mates are clearly audible through the plate glass window. I grab the chair I have been sitting on and throw it through the window. I want to help. The aggression building up inside could explain this unusual behaviour. I feel closer to my dying mates now that the window is removed.

As the glass and the chair fall away from my view, I see the Blackhawk on fire invert and plough into the ground upside down. I squeeze hard onto the wooden window frame, completely oblivious to the shards of glass that are now embedded in my hands.

'No, fuck no!'

The survivors' echoes pierce the night.

The reverberating screams traverse the room.

The physical pain does not register or resonate over the emotional pain I am experiencing. The other damaged Blackhawk lands hard on its skids. The burning remains of the first Blackhawk illuminate the rescuers who have reached the upright helicopter.

Men are pulling bodies out of the wreck. As they go to grab their mates, they find that only bits can be extracted from the wrecks. I turn away; I can't do any more than what is already being done.

I sit on the floor with my back against the wall. The screams slice through the dark night, overpowering the sound of metal as it crackles and buckles. Voices of the rescuers match the screams of our mates. I look down to my hands. There is still no pain. I decide that I am in shock.

Then I'm deposited inside a doomed helicopters before the crash, watching my mates' final moments.

All the operators are standing, kneeling and hanging onto the rope, ready to drop as soon as the first operator leaves the Blackhawk. All the others will be on top of him.

A flash of light. I see five strikes occur, each strike hitting metal and flesh. Obviously the flesh loses the battle. The first strike hits the fuel tanks and fuel is pouring in on them. It then ignites. The screams are deafening.

I'm suddenly flung back to the empty room where I witnessed the disaster.

I see someone trying to rescue someone else. The light of the fire gives me a visual image. A soldier is tugging at an injured mate. He falls backwards, pulling out what he has been struggling with, to realise he has only a set of human legs lying across his chest. The rescuer is violently ill. I sit down numb, no pain and no tears, totally bewildered as to why I can't express any emotion at this graphic loss.

I'm standing above the line of body bags.

The perspiration stings my eyes as I realise that I'm now back to the present. Panic rises as I assess if I have lost all advantage to execute my mission. Have I compromised myself?

I sit regulating my breathing to a slow, manageable pace and straining to hear any sound that would confirm my apprehension. An hour passes. I start to relax. I should've known better, for to relax allows my mind to wander and it wanders to wherever the PTSD takes it, for whatever time it wants to control me.

The colours flash and rotate in front of my eyes and the only solution to this chaos is to organise the kaleidoscope of colour and images into some order. The duration is always dictated by some force I have no control over. I smile as the first image to materialise is a soft, passive image of me standing at a door, excited, for behind this door is the selection panel for the SAS regiment. I am being given a chance to join the elite.

Chapter Three

My shot
(nine years earlier)

I waited outside the door quietly. I had just finished a conversation with a man who wore the sandy beret. The embellishment that he wore on his sleeve was the inverted parachute wings. The upside-down wings signified that this man belonged to a Special Forces unit. Through the door behind him was the SAS Selection Board.

Our conversation was brief.

'What unit are you from?' he asked me.

'10 RAR,' I said proudly.

'Infantryman, eh?'

'Yes.'

'Most of the regiment is made up of infantrymen. They usually get bored of doing battalion duties. They join the regiment to have some real fun. Good luck, Private.'

His conversation drained off as our focus of attention was given to the female officer who walked on the footpath below us. The door behind us opened. A hopeful applicant exited the door to move down the far stairwell. Just as he stepped on the first step, my name was bellowed out. I opened the door and marched from the door to the table, to be standing in front of the SAS Selection Board. I snapped to attention.

Sitting at the table to my front was the commanding officer of the Australian Special Air Services, his second-in-command and the regimental sergeant major (also known as 'God').

Their sandy berets sat so correctly on their heads.

The largest man bellowed, 'Private Roberts!'

He was sitting to the far right of the selection panel. In his hands he held my application form for attendance to the selection course for the Australian Special Air Services Regiment.

'Sir,' I replied and marched forward to stop sharply in a strong attention position in front of the selection panel. They were all smartly dressed in their summer uniforms. Campaign ribbons adorned their chests.

I was mesmerised by the collection on the large man, who by now I had correctly assessed to be the SAS regimental sergeant major (RSM), the rank most respected within any army unit. He continued:

'Private Paul Roberts.'

'Yes sir,' I replied.

I was still waiting to be told to take a seat.

'Age twenty-two.'

'Yes sir.'

'Completed Higher School Certificate at Linden High School, New South Wales.'

'Yes sir.'

'Infantry soldier.'

'Yes sir.'

He had an assortment of documents in front of him. The next document he raised to read was my platoon commander's report. He began reading it to the other members of the panel.

'Private Roberts has been a member of 9 Platoon for a period of three years. His position within the platoon is second-in-charge of his section. He is due for promotion at the beginning of next year. He has displayed sound leadership abilities. He is respected by his peers and has created a lot of firm friendships within the platoon.'

He lowered the document. The RSM looked at me inquiringly but said nothing. I just stared above their heads. The chair was to my front and I wished they would allow me to sit down. My legs were slightly trembling.

The panel started talking to each other, softly. I wasn't close enough to the table to hear any comments. The next person to speak was the commanding officer of the SAS regiment. He simply stated: 'Please sit, Private.'

I adhered to his request. They continued their murmured conversation. I sat and pondered whether my platoon commander's report was too good. We had compiled it together, for he was to face the same selection panel, and having allies on the selection process was a wise consideration. It was true: I was friendly with everyone, but I wasn't close. My real friends were now finishing their first year within the SAS regiment.

Over the past year I had dedicated myself to an extreme training regime and as a result had a hard body. I stood at a height of six foot, with a fair complexion, slightly tanned due to living in the tropics.

I worried about what I believed to be a flaw in my appearance: I had a baby-face, features which were smooth and cute. I shuddered as that word 'cute' resurfaced within my thought processes. 'Baby-face killer' was the nickname my platoon members had given me on my arrival to their platoon, which was three years prior, and it hadn't faded away as most nicknames do.

I had brown eyes and sandy-coloured hair framing my soft-featured face. I looked at each member of the panel with a hard stare. The RSM took notice of my attempt to look hard and cold. A smile crossed his lips as he studied my efforts more intently. As he looked at me he raised his voice above the hushed conversation that had continued through my self-appraisal.

'Private Roberts, if you ever get to my regiment I want you to assure me that on any operations, you wear a balaclava to ensure that the bad guys don't fall over laughing when they see your pretty face.' All members of the panel laughed.

I nodded my head, agreeing. They waited for me to react; I didn't, I just continued to stare into their faces one at a time. The RSM smiled at me, as though I had just passed a test. I returned a courtesy nod to his reaction to my non-response.

'How would you describe yourself?' he asked.

'I believe I'm happy most of the time, quite intelligent, a hard worker. I dislike lazy people, enjoy a beer with the boys, and I am totally committed to passing the selection course, sirs.'

The panel spoke softly to one another. When they were done, all members looked at me. The commanding officer spoke.

'Well, Private Roberts, I believe you to be an intelligent, articulate young man. We will see you in February.'

I showed no emotion and, rising out of the chair, saluted the men to my front. I was handed a piece of white paper, which was the authority for my commanding officer to sign, allowing me to attend the SAS selection course.

I about-turned and marched out of the office, trying to subdue the jubilation that was running through my body. I was finally getting my chance!

I ran back to my unit to get the commanding officer to sign that special piece of white paper. As I waited impatiently for him to sign it, he looked at me and said, 'They are finally giving you a shot, Private.'

'That's all I need, sir,' I replied.

I saluted him and marched out of his office.

I was so excited that on the two-level staircases, I didn't bother with the last flight, leaping over the banister to an eight-foot drop. Well, if I was joining the Australian SAS regiment, I would have to get used to that sort of physical activity. I landed safely and marched off with a grin that released a mantra.

'I won't blow my shot, I won't blow my shot.'

Chapter Four

Just twenty-four hours

I was dreaming, free-falling through the night in the new SAS patrol to which I had been assigned. My dream became a bumpy ride. Voices were yelling at me. I hit the ground hard. The realisation that my bed-end had been raised four feet and slammed down quickly snapped me back to reality.

The voices belong to our instructors. Commands were being screamed at us.

'Get out of bed.'

'Get your PT (physical training) gear on.'

'Line up outside on the road.'

I finally found my gym shoe that had eluded me since I had my rude awakening. Last in the hut seemed to draw additional attention.

'What's your name, Ranger?'

Holding the sharpest attention position, making a mental note that his accent was British, I refrained from mimicking his voice. (This behaviour to me was an enjoyable pastime.) Wrong place, wrong time. I replied in the strongest Australian accent I could muster.

'Private Roberts,' I shouted.

'Now it's Ranger Roberts, dirt-bag, don't forget it!'

A moment of stupidity, on my behalf, arose. The instructor had a watch on his wrist. I asked him the time.

'What do you want to know the time for, Ranger? Have you got a hot date? Just get your shit together and get on the road. Move now.'

I rapidly left the building, jumping off the entrance of the doorway, missing the five stairs. I landed on the ground, running to join the other men. It was bitterly cold and still dark; most of us were jogging on the spot to keep warm. I wasn't the last man to join the ranks, but definitely within the last five of the two hundred and seventy-five. I suffered for this lack of urgency.

'Ranger Roberts.'

My name was bellowed. I ran quickly to the group of instructors, immediately in front of me. There were about twenty men, of all ages, with extremely fit bodies. These were the SAS instructors for my selection course.

'Pommy' — the instructor that I had asked the time — moved me to the front of the group of men, still jogging on the spot to keep warm.

'Look at my watch, Ranger Roberts, and tell me the time.'

'It's ten minutes past four.'

I was starting to wish that I had never even seen his watch.

'Right, Ranger, you're ten minutes late. For every minute you are late, you owe me fifty push-ups. Can you add, Ranger?'

'Five hundred,' I replied.

'Good, start doing them. Do fifty, and when you have finished them I want you to run to the front of the pack. Let me know that you are there.'

I adopted the push-up position and started to count out loud. Everybody left; they broke into a light jog, disappearing into the darkness. I completed my fifty push-ups, started to run and tried to catch up to them.

They must be sprinting, I said to myself, as the cold air burnt my lungs. After fifteen minutes, I finally saw another soldier. The gradient of the road increased; I could see more soldiers, running slowly. The road just kept on going up; I couldn't see where it finished. My legs ached with pain, my lungs tried to regulate my breathing to ensure I had enough energy to complete this task.

I had reached the main pack. Some men were losing last night's dinner by the side of the road. Some spewed to their front, maintaining the pace required to keep up with the instructors. I was still to the rear of the pack, really hurting, and the road was growing steeper. I decided never to be last again, and to keep my mouth shut.

I put my head down and ran faster and harder, gradually moving past a large group of men. I had passed the slow ones, so this was the middle group. I reached the front of this bunch, to be disheartened when I realised the gap was another two hundred metres.

Dawn was breaking to illuminate my plight. I sucked a large volume of air into my lungs, and with my head down I inched forward of the middle pack. Alone now, I grunted from the effort it took to maintain this pace. My lips and mouth were dry. The only relief was fluid dripping out my nose onto my lips. I was beyond caring about what I looked like.

I made it! I had reached the front of the group.

My panting stopped me from being able to communicate; however, I was noticed by Pommy and he remembered that I still owed four hundred and fifty push-ups.

'Ranger Roberts, good to see you. You're my lead man for the next exercise.'

I had no idea what he was talking about. His panting made his accent even more difficult to understand. We had been running up a bloody mountain, and they wanted us to do another exercise?

'Ranger Roberts, do you see those pipes, to your left?'

I nodded in agreement, looking at the pipes, which were at least three feet off the ground, and six feet in diameter. I assumed they were used to transport water back to the coast.

'I want you to climb up on top of the pipes and run back to camp.'

I climbed the first concrete support, balanced on top of one of the pipes and ran a few steps. This feat was not easy; four inches of surface area had my total concentration. To not judge this correctly would mean that I would completely slip off and have to start again.

I started to run slowly. On the pipes behind me, men were clambering on to realise the difficulty of this exercise. I hadn't gone far when I heard a scream. I assumed someone had suffered an injury that would give them an easy out from this madness.

Concentrate, I kept saying to myself. The pipes developed their own madness. Conforming to the contours of the mountain, the gradient dropped sharply. No more running; now I was sliding! My shoes tried to remain in the four-inch safety zone. I dragged my back foot, inching forward with my front foot. Men were bunching up behind me.

'Who dares wins.' The motto of the SAS thumped in my brain. With no regard for safety, I ran faster. If I could get away from the others behind me, I couldn't be blamed for slowing the group. I had attracted enough attention for one day.

If I was well in front and I fell off, I could regain my lead position before the others could catch up. As soon as my plan was established in my head, I fell off the pipes.

I landed safely, ran forward to the next concrete support, climbed it and kept running, still in the lead.

An ambulance siren wailed. I decided that if I were to fall again, I would ensure that the distance to fall was lessened by sliding on my bum. A sore bum I got, but no broken bones. I finally made it back to camp. I was the first lined up as the others rapidly took their positions on the road, awaiting orders.

Pommy, who I was starting to hate, called me out to the front. I took interest at what he looked like this time. I was the same height as him. His age was between about twenty-five and thirty years. He had black hair, shortly cropped, and a hard face with hard dark eyes looking straight through me.

'You're not going to be late tomorrow, are you, Ranger Roberts?' he said.

'Not tomorrow, or any other day, sir,' I replied.

'Good, now move off to breakfast. When you are finished, prepare for your weapon to be inspected. You get breakfast first because you got back to camp first, so enjoy — after you give me fifty push-ups.'

I dropped to the ground and started to count. Ten was easy, twenty started to hurt, thirty my arms felt really heavy, forty my shoulders and arms started to stiffen from the pain. The last ten I did with my eyes closed, grunting, as I used every ounce of strength to inch up to the upright position. Fifty, my arms collapsed underneath me.

'Go to breakfast, Ranger Roberts'.

I raised myself and moved towards the mess hut. As I reached the door, the rest of the course swept me into the mess hall. I was pinned against the serving area. Not being hungry, I pushed through the two deep rows of men who were waiting impatiently to be served and out of the crowd. I felt extremely nauseous, needing two elements vital to the human body: fresh air and fluids.

Once I was in open space, I located the metal container that held cordial, and quickly downed four cups of the cold liquid. I felt my body responding, and moved to an empty table to enjoy some fresh air.

Two soldiers approached.

'Can we sit with you, Roberts?' one asked.

I nodded.

The other opened the conversation.

'Roberts, do you know you did really good this morning? By the way, my name is Troy Mills,' he said.

'My name is Paul,' I said. But I don't understand what you mean — really good? I stuffed up in a big way. I'm shagged, that proves it. If I get any more treatment like that, I don't think I will make it.'

The other soldier introduced himself as Nathan Walters, and as I shook his hand he continued. 'Paul, you and I are both from infantry units, and to us no one really knows what to expect on the SAS selection course. The gods must be smiling on us, because we have in our midst a signaller.'

He pointed at Troy, then looked me in the eye and raised his hand quickly to stop my mouth from opening. So what, were the words that screamed in my brain. I knew I had stuffed up. I didn't need some signaller patronising me.

Nathan kept on, though. 'Paul, we are both infantry soldiers and in our world we don't have any regard for those who aren't, except for the SAS soldiers.'

I nodded, ensuring I kept my mouth shut until he had explained how a 'chook' could know more than infantrymen.

The term 'chook' was used throughout the army as another name for a signaller, and referred to the fact that on exercises and operations the signallers would scratch around their tent, affectionately called the 'chook pen'. I was about to be educated.

Nathan looked at me as I studied Troy. I redirected my glance towards Nathan as he went on.

'There's a signals unit attached to the SAS, within the same barracks. Troy belongs to it; he has been working close to SAS operators for one year now. They are the people who recommended he apply for this course. Mate, I will let Troy explain to you what he meant when he first sat down.'

I redirected my eyes at Troy. He said, 'Paul, what Nathan said is true. I do belong to the signals unit that is attached to the SAS. Yes, I have worked with SAS operators, in a limited capacity. When you caught up with the lead group this morning, I told Nathan what I am about to tell you now.

'The operators that I have worked with have explained to me what to expect. This is not top secret, because knowing what to expect doesn't help you complete the phases.

'Phase One, one week, physically gruelling, mostly done in PT gear.

'Phase Two, one week, physically gruelling, mostly done in greens, with a belt and pouches (webbing) around the waist weighing ten kilograms, plus a rifle, and building up to carrying packs weighing thirty to fifty kilos.

'Phase Three, Sterling Ranges, up and down mountains with full gear, weight sixty kilograms.

'Phase Four, one week, challenges to be passed by individuals and teams. Only one meal over a five-day period, while completing the challenges. This meal is not very appetising; however, do not refuse it.'

I sat there stunned at the knowledge that Troy had shared.

'Would you please explain what you meant by telling me I had done a good job?' I asked respectfully.

'Paul, you did do a good job — you kept your cool. You achieved what they asked of you when they were expecting you not to.'

Nathan was smiling at me. I must've had a confused look on my face, for I was still questioning how I could have stuffed up, and these two blokes were telling me I did a good job.

Troy said, 'Mate, the instructors pick on everybody for a twenty-four period. It's designed to push individuals to their limit, to see how the individual conducts himself. This morning and for the rest of the day, they will ride you. My advice to you is to grin and bear it. Tomorrow it will be someone else's turn.'

'Okay, I've got that. Why is it that the instructors don't wear name tags and they don't call each other by name, just "sir"?'

'They won't tell us their names on the course. It's been done like that for years. Even though I know some of their names, if I told you I would be immediately removed from the course. Make up some nicknames so you can remember who they are.'

'Like the instructor that rode me this morning, with the British accent — I have named him Pommy.'

'You got it, and when we create another name for another instructor we will all identify him by that. Also, as the course goes on, some of the instructors will use nicknames they have given themselves, but never real names.'

We all rose from our seats. I quickly sat down in pain; my legs were cramping. The men waited for me to join them. I tried again, with the same result.

'Just twenty-four hours,' Nathan said.

'Tomorrow never comes,' I replied.

They both laughed at the comment that I had made through gritted teeth. While I staggered through the mess door assisted by my new friends, I took time to absorb their physical features. The new chook friend who had scratched his way into my world stood five feet and ten inches tall, with jet black hair that could only belong to an Italian. He also had the nose to match and a round face with red cheeks that too many grandparents would've squeezed, I dare say to his dislike. I made a mental note to have a dig at the enormous honker that shadowed his pouty lips and distracted from his blue eyes. I wondered if it was southern or northern Italians who possessed this feature. I would ask him.

Nathan was strong, carrying most of my weight as he flung the mess doors open. His six-foot frame, a classic thoroughbred, was all skin and muscle, not an ounce of fat. Anglo–Saxon and a hint of Sydney's western suburbs could be distinguished in his speech. There were scars on his knuckles, which were now visible because they were pressed against my cheek; his arm was around my shoulders, still waiting for my legs to stop cramping.

The sun stung all of our eyes and each of us protected them the best we could. I noticed that Nathan's face was clean of scars and blemishes. He had the model's face that the girls went crazy for, with blue eyes that were iridescent.

With scars covering his knuckles and a pretty face, he clearly didn't lose fights and he didn't mind hard work. I would eventually rib him for being a poster boy but not until I regained some energy. Nathan the infantry lad was going to be a challenge; I was feeling lucky an alliance was already made.

Nathan noticed the instructors paying us too much attention.

'Paul, we have to get back to the hut and strip our weapons for the inspection. Get back as soon as you can. I will get one of the blokes to act as a lookout for the arrival of the instructors,' he said.

I was left alone to travel the distance of fifty metres that they easily finished, sprinting. I didn't believe that they were fitter than me; it was just that I had expended so much energy on the morning run. I finally reached the hut, moved to my bed space, and started to strip my weapon. As Nathan had said, there was a bloke on lookout. I heard him say, 'They're fifty metres away.'

I shuddered.

I hadn't completed stripping my weapon and my hands were starting to cramp from the dehydrated state my body was in. Troy noticed the difficulty I was experiencing. He came racing over to my bed space, assisting me in this task.

'Twenty metres,' the lookout whispered.

Nathan joined us and helped too.'Ten metres,' the lookout whispered softly.

I looked at both of these men and commanded them to go. They continued stripping my weapon. The lookout at the door yelled, 'Stand fast.'

Now we were in the shit.

The instructor Pommy, who knew my name too well, started to ask questions that he had no intention of getting answers to.

'What are you two doing out of your bed space? How come that weapon is not completely stripped? Don't you men respect your weapon, as if it was your wife or girlfriend? How could you allow other men to touch your wife or girlfriend? Move back to your bed space and give me fifty push-ups,' he ordered them.

Once they had returned to their bed spaces, they both started doing their punishment. I bent down to join them. Pommy asked me what I was doing.

'They were helping me out. I'm responsible.'

'I dished out the punishment, and it didn't include you. You already owe me four hundred push-ups.'

A kind gesture, I thought.

* * *

We were lined up in three lines, known as ranks. When all two hundred and seventy-five of us were congregated, I once again heard my name screamed from the front.

'Ranger Roberts, here now'. There he was, looking through me with his dark piercing eyes. I returned his gaze, and screamed 'Sir!'

'Ranger Roberts, you are the duty student today. If anybody is late for a parade or activity, you will be the one who will receive the punishment. Do you understand me?'

'Yes sir,' I bellowed.

I'd had this task before in the infantry, but then I had only been in charge of a group that totalled thirty men. This was quite daunting, to be responsible for such a large group.

I moved to the front of this body of men, making my intentions clear. As soon as I opened my mouth, others would be calling me a wanker.

'My name is Ranger Roberts. I have been assigned to be the duty student today. Men, I'm not here for a popularity competition. I'm here just like you to complete this selection course. Unfortunately, if any one of you stuffs up today, I get the punishment.'

The instructors were still milling around behind me. I didn't care if they heard what I was about say.

'Men, I'm shagged from this morning's effort. I would appreciate that I don't get any more punishment. So if any one of you is dragging the chain, I will be right up you, booting your arse.'

I looked at the larger men in the ranks and realised that I had stated intentions that I would not be capable of carrying out. Fear started to rise, as I realised the dilemma I was in. I imagined a lot more painful sessions coming my way.

My concentration turned to a student who had raised his hand in the ranks. In a very undisciplined move, I started towards him, when my name was bellowed again.

'Stand fast, Ranger Roberts.'

This meant 'freeze'. I did just that.

'Who has got his hand up in my ranks?' my favourite instructor bellowed, and strode towards the soldier. 'What is your name?' He spat the words in his face.

'Ranger Griffiths, sir,' the overweight little man stammered.

'What's your problem, Ranger Griffiths?'

'I want to pull the pin.' He had gained control of his speech.

Pommy moved to the front again.

'Is there anyone else who wants to leave this course?'

From the position I was in, I could see six hands raised, including Ranger Griffiths'.

'No, men, you cannot leave this course. Unfortunately, you didn't read the fine print. You are mine for one week, not five working days; one whole week, seven days. Then and only then, gentlemen, can you go home to mummy. Put your hands down and expect a week of pain. Ranger Roberts, get your men inside and hand them over to the instructor who awaits you.'

'Parade attention, on my command … Dismiss, you will move into the building and sit down for the lectures to be given. Parade dismiss.'

Chapter Five

Battle fitness test

The parade was dressed in boots and green army pants with green T-shirts on. The instructor in charge of the next phase addressed the parade. We hadn't seen this instructor before and I thought that this eventuality was created to ensure that the rangers didn't become familiar with instructors. My assumptions were cut short as he hollered his command.

'Men, you are now going to do the battle fitness test, SAS style. The usual test you are used to is to run 3.8 kilometres in eighteen minutes. Today you will have to run it in under sixteen minutes, with what you are wearing, with ten kilograms on your webbing belt, carrying your rifle. When I have finished briefing you, an instructor will weigh your webbing.

'After the run, the test continues and you will complete a weight circuit. When your arms are tired you will have to climb a rope the distance of thirty feet, twice, up and down and up and down, without touching the ground. You must complete all tasks to qualify.

'Retest will not be conducted.

'Ranger Roberts, march these men to the building on the right side of the road about five hundred metres up the hill.'

'Yes sir,' I answered.

We marched up the road that we all had run up. This time we could see where we were going. The building that the instructor had referred to was huge. This structure was old in construction, World War II vintage. Corrugated iron went up one side and down the other. The peak of the roof was at least thirty feet high. I halted the men and awaited the next directive.

I didn't have to wait long. An instructor appeared dressed in green pants and boots. He was also wearing a white singlet with the telltale patch bearing the initials PTI (physical training instructor) sewn in the middle.

The man stood about five feet nine inches tall, was heavily tattooed, and had an extremely muscular body. His forearms were the size of my lower leg. His head had a thin patch of blond hair, which was receding. I thought to myself, I bet no one would take the piss out him for this slight imperfection. I waited for his instruction.

'Welcome to the SAS selection course gym. I will be putting you through most of the pain sessions during this course,' he stated simply. 'My name is Sergeant Davis. I'm the SAS regiment physical training instructor. I have been training rangers for five years. Most of you will not see me ever again in your life and you will be pleased about that fact. Those few who are selected will learn to enjoy pain. The session today ... I believe you have been briefed?'

'Yes, Sergeant,' I answered for the group.

'Good. About another five hundred metres up the road you marched on, there is a road on the right. This road leads to an airfield. You will run around the airfield till you come back to the entrance of the airfield. Get back onto the road and run back here. The course will be lined with instructors. Do you understand me?'

A chorus of voices bellowed, 'Yes, Sergeant.'

This instructor was the only one so far who had told us his name. I would have to ask Troy if he could explain this oddity.

Sergeant Davis set his wristwatch and simply said, 'Go. You have got sixteen minutes to complete the course.'

I was on the road pushing my limbs up the hill, saying to myself: it's only five hundred metres of hard slog. When I estimated that I had travelled about five hundred metres, there was no sign of a road leading to the airfield. Troy came up beside me. I grunted in pain.

'Where's the airfield?'

'It's another five hundred metres away, keep going. Never trust them when they tell you a distance to travel. It's always further away than what they tell you.'

'Thanks, mate. Why did the PTI sergeant tell us his name?'

'He's not operational.'

He increased his pace and moved in front of me. I tried to stay with him for three reasons. First, he knew where he was going. Second, if I could stay close enough behind him he could act as a windbreak for me. And third, at the pace he was maintaining I could do the first part hard, and rest on the downhill stretch, which would allow me to finish fast.

There was the airstrip: a flat section of land running between two mountain tops. It was a gravel strip but still big enough to land a Hercules C-130 aircraft on. Trust the SAS to have an airstrip in the middle of nowhere.

Troy was still just in front of me. He panted, 'Paul, we've got to pick up the pace. We're not going to make it at this rate. When we get to the down slope of the road, we're going to have to increase the speed. How are you doing?'

I wanted to say 'Like shit,' but I didn't.

'I'm all right,' I lied. So much for my plan to have a rest.

This course I could do easily in eighteen minutes. I had trained to ensure I could. But in sixteen minutes? If I completed the course in less than sixteen minutes it would be a personal best. This thought gave me more energy, surprisingly.

I estimated there were about fifty men in front of us. We came around the final corner and started heading down the road. I was watching Troy's boots, trying to maintain the same cadence. This allowed me to concentrate on something else other than the pain. We were really moving fast now. Images of men in boots and greens with their rifles flashed past me. I didn't raise my head to inspect those we had passed; I just kept focusing on Troy's boots.

'We are almost there, another three hundred metres, hang in there, Paul,' he panted.

The sergeant's voice drowned out the sound of boots slamming on the road, the only sound that I had been concentrating on. I was oblivious to everything else. He was calling out the time.

'Fifteen minutes and forty-five seconds.

'Fifteen minutes and fifty seconds.

'Fifteen minutes and fifty-five seconds.'

The voice was behind me now. Troy started to slow down. I did as well. It took us fifty metres to slow from the sprint we had just achieved.

'Did we pass, Troy?' I panted.

'Yep, we crossed the line in between fifteen minutes and forty-five seconds and fifteen minutes and fifty seconds,' he panted.

My legs collapsed underneath me. I sat on the road cross-legged.

'Troy, go and get our time. My legs have decided that they done enough today. I will wait till everyone is back and then I will join you.'

Weights circuit session, and then climb the ropes twice. My thoughts were not calculating what I had to do. I was convincing my tired and sore body that these tasks could be done.

The pain subsided in my legs. I raised myself and staggered back up the hill to the SAS gym. The lads who had completed the course within the set time sat separately. Troy came over to me and told me that only forty-three soldiers passed. Nathan, Ben, Tony and Peter from our hut had passed. Tom, Bill, Mark and Bruce had failed.

'Just the next phase to pass,' I said.

'You will do it, just give it your best,' Troy encouraged.

I was starting to like this man. It's always good to hear someone have faith in you when you are finding it hard to keep pushing on. As we sat in a group awaiting the next task I took time out to study Tony and Peter and surreptitiously Ben.

Tony Ridy was aged about twenty. His most notable feature was his striking red hair. He had a slightly freckled face with brown eyes. He was Irish, but didn't have much of an accent, which was a shame because I enjoyed listening to a deep Irish accent. He lay with his webbing under his head and his eyes closed, his breathing completely recovered. He looked the picture of a five-foot-eleven-inch elf, wearing his green army pants and green T-shirt that only showed sweat stains under the armpits. This man was fit.

Peter Chauci was a reconnaissance soldier from a Sydney battalion. With such a great start, he would already possess skills and talents we were yet to learn. He was definitely of Italian descent and was covered in coarse black hair. He would need to have two shaves daily. With a muscular chest and large forearms, large hands and solid legs, all remarkably packaged into his standing straight height of six feet two inches, he was a formidable sight. I wondered if he was from the north or south. I would have to ask him. Asset or liability, two Italians in the same group? Another question that I was sure would be answered.

And the last to go under my inquiring gaze was Ben Jones. This was done subtly, as his presence demanded you be intimidated. He hadn't spoken to anybody and he also was completely in control of his breathing well before the rest of us, and the past activity had not fazed him at all. Ben had dark hair with a short-back-and-sides haircut, and was an infantryman. He had large hands that were scarred and calloused. He was older; I assumed he was in his late twenties. He had a big chest, large arms, and was definitely of Australian descent.

I had just enough time to rest to be able to move into the gym for the next phase. The wooden floor creaked as we walked on it to get to an exercise station. Signs on the wall were there to motivate us, and they did.

The signs read:

Train hard, fight easy.

The only easy day was yesterday.

No pain, no gain.

The circuit was an arm and abdominal workout. For me it started with having to do sit-ups with a twenty-kilogram weight, then crunches, heaves, push-ups, hanging on a wall, raising my knees to my chest, and holding my feet above the ground until told to lower them.

Then my rest exercise was holding a five-kilogram bar out in front of me and doing exercises that the PTI chose.

Get through this, then it's only the rope climb to do, I encouraged myself.

The first time round I managed without too much bother. The second time round I was struggling at the last part of the rotation. If I were back at the battalion, the second circuit would be the finish. Learning from my last mistake, knowing now that this was the SAS, three or even four circuits could be demanded of us.

We started the third circuit. I was really hurting, and kept looking at the signs on the wall to distract me, repeating them over and over again.

It worked; I had completed the circuit phase. A rush of nausea interrupted my short-lived jubilation. I ran out the open door to propel my lunch onto the ground.

This was a blessing in disguise. Because I had to eject my lunch, when I had composed myself, I returned to the gym to find I was back at the end of the line waiting to climb the ropes. I could rest before having to attempt the next gruelling task.

The line I stood in had about twenty men in it, waiting to make their attempt. The first two men passed, the next three failed. Then five men passed, but there was to be a succession of failures next; ten men in total.

It was my turn. A senior instructor, I thought, due to his age, asked a simple question: 'Are you going to be the fourteenth solider to fail on this rope?'

'I will tell you when I'm finished, sir.'

'I like your attitude, soldier. Climb when you're ready.'

I liked to use the straddle technique. I gripped the rope high above my head and pulled myself up. The rope would be between my legs, my right leg would be bent and raised up to my chest. When my hands had pulled me up the rope and were level with my face, I would raise my left leg up and stand on the rope that lay across my right boot. In this position, I could rest standing on the rope. The completion of this process was known as a byte.

The rest position was still energy sapping, so I continued. Raising my hands again, pulling on the rope, raising my right leg, and then the other leg, I completed my second byte. Ten or twelve bytes later, I lost count; I touched the beam the rope was attached to.

The lowering technique was easier. Still gripping the rope, I placed the rope between my legs and crossed my feet over, locking the rope between both boots. I quickly lowered myself to not waste too much energy. The senior instructor had his back to me. I continued to climb for the second time.

The first two bytes were negotiated easily. I was feeling confident. Halfway up the rope, my hand started cramping. I stepped on the rope and brought the crippled hand down to my mouth, and bit it hard. The pain shot through my hand and down my arm.

This pain inducement created more problems: my other hand holding onto the rope slipped, giving me a friction burn. With both hands damaged, I lost confidence in my ability to complete this phase.

I was only six feet from the top. If I continued to stay stationary, I would fall twenty-five feet. I looked up at the top of the beam. I had to concentrate on something other than the pain. Peeling my blistered hand off the rope I reached up to grip a higher spot, moving my cramped hand up next to my other hand, a trivial, useless effort for now. This hand was clamped shut. I rested it on the burnt hand.

I straightened my legs. Now I was only four feet from the top, hanging on with one damaged hand. 'Look at the beam,' I said to myself. I locked the rope into my forearm to allow the functioning hand to reach further up the rope. My right leg bent; my trailing leg picked the rope up and stood on top of my right boot. I had only travelled one foot higher. My spirits dropped.

Then I heard a voice, encouraging me. It was Peter.

'Come on, mate, you can do it.'

Then there were two more voices, then three: Troy and Nathan and finally Tony's voices were recognisable.

'Come on mate, you can do it.'

I didn't dare look down; I just kept focused on the beam that the rope was attached to. I was prepared to do my next move. I used the alternative technique I had devised for the last move. I had covered another foot, deeply concentrating on the beam above. I prepared once again.

Then the sound bouncing off the walls of the gym was deafening. The whole course, two hundred and twenty men, yelled in unison, 'Come on, mate, you can do it.'

With the rope in the crook of my forearm, my burnt hand peeled off the rope again. I raised it above my head, and it gripped the rope. A stinging sensation returned to my cramped hand.

'I can feel something, I can feel my hand,' I yelled.

The voices rose again. 'Come on, mate, you can do it.'

Strength poured into my crippled hand. I reached up above my burnt hand and gripped the rope solidly. I brought my leg up and the trailing leg picked up the rope. I placed it on my boot and stood on it for the last time. I reached up with the hand that had done the least effort and touched the beam that I had focused on throughout the ordeal.

Loud applause erupted. I took the opportunity to look down at my audience. I was right; it was the whole course cheering, except Ben. I still had to be aware of the damage I had done to my hand. It needed to be peeled off the rope again. I rested it, allowing my now functional hand to grip the rope on the descent.

As I descended, the course filed out of the gym. Ben was the last to leave and held his thumb up against his huge chest; a sign that I had reached his approval rating and no one else would know that I had been bestowed that honour. I finally reached the bottom and had completed the task. The senior instructor was at the end of the rope when I touched the gym floor.

'Give me a look at your hand,' he asked.

I showed him. I was shocked to see the damage I had done. Across my palm was a red welt which covered the whole palm area. Skin was torn from its original position, exposing the tissue underneath.

'You are to go to the RAP (regimental aid post) and tell them I sent you. Ensure that you also tell them that you have probably suffered a heat illness today. Ranger, keep that wound clean. I have seen very good soldiers fail because they let their wounds get infected,' he advised. 'I will see you tomorrow. Good effort today. You have still got a long way to go.'

'Thank you, sir,' I simply stated.

I left the gym to walk alone towards the RAP.

The RAP was opposite the mess hall. There was a queue of soldiers wanting to be attended to. I took my place at the end of the queue. A medic addressed the men waiting. The badge on his sandy beret easily identified him; he belonged to the Medical Corps. The SAS regiment honoured the men who passed selection and who chose to not become operators by giving them the privilege of wearing the coveted sandy beret with their corps. badge attached. Respect was immediate for the owner of a sandy beret.

He inquired, 'Are there any men here that require attention, other than dressing blisters?'

I raised my hand.

'Move forward and I will assist you inside.'

Good bedside manner, I thought.

He had a clipboard resting on his lap and, pen in hand, he waited for me to take a seat to acquire my military details. I was slightly distracted by the muffled screams coming from another room. A pungent odour filled the room. He noticed my distraction and explained the medical procedure that was being carried out.

'Those soldiers are having feet blisters attended to. We drain the fluid out from under the skin using a syringe. Then we inject iodine into the blister, which is extremely painful. In about three days the tissue will harden from the iodine being injected.

'This has proved to be the quickest method that we have devised to get soldiers functioning at their optimum level.

'Okay, let's get some details,' he continued.

'Name?'

'Ranger Roberts.'

'Date of birth?'

'13 September 1968.'

'Hut number?'

'Ten.'

'Right, that's all I need. Well, what can we do for you?'

I hesitated. I didn't want to expose my blister, which spread across my palm the width of a five-dollar note. I could still hear soldiers screaming into their pillows from the pain they were experiencing from the blister treatment that sounded rather barbaric.

I stalled.

'I was sent down here from the gym. The senior instructor told me to inform you that I have probably suffered a heat illness.'

I gingerly slid my damaged hand behind my back.

'Have you vomited today?' he quizzed.

'Yes,' I answered.

'Have you had any cramping sensations today?'

'Yes.'

'Have you collapsed, or passed out today?'

'Yes.'

'Which one?'

'I have collapsed. My legs just collapsed underneath me for a short period.'

'How long?'

'For about five minutes.'

'Yep, you have suffered a heat illness. I want to take your blood pressure and temperature. Give me your arm.'

As he reached for my arm, he noticed that one arm was tucked behind my back.

'Where's your other hand, Ranger?'

The situation was hopeless; I couldn't avoid the barbaric treatment any longer. I showed my damaged hand to the medic. His face contorted.

'Nasty,' he diagnosed. 'Why were you hiding your hand, Ranger?'

'I didn't want to get the same treatment the boys next door were suffering.'

'Ranger, I would never do that. You have a severe burn on your hand. It will require two dressings a day, with a burns ointment. This is a deep tissue burn. The soldiers getting treatment next door have superficial blisters. If I was to give you the same treatment, you would pass out for a week and definitely rocket into shock, if you haven't experienced that already today.'

He dressed my wound skilfully as he explained to me that I didn't need to fear unwarranted treatments. Then I was shocked by what he said next.

'I have written an authority for you to rest for the remainder of the day and night activities. I will explain to your instructors. I want you to go and have a meal and then go straight to bed.'

I left the RAP and went straight to the mess hall. I had a large meal, by myself. Most of the other rangers had already eaten and were preparing for the night activity. I left the mess hall, moved to my hut, looked at my bed and imagined it to be a king-size waterbed.

I secured my rifle and webbing and took my boots off. I lay on the single bed with its loose springs that made the mattress bow in the middle. As I was falling into a deep sleep state I was still imagining that I was in a king-size waterbed. The image of one of the signs that I had seen on the gym wall entered my mind.

Train hard, fight easy.

Chapter Six

Battle efficiency test

Day seven finally arrived. We were told that at 1900 hours those who wanted to pull the pin (quit) could.

Today, we had an alteration to the program. We were given a set of scales for each hut to ensure that our webbing weighed ten kilograms and our pack thirty. We were required to do the battle efficiency test: a fifteen-kilometre route march in all our kit.

I was a bit concerned about the weight I was carrying. I hadn't trained for this challenge. In the infantry unit that I belonged to, this test was only done with webbing and rifle. Trust the SAS to make this task extremely difficult. They really wanted those who were not sure of their commitment to quit.

A route march is when a team of soldiers is told to travel a certain distance, carrying a certain weight. The objective is to get all troops capable of shooting effective fire to the destination together, no running allowed.

'Ranger Roberts, you are to lead this team throughout the route march. You must ensure that the team finishes together. I will be the instructor for this phase,' the senior instructor said.

'Yes sir,' I replied.

I almost added the name 'Kojak' silently to myself, as he wore his head completely bald. Have you heard the term 'six foot tall and two pick handles across the shoulders'? Well, this was the apt description of this man. Awesome. Another outstanding feature was his forty-four-gallon chest, and his shadow covered three rangers standing together.

I moved the team of ten men, including myself, to the start line. Then Kojak had something to say. My team fell deathly silent and completely motionless. Utmost respect was displayed.

'Men, the commanding officer, his second-in-charge, the regiment adjutant and some administration staff are out in front of you completing their battle efficiency test. This group left thirty minutes in front of us. I want this team to catch them and run over the top of the command group. One minute before we start.'

The pace would need to be extremely rapid and constant throughout the fifteen kilometres. To catch another group would be a huge feat; to catch one that was thirty minutes in front of us, nearly impossible.

I started the team off at three-quarter pace for five hundred metres, until their lower limbs were warm and stretched. I looked at all the variables that were against me.

Firstly, I didn't know the capabilities of these men. I didn't know who my weakest man was, so I could pace the route march off his pace to ensure we all finished together. I didn't know the terrain we were going to cover; when it would be good to increase the pace or slow down to give these men a rest so we didn't split and fail the objective.

I stopped myself from being negative. We had travelled about five kilometres and everybody was handling the pace. It was one responsibility to be the duty student. However, I knew that a team leader responsibility would be observed and assessed. Every student would get the opportunity to show leadership qualities. I wasn't about to quit on my occasion.

'That's the ten-kilometre mark on that tree,' Kojak said panting.

I looked at the tree with the white scar on it. Then I looked at my watch. It had taken an hour to reach the ten-kilometre mark; amazingly we were on time. I was at the back end of my team. They were in two lines: five on the right side and four on the left.

I looked at their clothes. Their shirts and trousers were drenched with sweat, and also water they'd poured over their heads during the march. It was important to keep body temperature as low as possible. Wet clothes indicated that no one was suffering a heat illness. If we were to complete this challenge, the last thing we needed was someone to pass out. Everything seemed to be going in our favour. I encouraged the team.

'Lads, we're on time to catch up with the command group, but we must remain at this pace. How is everybody feeling?'

Nathan up the front, not to allow a humorous situation to slip by, answered me first. 'I'm okay, how are you? I do need to do a poo.'

Before I could answer him, Tony, next to him, answered me in the exactly same way. 'I'm okay, how are you? I do need to do a poo.'

The same answer continued, from the other seven. They enjoyed laughing at me. They still maintained the required pace during this moment of joviality. I answered them back humorously.

'Put a plug in your arse. Make sure the speed is fast.'

They knew we would not stop for someone to do a poo. They all laughed. Even Kojak smiled back at me. I didn't need to tell these professional soldiers that we hadn't completed the task yet. They all quietened down and concentrated on the successful result we were collectively striding towards.

Everything was going fine. I was sure we had passed the fourteen-kilometre mark and had less than one kilometre to go. I looked up from the road that my eyes were glued to. This helped to focus on something else other than the pain I was feeling throughout my body. As I started my scan at the front of the team, I noticed one man's clothing was completely dry. It was Troy. He was suffering from a heat illness. As soon as I noticed him, he slowed down and the team surged forward, away from him. I dropped back to assist him.

The instructor, myself, and the team except for Troy were tripping on endorphins, the soldier's magical chemical. Perfectly natural, endorphins are released by the brain when the body is in too much pain. For Troy, the pace was becoming too hectic and he was losing coordination. Peter yelled, 'There, they are about two hundred metres in front of me. Hey Paul, the finish line is five hundred metres away.'

Great news, but I still had to get Troy over the line.

Troy was in Disneyland by now. He was all over the road. I grabbed his arm and pulled him up to the team and told him to watch me and get in step. He acknowledged he was trying, 'But the pain.'

'Switch off. Think of something else. The pain will go,' I replied.

He seemed to get angry with himself. With this new-found aggression, he knew the effort was required now if he was to finish. He started running, all his joints crying out with pain. He was slow and hilarious, struggling to get his limbs moving and working together.

We had dropped back behind the team and the instructor. His running was slow; it must've taken us two minutes to breach that ten-metre gap. I was trying to manage the pace with this individual who, by this stage, was running with a ridiculous shuffle.

Then it happened: the spaced-out look went from his eyes, his muscles tightened, and his coordination returned. With a determined effort, he moved to the front of the team and increased the pace.

The team was together, but we were still one hundred metres behind the Commanding Officer's group. Kojak's comment was, 'Right, Ranger, over the top.'

It was three hundred metres to the end of the fifteen kilometres and we were up their arses.

The problem with a lead group you have caught is that if they can maintain the pace, they can stay in front. You have to virtually walk on their heels to make them move out of the way.

This we achieved. My head was down, sweat was dripping off me, and I kept telling myself, 'Boots in front, hit their heels, they will move.' The command team couldn't maintain the pace and they peeled either side of our formation to let us through. The commanding officer made a comment to the instructor I didn't even hear, we were grunting so much. However, I will never forget Kojak's comment to us.

'You might be the commanding officer's rangers, but if you successfully complete the selection cycle, I would be proud to have you become my patrol members.'

Chapter Seven

The only easy day was yesterday

The deadline finally arrived: the opportunity was there to quit if you wanted to. One hundred and twenty-two men quit. The number still standing up in the knowledge-already-learned lectures was still the same. The relentless boredom of listening to lectures on subjects already thoroughly understood was designed to create fatigue, so to overcome the undisciplined act of falling asleep men would stand until sent to bed.

The instructors left the empty seats and still made us maintain our original seating. The empty chairs were a reminder that we could quit whenever we liked. 0000 hours arrived. I was knackered and looked forward to falling into bed. I awoke at 0330 hours to start another day. With my PT gear on, I awaited the instructors' arrival to commence our morning run. When 0400 hours arrived there was a shock in store for us. Another new instructor that I didn't remember seeing in the first week gave us this command.

'Men, I want you to go back to your huts, put on your boots and green pants and a T-shirt. I have got a surprise for you. Move like a bunch of startled gazelles. Go go go!'

I ran back to the hut, excited to be doing a different activity. I quickly put my gear on, when I finally noticed that there were four men missing. Tom, Bill, Bruce and Mark had pulled the pin even after a solid effort yesterday, when we all completed the fifteen-kilometre route march. Six remained: Ben, Tony, Peter, Troy, Nathan and myself. But there was no time to reflect on what I had no control over. I raced back to the parade ground, looking forward to the next activity.

I had a short memory. I should've realised the only easy day was yesterday.

We started off with a slow jog up the road that led us to the mountain. We ran up the incline that every morning tried to beat us. The 'last man to the front' exercise was easier now, as you would only have to pass a hundred and fifty figures in the dark.

We arrived at the entrance to the airfield. The 'last man to the front' was conducted on the flat, around the airfield. After the third rotation, when we had run the length of the airstrip, we were commanded to drop and do fifty push-ups and one hundred sit-ups. Due to my injured hands, I had to substitute the push-ups with sit-ups.

We did this at each end of the airfield for another three rotations. The promised surprise came next. Hidden off the end of the airstrip were telegraph poles cut into four-metre lengths. After being ordered into the bush to drag them out, it took six men to lift them. The instructors said, 'I want teams of six men on each pole.'

The original six men from our hut remained together. I was pleased with this. The result we'd achieved together yesterday made me feel confident that we would handle this task. The log lay at our feet. We awaited instructions.

'Good. These teams you are in will be the new teams you will stay in until further notice.'

A quick smile shared and some slaps on the back and verbal congratulations signified that we from Hut 10 were quite pleased to hear this. Ben's small upward crack of his lips, and his usual idiosyncrasy of his upward thumb across his chest and silence, made it unanimous.

'Pick up the log and put it on your right shoulder,' this new instructor bellowed.

Glee at this recent revelation bubbled within me, to the point where a smart crack escaped my lips.

'Hey Troy, use your nose and flick it onto our shoulders.'

It was extremely bad timing. Troy glanced at me as though I had escaped Ward B of the Psych Unit. He started organising us to ensure that the tall men were at the ends and the rest in the middle. This placed me two from the front, behind Peter, our tallest man. It was an effort just to get the log to our knees. With everybody straining, it finally rested on our right shoulders. The next command was, 'Raise the pole above your head, then shuffle forward. When the man at the front is not holding onto the pole, he is to run around the team and hold the pole at the rear, always moving forward. Go go go!'

It wasn't long before I was the lead man, holding the pole all by myself; that's how it felt. I was shuffling forward, trying not to let the pole crush my head. It took two seconds to reach the rear of the pole. I saw the lads' elbows buckling and then straighten once I had taken my share of the dead weight.

To date, I hadn't heard the course members grunt and groan with such exertion. Everybody except Ben was grunting and cursing just to keep the log up in the air. Ben's teeth were clamped shut, and an observer might have thought that in his vicinity a dentist drill was operating, as the unique sound was being imitated by Ben's teeth grinding together.

My turn again. I prepared myself for the additional weight I was about to take. Tony left the front of the pole. I tried not to allow my elbows to buckle as I shuffled forward. I was in a precarious position. My back was starting to arch. This left my hands behind my head and back.

This position was going to lead to a back injury. Fortunately, Nathan was behind me and offered support by placing his hands on mine to take the weight for a couple of seconds. This allowed me to straighten my back, and to once again take the load that was my responsibility. The pain was intense. When was this going to stop?

On the fourth rotation, the instructor finally said, 'Place the log down gently. I want you all to love your log — it's going to be part of your lives for the next three weeks.'

The log session lasted for ten minutes. I couldn't believe how exhausted I felt, with my upper body going limp. This instructor decided that our legs needed to hurt as much as our upper body. We were ordered to run around the airfield in our teams doing 'last man to the front'. After the fifth rotation, we were told to stop. My body ached for a rest.

After a brief pause, the instructor ordered us back on the road for the downhill run home. Every muscle in my body resisted. It took two hundred metres to loosen my muscles from their cramped condition. I couldn't maintain the pace that my team was managing.

I dropped back, forcing myself to keep going. An instructor noticed that I had fallen behind my team. A barrage of abuse followed, and phrases were screamed at me.

'You weak bastard,' he started. 'Letting your team down, you weak prick. Come on, catch up to your team. Are these men going to have to carry you when you fall apart on operations? When they're dead because you are not strong enough to keep up with them, are you willing to talk to their family about how you were a coward and let the team down?'

That last sentence cut deep. As I raised my head and the sweat rolled into my eyes, I looked at him and truly wanted to kill him. Call me a fucking coward, I thought.

For the first time that morning I found reserved energy to rejoin my team. It took a while but I was back in the formation by the time we reached the camp. We stopped and I collapsed. I heard a medic being called for, and then I slipped into unconsciousness.

I awoke, and realised I was in the RAP. The medic was attending to my injured hand.

'Your hand is healing well. How did you go with the logs today?' he asked.

'It hurt at first but I decided to block out the pain,' I replied. 'What happened?'

'You have suffered a heat illness. You have been here for just over an hour.'

My eyes had just started to focus, when I realised I was on an intravenous drip. The medic noticed my observation.

'Sorry, but this is your breakfast today. You missed breakfast. You are probably feeling nauseated right now. When we finish the bag's content, which is a saline-based treatment, you can rejoin the course to run yourself into the ground. Today, you will start to do navigation exercises. Be careful with your hand. You need it to heal quickly. Do not get it dirty and do not get it wet, understand?'

'Yes, I will do my best.'

I lay on the bed watching the fluid slowly drip into the intravenous tube. The next thing I remembered was being shaken awake to have some solid food. It was lunchtime. I was not connected to the intravenous line anymore. Instead, where the needle had been in my arm there was a sticky circular bandaid. I looked at the medic, inquiringly.

'I let you sleep. If I let you have too much rest, they would discharge you from the course on medical grounds. If you hurry, you can get some food into you and rejoin the course after lunch. The instructors will not pay too much attention to you.'

I thanked him and left the RAP. The mess hut was full of soldiers. The tables needed to feed the number of men who had started the course were now packed away. I found an empty spot with men I didn't know and ate my meal silently.

I went back to my hut to face the men I thought I'd let down.

'Sorry, boys, for letting you down,' I apologised, remembering what the instructor had said to me. Peter spoke first.

'No, mate, you have got it all wrong. You made it back into the team before we finished.'

'Did I?' I asked, totally confused; I only remembered that instructor calling me a coward. Nathan spoke.

'Paul, you went a shade of green before you dropped out of the team. Tony and I noticed that your colour was ash white. We commented to each other that you were in a bad way, but mate, believe us, you got back to the team before you finished. You lasted to the finish, and then passed out. The instructor moved everybody back to allow fresh air to you. He waited for the medic to arrive and said to the rest of the course, "That's what we want to see, a boots and all effort. One hundred per cent, gentlemen, that's what is required to get to my regiment."'

'You're bunging it on, Nathan.'

'What have I told you before? They push you if they want you. He obviously thinks that you can complete the selection course.' Troy joined the conversation.

'I really don't have any memory of finishing,' I admitted.

'It doesn't matter, as long as you realise you didn't let the team down this morning,' Nathan added.

'I guess I will just have to trust you.'

'You bloody better. Come on, grab your rifle, webbing and a green shirt. We are on parade in five minutes,' Troy informed me.

Ben waited until everybody moved to their own bed space and once again gave me the thumbs up across his chest. No one else saw this. I smiled; he turned and busied himself getting his gear ready.

They bolted out the door. I retrieved the items in the exact order that Troy had told me. As I ran to the parade ground, I was feeling fresh and had ample energy reserves. As I had looked forward to the change of routine this morning, I didn't want to underestimate the afternoon, which could turn out to be hell. I mentally prepared myself.

We were informed at the next parade that we would be doing a navigation exercise. The relevant lectures we had been given would now be put into practice. I felt confident I understood what was required of me. This was comforting, as the next directive was that all navigation exercises were to be done alone. To receive assistance from another course member would mean immediate dismissal from the course.

I waited in line to sign for my map, compass and protractor.

Troy approached me, and whispered, 'Remember you are in WA; always add your magnetic variation.'

I recalled the lecture when we had been informed of this anomaly. It had been explained that it was necessary on the western coast of Australia to add the magnetic variation to your calculation, and to subtract the magnetic variation on the east coast of Australia.

I was glad Troy reminded me, as I had clean forgotten. Once I had the equipment, Pommy told me the grid references that I needed. With pencil in hand, I jotted them down. I read back the references, to ensure I had heard them correctly.

Once again I had my pencil ready to correct any errors. A long pause. Pommy didn't answer me. I looked up from my pad. Pommy answered my bewildered look.

'Ranger Roberts, you don't get opportunities to ask and confirm. You must listen intently and act upon the directive. This is what the regiment requires of you. Now go, you are taking up my oxygen.'

I started to do my calculations. When confident that I had applied the correct calculations, I knew what direction I was to travel. I set my compass, and moved off.

The briefing said that the destination point I needed to reach before taking another bearing would be clearly marked. My first stop was at the end of the airfield, on the southern side. I was quite confident that I was in the right place. I looked around the area for something to suggest that it was clearly marked. It was taking too long — fifteen minutes too long. I was aware that this exercise was being timed and assessed. 'Be back before dinner,' they had said.

'Where's this fucking clearly marked spot?' I yelled.

How many times would I take them literally?

This was just one more time when I had gullibly believed their instructions to the letter. I readjusted my thinking. What would be clearly marked, I thought. Instead of looking for large objects, I concentrated on small. I was standing up and still couldn't see any object. I sat down and ensured I was at the spot where I needed to be. While I sat cross-legged I noticed something unusual: a brown piece of string attached to a tree one foot above the ground.

I went to investigate. The string tied to the tree was new. I pulled the excess string toward me. A blue marker was secured to the end. I quickly marked the plot sheet, verifying the first checkpoint. I plotted the next bearing and was ready to move, and then it hit me. These SAS instructors had an obscure sense of humour. 'It will be clearly marked …' they'd said. Coloured markers — textas! I giggled as I broke into a run, attempting to make up time.

Knowing the cryptic clues, the other checkpoints were easy to find on the mountain I had grown to hate. The next checkpoint was about two kilometres up and across the mountain, and halfway down a spur through the bush. The checkpoint after that was back up the mountain on the eastern side, once again halfway down a spur. I ran up and down the mountain throughout the afternoon.

I had reached all five and ran back into camp. When I arrived, Nathan, Troy, Peter and Tony were there, having completed the exercise. Tony was the closest to me. I asked him, 'Tony, how long did it take to find the first marker?'

'A couple of minutes. First I was looking for something more prominent, then I realised these SAS blokes have tricked us every time. So I started to think like them. I guess that's what they're teaching us in a cryptic sort of way. How long did it take you?'

'Too long,' I answered honestly.

Ben arrived and sat down next to us, quietly.

Tony had said something that had finally dawned on me. The sooner we grasped the concept of thinking like them, the sooner we would handle the selection course more comfortably. Instead of making assumptions about what was going to come up next, I should wait for the activity to begin and do my best.

I realised they were going to play with my head, just waiting for me to give up. I knew the key to passing the selection course: expect the worst they could do to my body and mind and that accept that every day was going to get harder. If I was to be selected, I had better get harder as well. I felt confident that I could do it.

On parade that evening the instructors once again offered the opportunity to pull the pin. I was in the rear rank, watching men move forward so they could be formally discharged from the course. It was a large group. One of the senior instructors commented, 'Count those men. I think this is an all-time record for pulling the pin on day eight.' He directed his command to one of the younger instructors.

'Forty-two, sir.'

He slapped his thigh.

'That is an all-time record. The last one stood at thirty-nine, for fifteen years. Is there anybody left in the ranks who wants to pull the pin to make my night?'

No one moved. Thirty seconds later a small man stepped forward and joined the other group. The senior instructor let out a holler.

'By gees, we are doing good tonight. That's it, no more offers or we won't have anything to do tonight. The rest of you will get your opportunity tomorrow. Bloody hell, forty-three! I never thought I would see the day,' he proclaimed.

'Tonight, men, we will be doing a night navigation exercise,' an instructor informed us.

'When the trucks arrive, you will put yourselves, webbing and rifle on board. Flash away now and get your equipment,' he ordered.

We ran into the hut. I told myself to expect the worst. The expression on my face must have given away my concerns.

'What's up, mate? You look like you have seen a ghost. Is it about tonight?' Tony asked.

'Yes, mate. I'm just preparing for the worst-case scenario.'

'Good thinking. But try not to scare the shit out of me while you're doing it.'

'Sorry, mate,' I finished.

Tony was closer to the edge than I'd realised.

We ran back to the parade ground, to wait for the trucks. When they arrived, we loaded ourselves and equipment onto one of them. Tonight we didn't have to carry our packs.

The rear flap of the tarp covering the truck was secured in place. Darkness enveloped us; the engine was turned on. As the truck drove, I asked Troy where we were headed. He answered, 'Paul, get some sleep. I have no idea where we are headed. I'll give you the same tip the operators gave me. When the instructors are not screaming abuse at you, sleep, because you are going to need the rest. Be prepared for an all-nighter. Now get your head down so the rest of us can do the same.'

I thought the last comment was a bit harsh. I was sure that everybody in the truck would appreciate the information that Troy had given out. Everybody was overtired; snaps and negative comments were becoming more frequent. I didn't allow that comment to affect me. I pushed my legs out in front of me, folded my arms, and quickly fell asleep.

I had no idea how far we had travelled when I woke, only that my name was being screamed at me.

'Ranger Roberts, if I have to call your name again I'm going to personally kick you off this course. Now get your arse off the fucking truck!' the unknown voice yelled.

Rudely awakened, I still didn't register that I was on the SAS selection course. While I was fumbling for my equipment, he hollered again.

'Look sleeping beauty, I left you to last so you could get some sleep. All your mates are out doing the navigation exercise. You're one hour behind already, so stop pushing my buttons and get off the fucking truck.'

It finally dawned on me where I was. The truck was empty. I hadn't been by myself since the course started. It was an eerie sensation, not having anybody in my personal space. That would soon change.

'Ranger Roberts, what is your major malfunction?' He spat the words.

I thought of answering back but that would just infuriate him. I stood there in a strong attention position, ready to receive the berating. He had convinced me that I deserved this attention for not being alert enough to carry out his directive.

'Ranger Roberts, sleep is a double-edged weapon to Special Forces soldiers. Yes, it gives you rest, but deep sleep can make you vulnerable. When you are vulnerable you can end up dead, or worse, a mate of yours can end up dead. Then you have to live with that. I suggest you learn to sleep lighter. Do you understand me, Ranger Roberts?'

'Yes sir,' I said quietly.

I looked this man in the eye to show that I respected him. I appreciated his words of wisdom. Although it was dark on the gravel road, I hoped this individual could see the immense respect I had for him. Here was a man who only knew my name as one of a list of names. I believed I had conveyed my sincerity.

He spoke softly. 'Well, that's the bullshit out of the way. Now let's get down to business. Here's a map, compass, protractor, torch and grid references. It's an all-nighter, which should be a cinch for you after all the sleep you have had.'

I looked at him humbly.

He continued, 'You have to be at the last checkpoint by 0600 hours. There are over one hundred men in this bush tonight. You are not to buddy up. If you see torchlight, you are to go to ground and turn your light off. There will be instructors trying to catch out soldiers who don't adhere to the rules. Are there any questions, Ranger Roberts?'

'No sir.' I spoke softly again.

He moved off, climbed into the driver's seat and drove away. I was all alone, and that same eerie sensation returned. After quickly plotting my route, I moved into the bush. The uninviting blackness swallowed me.

I followed the compass's luminous arrow. I was heading downhill through light scrub. The map indicated I was aiming for a re-entrant (a creek line). I was confident I was travelling in the right direction.

One hundred metres along the compass bearing, I fell down a thirty-foot embankment. Fortunately the embankment was soft soil. I covered the distance mostly on my bum. The momentum of the slide forced me into a forward roll. I didn't complete the forward roll, finding myself immersed in water. The clear night with stars shining confirmed the undisputed evidence that I was lying flat on my back in a creek.

I'd found the creek-line I had plotted to assist me onto my first checkpoint. I was required to get five checkpoints before 0600 hours. I raised my hand out of the water to read the time on my watch. It was 2230 hours. I remembered that most checkpoints had about two kilometres' distance between them: in total, ten kilometres or more.

The distance didn't sound like much but this was night. I didn't know what the terrain was like or what obstacles I would encounter. I sat in one now; this experience had wasted time.

I raised myself out of the water. A wet and uncomfortable sensation was also present. Picking up my rifle, which fortunately didn't end up in the drink, I followed my plotted bearing. The luminous arrow pointed straight up the creek-line. I remained in the creek, walking in water up to my knees.

I calculated how far I'd travelled by counting my paces. Every thirteen steps meant I had travelled ten metres. Still in the creek-line, I finally reached one kilometre. This wasn't easily achieved. I had tripped over logs that were submerged, and had been whipped in the face by low-hanging branches. A collection of cuts and bruises verified the truth.

I moved up the bank of the creek to encounter another obstacle. Dense brush stopped me from breaking free of the creek-line. I expected this; nature was predictable around any watercourse, where plants grew thicker and stronger. I burrowed underneath the foliage, as a rabbit would, to make my escape. I was able to move more freely. I covered a distance I calculated to be twenty metres. I was totally engulfed by the blackness of night; no light penetrated this small space of the earth. As it would take at least twenty minutes to regain night vision, I refrained from using my torch.

I quickly made an assessment. Brush this thick, this distance away from the water source, was unusual. I couldn't go around this obstacle; I had no idea how far this density of brush continued ahead of me. I knew I had to stick to the bearing.

The checkpoint I was heading for was five hundred metres up the re-entrant I was in, one of many that fed the creek and meandered down this mountain that I was desperately trying to ascend.

'How do I get out of this thick shit?' I questioned myself.

The obstacle was wearing me down. I had to come up with a positive answer to the questions that were swimming around in my head. I stood up, breaking all the branches that had cocooned me.

The foliage intertwined at head level. With my eyes slowly adjusting to the light, I realised my predicament. I had at least one hundred metres to travel. I felt disillusioned.

I started ripping leaves and branches from the foliage to my front. I was furious. I started to imagine being removed from the course because I failed this objective. The pain from my hands ripping on the sharp components of the brush didn't even register.

My footing slipped during the frenzied attack on the adversary that seemed to be determined to make me fail this assessment. I slipped over trying to give the brush a roundhouse kick and fell forward. A new insight dawned.

As my weight came to bear on the brush, it collapsed, supporting me two feet off the ground. The brush was so thick I could walk on top of it. By throwing my body forward, I could stand up and continue the process until I reached open ground.

My adversary was whipped. However, when I got to the other side I thanked the brush for the challenge. Why not? If I faced the same dilemma again tonight, I would have the solution.

I looked down at my watch; it read 0030 hours. I was angry with myself for not coming up with this solution sooner. I had wasted two hours in that creek-line and brush and had only travelled one kilometre. The going became easier as I rapidly walked to the checkpoint. I saw a cylume light stick hanging in a tree. I assessed it to be the checkpoint.

I froze. Two torchlights came on at the checkpoint, and I remembered what the instructor had said at the truck: if you see any lights, avoid them. The torchlights remained on. If this was students banding together, I was getting pissed off. I wanted to get this checkpoint verified so I could make up time. Twenty minutes passed; finally the torchlights were turned off. I moved in. Two instructors sat against a large tree. One spoke to me.

'How many checkpoints have you got, Ranger?'

'One, sir.'

They both broke into roars of laughter.

'Do you know what time it is, Ranger?'

I looked at my watch; it said 0110 hours.

'0110 hours, sir.'

'You better get a wriggle on then, hey Ranger?'

'Yes sir.'

I moved out of their vision, sat down and plotted my next route. The time and space problem needed to be addressed. I had approximately eight kilometres to travel in darkness and less than five hours to do it in. I looked at the grid references I had been given: five checkpoints, one already achieved, and the last one would be the finish.

After I studied them carefully, the locations of these checkpoints told me the direction of travel that the SAS instructors dictated by numbering the checkpoints. I was supposed to complete the remaining checkpoints in sequential order. The time and space issue demanded that I find a more expedient solution.

'Who dares wins.' These words rattled my mind. I needed to adopt a new plan to heighten my chance of completing the selection course without failing any assessments.

My simple plan.

The second checkpoint was one kilometre to the north of the position where I came out of the brush, back in the same creek-line. The third checkpoint was at five hundred and fifty metres north of the first checkpoint, back up this feature (mountain). The fourth checkpoint was one kilometre north of the second checkpoint in the creek-line. The final checkpoint was on the same creek-line, at the point where the road and creek met: approximately three kilometres.

The course dictated that I would be travelling up this feature and down to the same creek-line all night.

My expedient solution.

I wanted to get the next checkpoint (checkpoint three) that was on this feature (mountain), then race back to the creek-line to get checkpoint two, and move swiftly down the creek to get checkpoint four. Checkpoint five, the final checkpoint, was on the same creek-line, at the point where the road and creek met.

I plotted my course to checkpoint three on the feature. It was easy walking, and I made good time. Three cylume light sticks hanging from a tree identified it as the third checkpoint.

If asked by an instructor how many checkpoints I had completed, I would lie and say three, hoping that further investigation didn't catch me out in the subterfuge I had created.

The light sticks were still fifty metres away from me when I heard a voice.

'Who's there?'

'Ranger Roberts,' I said quickly.

'Right, you have been here, now piss off. I want to get some sleep.'

My eyes saw a shadow under a tree that moved to turn a torch on, write something, and then turn the torch off. I was still fifty metres away from the three cylume light sticks.

I couldn't believe my luck.

I moved off swiftly in case I was called to verify checkpoint two, which I didn't have. I quickly found the route I had originally used to move to the first checkpoint. The moon was now high above me, aiding my progress. I rested before moving to the creek-line.

I needed fluids. I took one of the water bottles from my webbing and drank the contents. I looked at my watch to read the time; it was 0230 hours. I had five kilometres to travel in a creek-line before 0600 hours. I felt confident this could be achieved.

I started with a slow jog, ducking under low branches and dodging tree trunks. I emerged in an opening and spotted the path I had thrown myself into, literally. I covered the distance to this scar in the brush quickly.

I chose to return to this spot so I wouldn't have to create another entrance to the creek-line, wasting valuable energy. Also, if I raced down to the creek-line directly below checkpoint three and created another scar in the brush, astute SAS operators would notice this anomaly. An investigation would probably unwrap my subterfuge, a situation I did not desire.

I moved into the damaged foliage to access the creek-line. Eighty metres into the one hundred-metre journey, I came to a wall of brush. I had forgotten that I had originally crawled the first twenty metres. I was at the same spot where I had spat the dummy. With no other choice, I threw my body into the brush once more. It was slow going but I persisted. I told myself that once I reached the creek-line I would give myself a rest. Then I could pursue the other checkpoints.

I bashed at the brush, throwing myself forward into the thicket. I had lost a lot of energy. I was operating on pure aggression towards this adversary. With the next body lunge the brush gave up. I flung myself head first into the murky creek water, again!

I was relieved, but bloody uncomfortable; I was cold and wet. I told myself to think like a soldier and not be concerned that normal people would be at home right now, dry and comfortable. The soldier in me won the argument. To apply to join the SAS is not normal. I made a decision to walk up the creek-line.

Let's concentrate on the task ahead, I told myself. With body and mind working in unison again, I continued north to checkpoint two (my third checkpoint).

Boots sloshing through the water, I counted my paces by looking at the bank, measuring what I believed to be ten metres. When I had travelled that distance, watching the bank and moving through the water, I had some idea of the total distance I had covered. When I had completed ten metres I would do the same thing, adding the lengths together.

I had reached nine hundred and sixty metres when I heard a noise.

'What's your name, Ranger?' I heard the muffled question.

Above me came an answer that I couldn't understand due to the noise of the creek. Others were obviously still out here with me. I continued to move up the creek. Suddenly a torch was on me.

'What's your name, Ranger?' the owner of the torch asked.

'Ranger Roberts,' I answered softly.

He sat on a fallen log that reached to the other side of the creek bank. Hanging from a branch were two cylume light sticks that were obscured briefly until he moved.

'Righto, Ranger, keep going, it's not over yet.'

I obeyed and kept walking in the creek with water up to my knees. The third checkpoint was accomplished. It was 0350 hours and I had one kilometre to travel in the uncomfortable environment I had chosen to reach the fourth checkpoint. Two more checkpoints and I would be home. Once again, I used the bank to measure the distance that I had travelled.

My legs were aching from the cold. I talked to myself, encouraging my body to work with my mind. Together, they shut out any uncomfortable sensations, putting me into a euphoric state. Sleep deprivation was rearing its ugly head.

While experiencing this euphoria, I decided to run in the creek-line, and fell over frequently. I continued this type of activity for about thirty minutes. I then realised that I hadn't been judging the distance that I had travelled.

I gave myself a dressing-down. I stood in the creek-line and abused myself for being incompetent. How could I be so dumb? Fatigue had its grip around my usually stable functions. Yelling at myself gave me an opportunity to pause.

This allowed my normal functions to return. It's all right, I said to myself, just move down the creek-line quietly and listen for noise like you heard at the last checkpoint. Just get this one, then you're home. No one can miss a road–creek junction. I felt relieved that my brain was feeding my body sensible directions.

I moved off along the creek-line, trying to be as quiet as I could. I heard a noise; it wasn't near me; in fact, it was behind me. It was another confirmation that I wasn't out here alone. I needed more information if I was going to change direction. It could be just another ranger giving himself a dressing-down. Then I heard the words that I was waiting for.

'What's your name, Ranger?'

I couldn't hear the reply over the noise of the creek and my boots sloshing in the water, so I froze to identify the correct direction that this muffled conversation was coming from. The voices were behind me and on the bank of this creek-line.

I turned around to locate the fourth checkpoint. Moving slowly, aware that I had already foolishly passed this checkpoint, I told myself to remain vigilant.

Ahead of me were eight cylume light sticks tied to a piece of string hanging from a branch above the creek-line. I focused harder on the light sticks, which rapidly became blurred, and the illumination of them was now forming a single solid glow. In my fatigue, the sight held no rationale. From eight lights to a big single glow, when my objective would be identified by four light sticks? I utilised my training to observe objects at night.

'Look to the right and focus,' I ordered myself.

Immediately the glow lessened. I finally focused on four cylume light sticks slightly swinging in the breeze. I realised then that I had walked right under them when my mind had engaged the body into high gear. The running effort was extremely foolish, almost causing me to fail. I would have to be careful not to lose the plot again.

I pulled my wet boots out of the water to climb the bank to the instructor. Consistent with the vigilance of the other instructors, he noticed me before I had even seen him. I was looking straight ahead when a voice five metres to my right asked the most frequent question I had been asked throughout the night.

'What's your name, Ranger?'

'Ranger Roberts.'

'Get going, you are running out of time.'

'Yes sir.'

I checked my watch as I ran the short distance back to the bank of the creek-line I had recently crawled up. The time was now 0445 hours. I was shocked that this time was a reality. I must've used more time than I thought locating this last checkpoint.

The creek-line was only lightly wooded. I decided to run along the bank. If the brush grew denser, I would enter the creek to continue my journey. I still had to judge the distance I was travelling, so all my concentration was directed to this factor.

To gauge distances at night and on the run is extremely difficult. As the moon was still illuminating the ground, I was able to employ a system to ensure my judgement was accurate. When I had travelled what I calculated to be fifty metres, I would stop and look behind to check that this seemed right.

By the system I was using, I had travelled fifteen hundred metres. The time was 0515 hours. I had travelled fifteen hundred metres in thirty minutes. At this rate I would finish with fifteen minutes to spare, barring any further obstacles.

Then suddenly, I heard rapid gun-fire.

The noise was deafening. The breaking dawn rapidly turned to mid-morning just for a few seconds as flashes emitted from weapon barrels. I instinctively hit the deck, confused as to if these weapons were shooting at me. I needed to assess the situation rapidly.

No bullets cracked past my ear; the gun-fire sounded like blanks. The direction of the gun-fire was to my left, about one hundred metres away. The lack of shadow on the ground where the gun-fire originated indicated to me that it was an opening in the bush or a road slicing through the bush. The amount of quick gun-fire indicated an ambush had just been sprung. Was I in the ambush?

Still lying flat on the ground, I heard somebody speak.

'Stand up and move over here,' the command was bellowed.

Automatically I stood to my feet and moved towards the site where the training ambush had been sprung. The next conversation confused me.

'We don't walk on roads in the regiment. Your exercise is finished for tonight.'

I was about twenty metres away from the road when it finally dawned on me that I wasn't responsible for springing the ambush. I lowered myself and crawled away, in case these instructors assumed that I had been walking on the road, so I would not face the punishment that was handed out to the men caught in the ambush.

I moved back to the creek bank. I had reassuring information now: the road did exist. I reached the road–creek junction at 0550 hours. I sat down with the rest of the men. About thirty had completed the task so far. Peter and I were the only ones in this group who belonged to Hut 10. He asked me a simple question: 'How did you find that, mate?'

'Up and down,' I replied.

We both giggled.

I wasn't about to tell him that I only went up the mountain once. I never told anyone.

Troy, Nathan, Tony and Ben came in separately just before the 0600 hours deadline. Together we had completed the challenges that were set for us. We, as a hut, having been reduced down to six men, had a one hundred per cent pass record for all tasks assigned. At 0600 hours, Kojak called out the names of the rangers who had failed one or more objective. Hut 10 personnel remained seated as a group.

Kojak spoke to the other group.

'Men, unfortunately I stand in front of a fine body of soldiers who are now given the opportunity to leave this course graciously, with their heads held high. Individually you have done your best and I am proud to have been one of your instructors. Unfortunately, the regiment only requires a small quota of recruits for this year's intake.

'You have all failed one or more of the challenges set.

'At this stage, I must inform you that you will not be considered to continue with the selection cycle. This group is now required to hand in their equipment when we return to camp. I know that this is disappointing; however, you will be considered for selection next year before newcomers.

'Thank you for your effort. I hope to see you all attempting selection next year. Dismiss and await the buses.'

'Wow, what a bombshell!' I said.

Troy answered us all.

'This has never happened before. They're sacking over eighty men in one fell swoop. What's this about?' he asked himself out loud.

'Maybe they're bringing the interrogation forward. No …' he laughed at himself, 'that's ridiculous.'

Peter took this speculation seriously. He got a piece of gaffer tape and stuck it to his knife, then secured it under his armpit with a cord tied to it.

'What do you reckon, Peter?' I asked.

'Be prepared. I was once a boy scout. That's my motto.' We both laughed.

Chapter Eight

Man against mountains

I looked at the grid references given to me. There were six altogether. I looked at the map. Each of the grid references indicated a spot-height on five mountains. The last one was where the Land Rover had met the bus.

I looked at the map. The first peak to climb was called Abbey. The height I had to go to was twelve hundred metres. The equipment I was carrying weighed fifty kilos.

The map would be of use when moving across the ground to another mountain, but right now it was plain to see that I was looking at Abbey and the map could not give up any secrets to make it easier to climb.

I attacked this monster, straight up. The going was easy for the first three hours. I then hit the base of Abbey and decided to have something to eat to give me enough energy to move forward. I commenced my ascent again. The gradient rose sharply. I slung my weapon over my shoulder, enabling me to use the smaller trees to pull myself up.

I used a system: for one hour I would pull myself forward, and then rest for ten minutes. I disciplined myself to this system for three hours. Then, unavoidably, I needed to lessen the work rate. I walked for fifty minutes and rested for twenty. This again changed. After a further two hours the system became walking for forty minutes, resting for thirty minutes. After another two hours, the system was walk for thirty minutes, rest for thirty minutes.

I was resting too much, so I gave my body a rest for fifteen minutes and walked for thirty minutes. With this routine, I decreased the rest period down to ten minutes and managed to walk for thirty. Enduring this thirty-minute period became extremely strenuous. The time was slipping away on me; I had to push at this rate.

It was 1400 hours and I still had not reached the spur-line that would take me to the spot-height. I kept pushing the rate I had set myself: thirty minutes walking, ten minutes resting. I calculated the rate I was achieving; this would get me to the top of the mountain by 1600 hours. After another rest, I picked myself up to do the last thirty minutes' push and finally saw the instructors on top of Mount Abbey. I reached their position.

'Oh, it's Ranger Roberts,' one of them said.

My name was becoming overused. Now they were recognising me before asking me to identify myself.

'Ranger Roberts, do you know the next grid reference that you have to go to?'

I raised my arm and pointed to the mountain west of this position, about seven kilometres away in the sunset.

'Mount Trio, behind which the sun will set, sir,' is all I said between rapid breaths.

'Leave here and go as far as you can before dark. You must contact base on your radio when you stop, to give them your night location. Do you understand this directive?'

'Yes sir,' I bellowed.

'You don't have to yell at me, we are all on the same mountain.' He finished speaking, pointing his finger to the west.

It had taken from dawn to dusk to achieve the first checkpoint. I moved swiftly down the mountain, heading west. I had two hours of light left to travel in. I was about a third of the way down when I noticed the sun slip behind Mount Trio.

I looked around to find a spot to sleep. I was on a forty-five-degree incline. I found a flat rock to sit on, pulled my radio out of my pack and turned it on, and looked at the piece of paper that had my call sign written on it. It was BC10.

'Base, this is BC10. Over.' Pause.

'Base, this is BC10. Over.' Pause. My radio crackled into life.

'BC10, this is base. Over.'

'Base, this is BC10. Night location grid 336872. Over.' This was the location I was at on the side of this mountain.

'BC10, this is base. Roger. Over.'

'Base, this is BC10. Roger. Out.' I turned the radio set off to save batteries.

After that short conversation, base now knew my location for the night. A pin in a plot map would mark the spot. The instructors would be laughing at my uncomfortable position. I needed to tie my sleeping bag to a tree, to not have it slip away in the middle of the night. I decided to get my bedding sorted before it got too dark.

When this was done, I prepared a meal from my ration pack. It was good to be by myself, without the instructors abusing me. Darkness fell quickly, as did the temperature. I got into my sleeping bag and listened to nothing. It was bliss. I fell asleep quickly.

It was 0500 hours when I woke. The darkness of night became lighter, as the sun took its usual position and started to rise behind me in the east. I was still facing westwards toward

Mount Trio. I looked at the map to study my route to the top of the mountain. I realised that I had underestimated the distance to the foot of Mount Trio. Last night I thought it was only seven kilometres, but now looking at the map, I saw it was at least thirteen.

With this information, I quickly packed my gear away and briskly walked down Mount Abbey. I decided that I would eat breakfast and lunch when I reached the foot of Mount Trio.

I finally had left Mount Abbey behind; it had taken four hours to descend altogether. I still had to travel eleven kilometres to begin scaling Mount Trio.

The going was easy. Lightly wooded areas and the creeklines were mostly empty of water. I could just plough through, not having my pace dictated by obstacles. The rate I was achieving was quite fast. Sweat was dripping off me, and my heart was pounding with my lungs heaving to get as much oxygen as I could handle. The only rest I took was to stop moving, to take the opportunity to flick my pack up to my upper back to give my lower back a brief reprieve from the weight it had to bear.

I had travelled the thirteen kilometres in three hours. It was now 1200 hours. I was at the foot of Mount Trio. Her skirt was filled with fresh-flowing creeks. There were smaller pine trees moving into a forest of larger pine trees. Underfoot was littered with pine needles. The surroundings were magnificent. Unfortunately I couldn't admire her beauty.

I stopped and had lunch and made a cup of coffee. When I finished, I lay back on the pine needles, which massaged my aching back. I'd been resting there for ten minutes when the serenity of this mountain overcame me. I fell asleep.

I awoke with a shock; I had not intended to fall asleep. My left arm shot in front of my eyes to check the time. It was 1300 hours. I was angry, so I took it out on the mountain.

'You seductive bitch! You use your beauty to bedazzle those who are not aware. I can't sleep at your feet. I must climb to the top and face you eye to eye,' I yelled.

I had no explanation for this outburst, or why I would imagine this mountain as a female. A movie I enjoyed as a child, *Picnic at Hanging Rock*, came to mind. The story revolved around four girls' disappearance: it seemed the mountain that they were on had swallowed them up. Mount Trio had the same mysterious capabilities, or so I thought.

The direction of travel was really simple: follow the spur-line; when that is finished, follow the next one. The spur-lines were not steep at all. The gradual climb just moved left to right. I started out on my ascent, feeling rather refreshed by the unwanted sleep that I had.

'Thank you, Mount Trio,' I softly spoke.

The mountain was invigorating; her beauty just went deeper as I moved into her forest. The colour of the bird life was stunning. The oxygen she produced was pure, fresh air that is only found where man has not intruded with development. Butterflies fluttered around me. Moss grew on the mature trees. She was seducing me to stop and enjoy her. I kept walking without resting; I couldn't stop. She would put me into a deep slumber, one from which I would never awake.

I broke out of the forest to see that the mountain top did not nurture any trees. A carpet of healthy grass grew on it. I was four hundred metres away from the instructors. I moved quickly towards them. It was now 1530 hours, and I wanted to be off this mountain by dark. The wind hit me hard; I was walking straight into it. The hardest leg of this journey was to be the end. I finally made their campsite.

'Ranger Roberts, it's good to see you. You are the first one to make two checkpoints.'

I didn't believe him.

'What are your future intentions?' he asked.

'Mount Hassle is my next port of call.'

'Do you know where it is?'

I looked at the map to orientate it to the ground. I had not yet looked at the view, as I had had my head down fighting the wind, walking into the checkpoint. I looked up to see an awesome sight: about ten kilometres away was an enormous, jagged, rocky-faced mountain.

That was all it was, a mountain of rock. No trees, no creeks, no life, just rock which went as high as Mount Abbey. I remembered how difficult Mount Abbey was, but at least there were trees to pull me up the mountain. Mount Hassle was just that — a hassle.

I left the instructors to make my way down Mount Trio. What lay ahead after this terrific experience was just pain. No pain, no gain, I reminded myself.

I was off Mount Trio in just an hour. As I moved away from the instructors, I found a well-used bushwalkers' track, which gave me the opportunity to run to the bottom of Mount Trio. As I walked out of her skirt of smaller trees the quality of air changed.

Mount Hassle was in front of me. I was going to get as close as possible before dark. I travelled the correctly estimated ten kilometres by running and walking. There was a small creekline at the foot of Mount Hassle. This was where I would stay the night. I had a big meal and radioed my position to base.

Once again, they would be putting a pin into the plot map to indicate my position. 'Look, he's got Mount Hassle in front of him.' I imagined laughter as they did this. The serious side, however, was that they had a responsibility for my safety.

Having conquered Mount Trio without too much rest, I quickly fell asleep. I awoke about 0300 hours, the time I was used to getting up at the selection camp. I made a quick cup of coffee, had some breakfast and packed my gear away.

I started the assault on this rocky mountain. I had travelled up the face about one hundred metres when it got extremely steep. Every time I moved forward, I would slip back the same distance — at times more.

The weight in my pack was becoming an issue. I had to work out a solution to this problem. I tried tying a rope around my waist, dragging it behind me. This worked for a short period, but the higher I went, the larger the boulders became. The rocks gripped my pack, once again impeding progress.

I tried another technique; crawling forward I pushed the pack in front of me. Although painful, tedious and seemingly futile, I found this to be the best method to conquer this 'Barren Bitch'. I continued this action, a bit at a time, slowly creeping my way up the hill.

On the side of a spur-line, I headed for the ridge. I was hoping that the ridge would be wide enough to walk on. I kept pushing my pack forward, and then crawled to it. I looked back on the progress I was making. I was four hundred metres up, about halfway to the spur-line ridge.

I looked at my boots. They had the toes kicked out of them, so that my socks could be easily seen. The colour of my sock toes was red. Until now I had no idea I had damaged my feet.

The pain reached my brain. I had not suffered any damage to my feet until now. All the dragging of my feet had destroyed my boots. Now my toes had an extra inch to move in my boots before being snug and safe. No pain, no gain, I repeated to myself.

I continued up the rocky slippery-dip of a mountain. I finally reached the ridge of the spur-line. Below me were three small figures using the same technique I had devised, each of them at different heights, taking different routes to the ridge of the spur-line that I now stood on.

The ridge offered a small area to walk along, two feet wide. As I took my first step, the pain of my damaged toes was excruciating. I told my brain to stop feeling the pain so I could complete this phase. It didn't listen. I limped forward to the summit.

I was beginning to adjust to the pain in my feet; however, as I had resumed carrying the pack, my back was crying in pain. I desperately needed to rest. There was a noisy battle going on in my head, every pain receptor screaming for attention. My body was demanding relief, my mind demanding I go on. I just kept saying to myself, 'No pain, no gain', the mantra of necessity.

I finally reached the summit. In the distance I saw a figure pressed to the earth. I assumed the instructor's voice was incoherent due to the wind that blew over this desolate ridge-line. As I neared their position I realised I was wrong.

'Ranger Hardman, how many is that?'

'Fifty-five, sir.'

It was Tony, who was being ritually punished by an instructor who was determined to break him. Tony turned his head and smiled at me. I smiled back. He was, as we all were, getting stronger from the extra attention and physical punishments. I left him bouncing up and down with ease. The instructors took my name and I left their presence rapidly. I wasn't going back the direction I had come from. The next mountain to conquer was called Mount Henning. It was to the east of me. As I got to the eastern side of Mount Hassle, I saw my objective.

Mount Henning didn't have mature trees on it. It looked like it was covered in brambles, from the bottom to the top. I stopped looking at it. I would be there soon enough. I followed another ridge that led to the east. When the mountain got steep again I started sliding down, not paying too much attention to the pain in my feet and back.

I was at the bottom with a couple of hours of daylight left to get closer to Mount Henning. I was moving swiftly, ignoring the pain. A thought entered my head: 'You haven't been drinking much today.'

Looking at the ground, I noticed an anthill, and then heard my weapon crash to the ground. 'That's strange, I'm carrying my rifle.' A grey mist overcame me.

I came to, my eyes level with the anthill. I was totally disorientated; I had not accepted I had passed out. I was still wondering how I ended up in this strange position. My faculties caught up with the event that just happened. Wow, I must've passed out.

It was late enough to call it a day. I prepared an evening meal. I also poured two sachets of electrolytes into each water bottle and downed them. I called base on the radio to let them know of my location for the evening. This done and still daylight, I fell asleep.

I awoke to hear two voices having a conversation as they walked past my position. I paid no further attention to this incident, falling back to sleep. My body clock was working again. I rose at 0300 hours to have a full breakfast out of a tin, and coffee to follow.

I pulled out my medical kit to dress my damaged toes. I squeezed my feet into each boot gingerly. Then with tape, I repaired my boots the best I could. I was ready to walk again.

As first light hit the range, my body complained of cramps. I kept walking to allow the limbs to loosen up. Within the hour, my body was limber and not stiffening up to cause distractions.

My focus was on Mount Henning. 'Two to conquer,' I said to myself. First I would need more water. I looked at the map. There was a spot marked where I was headed that indicated a water resupply, especially placed there so the rangers could refill their empty water bottles.

I found the water resupply spot. It had two plastic bottles holding twenty litres each. I filled all my bottles, plus drank one water bottle, then filled it again. With this done, I had all my water bottles full.

I started towards Mount Henning. The walk was easy and not too taxing on my feet. At 0900 hours the temperature rose sharply. The ranges had been quite mild during the day; however, today it felt like I was in heatwave conditions. I was thankful that I had replenished my water bottles. I had already used one water bottle, leaving me with five.

Three hours of solid walking would get me to the base of Mount Henning. Then I would have to scale it. If I could get up and down it today I could get to the next mountain before time ran out.

At 1200 hours I was at the foot of Mount Henning. The perception I had about Mt Henning being covered in brambles was correct. One hundred metres into this terrain, the thorns on the small twisted trees dug into my flesh. My clothes and skin were being sliced constantly.

I pushed up the mountain. It took fours hours to reach the ridge-line, which led to the summit. The ridge was bare, as I had experienced on the other mountain tops. I finally reached the position of the instructors, where I was told something unusual.

'Ranger Roberts, we have been ordered to keep you on top of this mountain with us tonight. Tomorrow morning a helicopter will lift us off. That's the finish of the Sterling Range phase.

There's a storm front coming in and it's too dangerous to continue the exercise. These are orders from the senior instructor.'

I didn't believe a word they said. They were trying to fuck with my brain. I went and prepared my sleeping spot and had some dinner. I was thinking that tomorrow I would have to move swiftly to complete the challenge in its entirety. I knew I needed a solid sleep, so I did just that, and fell asleep.

At 0130 hours I was suddenly awoken by fierce winds and heavy rain. I thought for an instant that maybe the instructors were not lying. I discounted this thought by assessing the storm to be coincidental. I fell back to sleep.

The noise of my shelter, flapping severely, woke me up. It was daylight. I looked at my watch, which read 0630. I must have needed that sleep. At first I thought the commotion belonged to the storm that had arrived last night. I got out of my sleeping bag to find out where the commotion was really coming from. It was a helicopter, just as the instructors had told me. They didn't lie. I quickly packed my gear up and hobbled to the helicopter. My feet were extremely tender this morning. The helicopter ride back to base camp took twenty minutes. It was great to get a bird's-eye view of the places and routes I took on this exercise. I alighted from the helicopter to face Kojak.

'Well done, Ranger Roberts. You achieved the best result,' Kojak congratulated me.

I sat down on a log, looking at him disbelievingly. I removed my boots to see the damage I had caused to my feet.

'When we get back to camp, I want you to get the RAP to fix your feet,' he commanded.

'Well done again,' he finished.

I still didn't believe him. I felt sick to the stomach when he ordered me to have the barbaric blister treatment. The other rangers soon were delivered to the base location, by the same means of transport that I had enjoyed. For some of them, the helicopter ride would have been thrilling, most likely their first such experience. I awaited the arrival of the men from Hut 10.

Ben returned first, and we had a short conversation.

'Ben, how did you go mate? I asked, not expecting an answer.

'I only got three: Magog, Henning, and Trio. I was about five hundred metres up Hassle when I got told over the radio to stop where I was; transport would pick me up in the morning. I was spewing. I could have got Hassle if they let me continue. Instead, I had to be winched off the side of the mountain this morning. Do you know what's going on?'

'No idea, mate. I got taken off Henning this morning.'

I was surprised that Ben offered me so much information. He must have missed human contact, for when he got the first opportunity to share he couldn't refuse.

'How many did you get, Paul?'

Ironically, I wasn't able to answer his question straight away, which did lead to a facial expression that Ben had not offered to date. He was disappointed. As the helicopter rotors ripped through the air, no one could hold a conversation. The helicopter finally departed to pick up more rangers as Tony, Peter and Nathan arrived at our log.

'G'day Nathan, Peter, Tony.' I greeted them individually.

'How did you do, lads?' I asked, using the question that Ben had asked me — who now sported a pained expression as I avoided his rare attempt at communicating verbally.

'I got three: Abbey, Trio, Hassle. I was just about to climb Henning when I got told to wait where I was, and that I'd be picked up in the morning,' Peter answered.

'Me too, I got three and was about to climb Trio,' Tony answered.

'Well, I got three too. I was just about to climb Magog.' Nathan's voice was drowned out by the return of the helicopter.

Troy walked over to us with his body slightly bent to balance himself against the force of the downwash caused by the rotation of the blades. He joined our small group.

He looked relieved to be among friends. Tony asked the most repeated question of the morning.

'How did you go, Troy?'

'I think I got four. I reached the top of Mount Trio at about 6 pm. I was told that's the end of the exercise and await pick-up in the morning. What's going on?'

No one answered. We didn't know. I knew that I had four mountains completed; however, I wasn't going to brag about it. Troy and I had the same amount of peaks accomplished. I wondered why we had this challenge cut short. We were about to find out.

Kojak called everybody together: the instructors, the cooks for the instructors, the helicopter crew, and the rangers.

'Who're those blokes?' I asked Troy softly.

'They're the surveillance teams who catch rangers who cheat on this phase,' Troy answered me.

There were ten men in this group, unshaven and just as filthy as us. They joined the group that waited to hear from Kojak. He commenced his brief.

'Right, men, we are vacating this area immediately after this brief. The Sterling Ranges are about to experience severe winds and thunderstorm activity. The surveillance team thank you for your effort, and to the two rangers caught walking on roads, well done.

'You will travel in the vehicles you came down in. Instructors will travel with the rangers, who will travel on the bus that is expected in this location shortly. Cooks and support staff will travel in their own vehicles. The next three senior instructors will travel with me on the helicopter. Are there any questions?'

A short pause.

'Good, now move to your designated mode of transport.'

As Kojak finished his brief, a touring bus pulled to a halt behind him. As if he had a direct line to the one who controls the weather, the wind speed increased and a torrent of rain belted us heavily. We quickly gathered our gear and loaded it onto the bus.

The same base camp that was fully functional one hour ago returned to its natural state. The vehicles departed in convoy with haste and purpose.

The bus trip took hours. We stopped for morning tea at a garage, where the bus refuelled. We journeyed on to a destination unknown.

Troy advised us, 'Eat big, lads. This will be the last opportunity to eat for five days. We are about to begin the challenge.'

We followed his advice and ensured that we still had food to eat on the bus.

Chapter Nine

The challenge: the stretcher carry

Another stop and darkness had caught us. We were awoken for another food and piss stop. The garage was in an isolated area, the toilets separate. While waiting to use the amenities, I thought of how full of food I was. Maybe by excreting some of the waste in my body, I might feel like eating again.

The toilet journey had not given me the desire to eat. I returned to the bus to try and sleep off my upset stomach. I was to rue this foolish decision.

The bus stopped again. I woke up to notice that we were in the middle of nowhere; the pitch-blackness surrounded the bus. An instructor stepped onto the bus screaming at us. I had forgotten the screams of abuse. It had been almost five days without it. I missed the silence that I had appreciated when I was alone.

'Get off the fucking bus. Line up beside the bus and strip,' he shouted.

'Strip, is that what he said?' I asked myself. The answer was in front of me when I left the bus: men were starting to strip.

'Put your clothes out in front of you,' he added.

'Sir, all the way?' a bemused Nathan questioned.

'Yes, Ranger, all the way. We want to look up your bum crack to see that you haven't got a Mars Bar up it.'

He's joking, I thought. With my clothes crumpled in front of my pack, another instructor searched every item of clothing I had, my webbing and my pack. Feeling the cool breeze on my body I hugged my chest to try and keep warm. Looking down the inspection line I saw others doing the same. When the instructor had finished searching my clothes and equipment, he ordered me to leave my gear and move to the torchlight. Nathan was still in his trousers and was quite agitated that he had to expose himself. He had nothing to fear, for when he finally disrobed and joined us his own hands couldn't hide the extra length of penis that hung against his thigh. I was shocked. A glimpse was enough; now I understood why he showered in shorts.

We reached the vicinity that the torch illuminated. To our horror, the torch was being used to inspect bum cracks. A couple of the lads were making jokes to deal with this invasion of privacy.

'Sir, that torch is not big enough. If you're going to put a torch up my arse I want a big one,' one ranger said.

'I hope you got K-Y Jelly to go on that torch, sir,' said another.

Big bravado, for when it was their turn to spread their cheeks, they were both quiet as mice.

My turn; I hoped a dag was not hanging out. A silly thought, but that was what I was thinking as I bent over and pulled my cheeks apart so the torchlight could inspect my nether region.

'Move back to your gear,' I was ordered.

'Jesus, Ranger, have you got a licence for that?' Nathan's face went crimson.

When we returned to our equipment it was in complete disarray. Every pocket in our clothing was turned inside out, our packs were completely empty, and the pouches that could be turned inside out had been. My webbing was stripped and I had to put it back together. Its pouches were also turned inside out.

All the rangers had gone through the crack inspection. We had finished putting our gear back together, when we were given the next directive.

'Rangers from Hut 10, over here.' He pointed to where the bus was.

'The rest of you men, listen for your name — that will be your team for the next phase.'

I didn't listen to the names being called. I was just overjoyed to be with the same crew that I had started with at the beginning. I knew everyone of us was totally committed to passing the selection course. Everyone of us would do our best to complete this phase.

'You know your teams. Get some sleep now. You will need it,' he commanded.

After having a lot of sleep on the bus I still felt fatigued. I watched my mates all rest their heads on their pack and fall asleep. I was tired; unfortunately I was hungry as well. I settled my head on a comfortable part of my pack and fell asleep.

All too soon I heard the command: 'Get up and move in to me.'

We picked ourselves up and moved towards the voice.

'Hut 10, here are your instructions. You are to follow them to the letter. Any deviation from these orders and the whole team will fail this objective. Ranger Ben Jones, take charge,' he directed.

* * *

Ben had the sealed envelope that the instructor had passed to him during his brief.

We huddled together to read the instructions. I held a torch on the papers. Ben read the orders to all of us, still only speaking when spoken to or to give orders. Most Hut 10 members followed his example, keeping idle chit-chat to a minimum.

'You are to move to grid location 33467291 to meet an agent at 1200 hours,' Ben finished.

Peter had already located the grid reference, and informed us, 'That's fifteen k's away. We better get moving.'

We collected our gear and were walking in the direction of the grid location where we were to meet an agent, when the instructor called us back.

'Come here, I got something for you. Go around the back of this tent and put a sandbag into your packs.'

We did as he asked. I picked up my sandbag and it weighed about thirty kilos. I put my pack on feeling the extra weight. My knees almost buckled.

'That's an extra thirty kilos, men. Now you are carrying a simulated operational load, with the twenty kilos in your pack already and ten kilos on your belt, and your rifle weighing five kilos. That's sixty-five kilos per man. If you want to come to my regiment, this is the softest load you will ever carry. If this is too much for you, quit now and save me some time.'

Nobody spoke.

'Go,' his final command.

We headed off in the direction that we had started in before being called back for the additional weight. The first I noticed was my feet. I had done a minor repair to them, but the state of my boots caused more problems. The hole in the toes was allowing my feet to move forward an inch.

This problem caused friction burns, due to my feet having so much freedom of movement instead of remaining snugly in the boot.

The dressings I had on my feet were starting to peel away from my toes. My feet were getting more damaged again.

I had to get the pain out of my head. I moved to the front of the team, with my compass set on the bearing. I concentrated on ensuring we were going in the right direction. We stopped at the five-kilometre mark to rest. Fifteen minutes later, we were up and moving again. I remained in the front, telling myself to keep going and not feel the pain.

I maintained the pace that everybody was happy with. I still took responsibility for the direction that we were heading in. I needed to think about something else other than the pain.

At the ten-kilometre mark we stopped and had another rest. This time I got a roll of tape that was in my webbing and used the rest period to tape my toes and the holes in the ends of my boots. I was trying to limit the amount of movement my feet had in my boots. I felt certain this repair job would last another five kilometres. We started again. I remained in the front to allow responsibility to distract me from the pain.

I saw the agent first.

'Quick, come with me. I have an injured man who has got information for your government,' he said.

This was the scenario to be played out: an injured man, who we would obviously have to stretcher carry for whatever distance they wanted. With equipment weighing sixty kilos and an eighty-kilo man, I wasn't looking forward to this activity. The pretend injured man started screaming. I moved to where he was on a stretcher, took my bush hat off and shoved it in his mouth. I looked at him seriously, directly into his eyes, and raised my first finger to my mouth, indicating for to him to shut up. He went quiet.

Ben was in charge of this challenge, so we let him move away to collect his thoughts while the rest of us worked out the best way to carry this malingerer. Ben returned and gave his orders.

'Four men will carry this bloke for two kilometres. The two rear blokes will change and become protection for the stretcher party. The front blokes will move to the rear, carrying the stretcher for a maximum distance of four kilometres. The first change will be at two kilometres, which will be a rest as well. Those who start as protection will move to the front and carry the stretcher for a maximum distance of four kilometres. Any questions?'

There would be no questions. He was under assessment and we would all work together to make his period under scrutiny flow with ease.

I moved quickly to the front to disappoint Tony and Peter as they jockeyed for the position I claimed. I still needed to concentrate on something else other than the pain in my feet. I was up the front and I had four kilometres to carry additional weight. I jumped a couple of times to try and get the stretcher to sit comfortably on my pack.

It didn't; it was pinching my shoulder flesh into my collarbone, forcing my head down. I tried again with the same result. I was happy: there was more pain than in my feet. The pinching in my shoulder was definitely distracting; however, it wouldn't debilitate me as my feet would if I allowed myself to concentrate on the pain that they were in.

We started to move off, with Ben ordering Tony to call the time.

'Left, left, left, right, left.'

He was calling the time to ensure that carrying the stretcher would be comfortable for those involved. If we didn't put the correct foot down at the same time, the stretcher would bounce, making those carrying it extremely uncomfortable.

We had gone about five hundred metres, walking on a gravel road. The gradient was flat, but that was about to change. I forced my neck to straighten briefly, looking down the road. Two hundred metres ahead it started to climb. My head returned to its locked-down position uncontrollably quickly. This enforced body position did not allow my eyes to follow the gradient upward, due to the weight I was carrying and the pinching I was suffering. I could only wait until I reached the base of the rise to know how difficult it was going to be. Troy, up the front and to my left, gave me some indication.

'Fuck me! It goes on forever.'

'Come on, boys, let's get over this mother,' Ben encouraged. The shock of hearing him speak motivated us unexplainably.

Then the two blokes who had ended up doing protection party encouraged us also.

'Come on, lads, you can do it,' one of them said.

'Dig deep, lads, you can do this,' said the other.

I didn't recognise their voices. I was panting too much and the cries of my fellow stretcher-bearers drowned out further encouragement. We were hurting; just putting one foot forward became a monumental task. Ben called the time, another shock.

'Left, left, left, right, left.'

I pushed forward, holding the growls of pain between clenched teeth. Ben called the time again.

'Left, left, left, right, left.'

I listened to the time to remove myself from the effort that was being asked of me. Then Troy said something that lifted my spirit.

'One hundred metres to go, then it's downhill from there,' he informed us.

I just kept putting one foot forward. My leg muscles strained from the weight that I was carrying. There were three others that I told my brain not to let down: the other stretcher-bearers. I had to carry my load; to collapse now could seriously injure one of them and they would have their chance of being selected stripped from them. Just get to the top of the hill, I told myself. Troy enlightened us on our progress.

'We've made it!'

I looked in the only direction that the weight of the stretcher would allow: down at my feet. The gradient of the road started to dip; we were moving downhill. The exertion required getting up this hill needed to be redirected. The decline in the road started to increase the pace of the stretcher team.

The fear I held for the stretcher team if I was to pass out was now a reality for each team member. To slip over at this pace would create a disaster; someone would be seriously injured. Boots were slipping and sliding, as we did whatever it took to maintain our balance.

The concentration required to keep in step with the team was almost insurmountable. Ben noticed the difficulty we were having. He called the time for us. His call started off at the pace our tired limbs were experiencing, quickly.

'Left, left, left, right, left.'

The words shot from his mouth at the speed of rapid gun-fire. We were in step again, but at a rapid pace that could not be sustained. Ben slowed the call down again.

'Left, left, left, right, left.'

Still in step to the time Ben was calling, the stretcher team managed a slower pace. The cohesion returned to the team. No longer out of control, we marched purposefully down the rest of the hill. The changeover came a further five hundred metres along the road on a flat section. Ben simply commanded us, 'Stop and rest. Move in fifteen minutes. Position changes are as I informed you at the beginning of the task.'

I was assisted to have the stretcher taken off my shoulder that was now numb. The end of the length of wood running alongside our patient was in my hand. The team waited for all bearers to be in this position to lower the stretcher gently. We moved off to the side of the road for a well-earned rest. No one spoke a word except to utter the odd groan.

The rest time elapsed quicker than I'd expected. But I was quick to close down this thought. Ben was in charge and it was better to accept the way things were than to create resentment. Resentment festering away could ruin the team's effort. We had to stick together. Ben was the boss and we had to let him lead.

Even though I thought I only had four minutes' rest, I knew that once I returned to the stretcher this thought would lose its credence. The pain would be back.

I was at the rear of the stretcher, with Troy beside me. We looked at each other, nodded our heads together and raised the stretcher to sit on our shoulders in time with each other. The pinching began again, and the pain followed immediately. Our patient was asleep, then awoke when he found himself five feet off the ground.

We moved onto the road to recommence the task. Two more kilometres were all I had to do, then a four-kilometre rest, I encouraged myself.

The new stint on the stretcher was relatively easy compared to the first horrific experience. The ground was consistently flat. The only break from the monotony of the flat gravel road was the slight bends to the left and right.

'Stop and rest. Move in fifteen minutes,' Ben ordered.

Troy and I lowered the stretcher off our shoulders down beside our bodies. When the team was in position, with all of us having fully stretched arms holding the weight of the stretcher, someone said 'lower'. I complied; breaking out of the daydream I was in. It was better to be having a fantasy than to be feeling this pain.

The rest felt longer this time. I took the position of protecting the rear. Troy and I would change at the next one-kilometre mark. My feet screamed in my head of how much pain they were experiencing. They no longer had a distraction to confuse my brain as to where the pain signals should be sent.

We walked for another two kilometres. I had finally gripped control of my brain trying to tell me to stop and relieve this pain I was suffering. The stretcher lowered. I kept standing to not allow my feet to get too comfortable. I didn't want them to seize up and become useless. The rest stops were becoming longer than I thought. I was growing impatient and desired any distraction to ensure that I completed this phase.

I took the front position again. The wooden pole dug into my shoulder with the same intensity that it had before. The walk continued to be easy going; the next two kilometres went quicker than I expected. I reminded myself to keep my mouth shut. I had been wrong every time when it came to judging the time it was taking to complete rest stops and the duration we were working at. We rested, after the familiar routine of lowering our patient.

Two more kilometres, then the long rest. Keep going it, will soon stop. Another leg completed, followed by a fifteen-minute rest. Ben called us together to give us a brief.

'Men, we have travelled ten kilometres. We are to meet another agent at this dam to give us further orders.'

Then he pointed to his map.

'That's two more kilometres to go. How's everybody holding up?'

Everybody acknowledged him verbally except me. I didn't dare open my mouth in case a whimper of pain escaped. I looked him in the eye, nodded my head and raised my thumb up to acknowledge that I was okay.

'Good, that's the rest period over. Back onto the stretcher.'

He was in the stretcher team as well. Like all good leaders, he didn't ask his men to do what he wasn't prepared to do himself.

We lifted the stretcher together to head for the next part of our task: meet with an agent at a dam. It was bloody obvious to me what task we would be given: a dam crossing with the stretcher. The crossing and getting the stretcher across wasn't what was concerning me. The infection I could get, having to swim in stagnant water with the flesh of my feet exposed, was. I was really starting to get distressed at the thought.

The dam was in front of us, one hundred metres ahead. We travelled this distance quickly; it was getting dark as the sun sank over the horizon. The challenge was to get the stretcher across this filthy body of water without drowning the patient. The equipment we had to do this challenge consisted of four plastic jerry cans, each with a capacity of twenty litres, and a length of rope that would reach the other bank of the cesspit.

Ben took control and gave his orders.

'I need the water jerries filled to one quarter of their capacity. Then, using your issued ropes, secure them so they are in a line the length of the stretcher. When that is done, secure your pack and webbing inside your hutchie (plastic sheet). Secure your equipment onto one end of the rope you were issued; it should float next to the stretcher. Then I will need four men, one on each corner of the stretcher, to ensure that the patient doesn't drown. I need one man to swim the rope over and then pull the stretcher over using the rope. We will take his equipment with the stretcher. The odd man out can provide rear protection until we are on the other side, then we will provide his protection as he crosses. Any questions?'

As before, there were none. It had been a detailed brief, and everybody knew what to do. I still hesitated to go near the dam edge. I was to be relieved of my apprehension when Ben gave me an order.

'Paul, I want you to be rear protection. Leave your pack; we will take it over on the stretcher.'

My pack had the privilege of staying dry. I moved down the road to ensure nobody snuck up on the team while they were preparing the stretcher for a water crossing. I had to wait until the preliminaries were completed. When they were ready to go into the water, I was called to their position to provide protection and assistance if anything went wrong.

The crossing went smoothly and successfully, then it was my turn. The logical part of my brain said, walk around the outside. The rational side said, if you do you will fail. I emptied my water bottles onto the ground to create as much flotation as I could. I rested my rifle on my webbing and kicked with my legs.

Logic was forgotten. I entered the dam and kicked furiously to remain afloat. I was surprised how quickly I achieved the crossing.

When I rejoined my mates on the other side, they were congratulating each other on a job well done. Ben smiled as I approached and I gave him the thumbs up as he had done for me during the selection course. He moved into my personal space and picked me up and gave me a massive bear hug. The instructor assessing us, who had kept hidden throughout the challenge, appeared.

'That's the stretcher challenge completed. Now as a team you will travel ten kilometres to your next stand, which will commence at 0500 hours. The new team leader will be Ranger Troy Mills.

'Move out in five minutes. Any questions?'

There were none.

Chapter Ten

This is going to sting

The instructor started to walk away, when he turned sharply on his heel and ordered, 'Ranger Paul Roberts, come here.'

I moved in his direction, doing my best to cover up the pain I had in my feet, which was hopeless. It didn't matter if I walked on my toes, heels or sides of my feet; I was limping and couldn't disguise it any longer.

'You look like you have a little trouble with your feet,' he stated.

That's the understatement of the century, I thought. 'Yes sir, they got damaged at the Sterling Ranges,' I said.

'Follow me.' He moved off to the right of the dam.

I shuffled beside him, trying to match his pace. I was beginning to worry, and voiced my concerns. 'Sir, are you removing me from the course on medical grounds? If you are, I can assure you that I can complete this course with my damaged feet.'

'Ranger Roberts, the senior instructor assured you that you would get the chance to have your feet attended to. The senior instructor is a man of his word. So now you will have your opportunity to see the medic.'

Before he had finished relieving my anxiety, I stood, amazed at what I saw in front of me. There was the base camp, with four large tents, trucks, Land Rovers, an ambulance and a fully operational medical tent, just two hundred metres from the dam. The camp came alive when they saw the instructor and myself return from the dam activity.

They must've been completely silent to maintain this position in such secrecy. This place was a hive of activity. Vehicles were being started up to drive to destinations unknown to me. Fires were being lit, which would have been doused to ensure that the rangers didn't know this location. Everybody was moving with haste in a direction that they only knew. No one spoke a word.

No one paid any attention to me. I moved towards the tent with the big red cross on it. I shivered at how eerie this scene was. I entered the flap of the RAP tent and sat on a wooden chair waiting for arrival of the medic. He arrived to notice my dumbfounded look.

'Yes, it's amazing, isn't it?'

I wasn't sure if we were talking about the same subject. He clarified. 'These men get told what to do. They know immediately what is required of them and go and complete the task silently. I find it quite eerie at times.'

My sentiments exactly, I thought.

'Right, get those boots off, we are throwing them away. A new pair arrived this morning. Your size is 10G, isn't it?'

'Yes sir,' I answered.

A thought crossed my mind. They were one hundred per cent right with my boot size. I wondered if they knew my jock size. I laughed to myself, for I wasn't wearing any jocks. The joviality was short-lived, for I was shocked back to reality when I went to remove my boots.

The medic could see the trouble I was experiencing. A sweat broke out over my whole body. He stopped me from putting myself through too much pain.

'Since we've got new boots for you, we will cut the old ones off,' he offered.

'Please, please, we would like that,' I answered for my feet.

He got some surgical scissors and sliced through my boots with ease. His face told the story. It was a slight sway from professionalism, as he would have been trained not to react to the sight of injuries. His face contorted for a fraction of a second, enough for an astute patient to really know the truth.

'That's not too bad. We will have you fixed up in a jiffy,' he lied.

I didn't question his honesty. I made real sure that I didn't look at my injuries, which were now exposed to the air. His next comment to me confirmed that my feet were not a pretty sight.

'I'm going to give you a penicillin shot, so drop your pants and get on the bed and lie on your stomach.

'This is going to sting a little,' he said nonchalantly.

He wasn't wrong. The process took at least one minute. With that big needle in my butt for that period of time, I thought it was to become a permanent fixture in my body. He finally removed the needle to allow me to sigh into the pillow. When the colour returned to my face, he spoke to me again.

'I'm going to have to scrub your feet with a disinfectant solution. It's going to sting like hell,' he advised.

'Then you're going to inject iodine into my blisters, right?' I asked.

'Wrong. Your feet are no longer blisters. You have worn the skin off what used to be blisters. Now the injury that you have is exposed flesh without any skin covering it. The soles of your feet are almost completely skinned.'

I put up my hand to make him stop. I didn't want to hear any more. I was starting to become nauseated by his detailed description. He noticed my distress and completed the mend job in silence. One hour later, he was done.

My feet were two bandaged socks. He had padded the injury area with thin foam. I pulled a boot on, expecting the same pain that had become prevalent. The boot fitted extremely comfortably. The other boot gave me the same joy. I stood up; the padded bandaging gave an excellent result.

With my feet comfortable in their new boots, I walked around the tent. No pain! It was such a relief.

'Thank you, thank you.' I shook his hand vigorously. It was hard to subdue the jubilation that was within me.

'Okay, Ranger Roberts, settle down. You still have to complete the challenge. I want you to report to the instructor who brought you in. If you go over to that tent jumping out of your skin, they will think that you have ripped off some happy drugs. They'll about-turn you and send you back to me for the urine test. Good luck with the rest of the course.'

I left him with the biggest grin I'd had in a very long time. I turned around to look back at the RAP; he was smiling at me. He quickly turned around and moved back into the RAP tent.

I found the instructor who had brought me to this eerie location. Still, there were no voices to be heard. Being caught up within this environment, I obeyed the rules. I whispered I was ready to continue the challenge.

'Is that right, Ranger Roberts?' He answered loud enough for me to just hear his words.

'Go back to the dam. You will find your team there. I will see you in the morning.'

'Yes sir.'

I returned to the dam to find every member of my team sound asleep. I placed my head on my pack and drifted off into a comfortable sleep.

Chapter Eleven

Land Rover recovery

My boots were kicked to awaken me. Twenty-four hours prior I would've jumped from the pain. This time it didn't register within my pain receptors. I greeted the morning with a smile. Day two of the challenge. The rest of the team must've thought I had gone mad. I'd slept in my uniform, with my comfortable boots on. I was happy, noticeably.

'I will wipe that smile off your face today, Ranger Roberts,' an instructor promised me. Another new face. A strange thought entered my head: did the SAS operators share their workload around so they wouldn't get attached to anything? I had long given up trying to remember who each individual was.

'Gather around for orders,' Peter commanded.

It was his turn to lead the team. Troy had been assigned to lead and then, when the instructors ordered my feet be repaired, they had used the opportunity to remove this status and play with his head. Peter explained the task.

'There's a Land Rover five hundred metres away from here. It has lost a wheel in a contaminated area. The wheel has to be put on and we have to push it for a distance of twelve kilometres.

We are to provide our own protection, front and rear of the vehicle. I will brief you further when we are at the vehicle.'

My smile was removed. The instructor looked pleased. Immediately, I realised that the vehicle would only be pushed by four of us at a time. This was going to be hard work.

We rounded a corner on the gravel road that we had walked five hundred metres on. There it was: a Land Rover with its right rear wheel missing.

The instructor spoke.

'Men, the rear wheel is in the back of the Land Rover. How it got there is a tragic tale. The first party sent to retrieve this vehicle didn't complete the job because the ground is foul. Two men have been sent to hospital with mustard gas poisoning. The tape around the area indicates the foul ground. If one of you touches the foul ground in this recovery operation you will be sent to hospital as well, leaving your team one man short. Have I made myself clear?'

'Yes sir,' we hollered in unison.

'Good. Ranger Peter Chauci, take charge.'

'Sir,' Peter replied.

He looked at the task in front of him for about ten minutes, approached the instructor and asked a question.

'Sir, the rope in the Land Rover, is it contaminated?'

'No, Ranger Chauci.'

He moved away from the instructor and studied the scenario again for a further five minutes.

'Come here, lads, and line up along the tape so you can see what I want you to do.'

Everybody was lined up and awaiting his instruction. I heard my stomach rumble. Two others joined the chorus. Pain had diverted my hunger. Now I was really aware that I hadn't eaten for almost two days. Food gives you energy. I was using a great deal of energy without being able to restock with food. There was nothing to smile about. I listened intently to Peter's directives as he gave his plan to us.

'With the ground being contaminated, we are going to build platforms to walk on. The first will be from where we are standing to the rear of the Land Rover. Once that is completed, we will build another platform out from the wheel hub. This will have to be wide enough for five people to stand on. So, we'll lay those two straight logs parallel to each other, out from the hub, with a gap of six feet, which we will fill with dead wood. When these platforms are built, Nathan, I want you to climb that tree and move out onto the branch hanging over the Land Rover. The rope will be tied to the hub and swung over the branch. As the rest of us lever the hub up, Nathan, you will pull on the rope and tie it to the trunk of the tree. When the vehicle is secure at its new height, we will use sticks and rocks to ensure it doesn't slip down. When we have the vehicle high enough to put the wheel back on, four of us will hold the rope to ensure that the man putting the wheel on doesn't get injured. Are there any questions?'

No one asked any.

'Good. There's a lot of work to do, so let's get cracking.'

It was a good plan. We all went about our work with gusto.

The laborious task of collecting wood for the platform took hours. The sun was high above us when we had finally completed the walkway and platform. The newly created platform ensured that we didn't step onto contaminated ground, as the scenario dictated. A log was found that was strong enough to be utilised as the lever to raise the vehicle. Positioned at the hub was more wood and some rocks to act as a jack.

We were ready to start levering the rear of the vehicle upwards. Everybody was in position; Nathan holding the rope, which was tied to the hub and slung over the tree branch; the rest of the team standing on the dead wood platform, ready to lever.

Peter, being the front man, gave the command.

'Lever ready, raise, raise, raise.'

Every time he said 'raise', the vehicle went higher into the air. This technique was extremely successful. As the vehicle went higher, Peter piled wood under it so none of the hard work would be wasted. If by chance the lever snapped or slipped, the wood pile would maintain the height we had already arduously achieved, a precaution that wasn't necessary as the recovery operation went smoothly.

With the vehicle now sitting on a pile of wood, it was ready to have the wheel replaced.

'The rest of you jump on the rope with Nathan and keep it up in the air long enough for me to tighten the nuts,' Peter commanded us.

With four of us on the rope he felt assured of his safety. He quickly placed the wheel on the hub and tightened the nuts onto the studs. He stood up from a position where we couldn't see him, raising his fist in the air, yelling one word.

'Success.'

We let go of the rope and congratulated each other on a job well done. I looked at the instructor. He didn't seem impressed. I walked around the tape to where Peter was studying our next problem: how to get the vehicle out of the contaminated ground. I now knew why the instructor didn't look impressed; it required the same process as we used before. Peter mouthed my thoughts.

'We will need to build another walkway on the other side of the vehicle. Quick as you can,' he ordered.

We collected as much wood as we could carry, then dumped it near the taped-off boundary. Peter was building the walkway. It took hours again to build a walkway on the other side of the vehicle. The sun was setting when we finally pushed the vehicle out of the contaminated ground. We still had to travel twelve kilometres.

I started out pushing the vehicle. The road was flat and once we gained some speed, the momentum carried the vehicle forward. We travelled two kilometres and then rested. It was now my turn to do protection for the next two kilometres.

The going was still relatively simple. The sky was black, littered with stars. The team pushed again on the road, now slightly rising.

The down slope was the reward, as the vehicle, moving forward with its own mass, allowed everybody to rest.

The night sky didn't allow us to recognise any features of this area we were in yesterday. We were all oblivious to the mother of a mountain that was just ahead of us, the one we'd experienced doing the stretcher carry.

I was still doing rear protection when I heard the abuse that was like a recording of yesterday's events.

'This fucking mother goes forever.'

'It's the same one from yesterday, I'm sure. Fuck it!'

'By fuck, not again.'

The chorus of abuse was mixed and rapid-flowing. Peter, between grunts of exertion, tried to encourage the boys.

'Come, lads, we can do it,' he encouraged.

The boys were really feeling the pain that was required to keep pushing themselves. The vehicle inched forward; at times a whole foot would be achieved. However, when two to three metres were gained, the handbrake had to be applied because the boys had lost their steam to keep pushing up.

Everybody rested when the handbrake went on for a short period of time, just long enough for those who were pushing to get their breath back. Collective long rests were redundant.

They had made it one-third of the way up the hill. The changeover happened quickly, to avoid losing any ground. The movement forward was increased. With fresh pushers, we could travel ten metres, then have a short rest. Sticking to this disciplined routine, we had only covered two-thirds of this mother of a mountain.

Another changeover, and the speed increased again. The incline now wasn't as steep; we could do twenty metres before we needed a rest. We kept on swearing at the mountain. Aggression was all we had left. Every man pushing that vehicle expended all of his physical strength. Their hearts got the vehicle over the lip of the mountain.

The vehicle started rolling on its own.

'Everybody in the vehicle,' Peter ordered.

I ran, increasing my pace to match the freely coasting vehicle. I jumped in, landing in the passenger seat. The rest of the pushing team climbed aboard. The protection boys were cheering our collective effort, sprinting after the now speeding vehicle. The down slope of the mountain finally finished. Peter, who was in the driver's seat, nudged me and pointed to the trip meter. It read 12.7 kilometres. We had done it!

The sun was just beginning to rise. It had been a twenty-four hour effort. The instructor finally caught up to us and checked to see what the trip meter read.

'It's a new day. Your next challenge will begin when you get off the vehicle. Ranger Tony Ridy, come with me and I will brief you. Men, today you will get a feed,' he advised us.

Chapter Twelve

A culinary delight

I wished the instructor hadn't mentioned food, because now I was really hungry. It had been over two and a half days since I had eaten.

Tony returned from his brief. We gathered around him to listen to his orders. They were simple and concise.

'Lads, we are to go to a grid reference where we will be given food. The location is twenty-five kilometres away. We must be there by 1200 hours or we will miss out on this meal. It's now 0600 hours, so we have six hours to cover the distance and earn our meal. Any questions?'

There were none. We still held firm to the code: support the mate who was placed in charge. Twenty-five kilometres was usually hardly a challenge, but now we were physically depleted and additionally dealing with hunger pains.

The team knew that the deadline was obtainable; however, it would require a superhuman effort. This is what the SAS instructors demanded. Anything less would not be tolerated. From now on, the instructors could remove individuals from the course who they believed were not giving and maintaining a superhuman effort. The pressure was on.

We walked for five kilometres through the bush; it took us an hour. With a ten-minute rest, it was easy to calculate how long it would take to complete this challenge. Every five kilometres would take one hour, with a rest stop of ten minutes. Four stops, calculated at ten minutes each, meant we should cover the distance in five hours and forty minutes. To ensure we reached the location before the deadline, Tony would need to push us hard to allow extra time for any misadventures. But it was hard to push an exhausted team. We did our best, but throughout the walk we didn't increase the pace. We maintained our rate of five kilometres every hour and our well-deserved ten-minute rests.

Exhausted, and still carrying sixty kilograms, we would move off after each rest stop by leaning forward; the weight of the equipment and our own bodies created the momentum.

Tony would set the pace. On occasions, team members found the rate too hard to handle and would drop back from the team, as far back as the instructor, who was assessing us from the rear. Seeing the instructor would spur the individual into rapid forward movement.

At one stage, I found myself looking at the instructor, totally oblivious to the fact that I had left the team's formation. I ran back to the team, but had a complete blackout as to how I had left it in the first place.

It was a bloody long walk. The dressing on my feet had worn away. The pain returned and I wished for the finish.

The terrain changed, and we were now walking on a road. As we rounded a corner, we were greeted with a pleasant sight: a vehicle with two hot-boxes to its rear containing our meals.

The cooks opened the hot-boxes as we approached the vehicle. It smelt like soup. Trust the SAS to serve soup on a thirty-five degree day. With the arduous tasks that had been set, two of which were yet to be completed, I expected that we would be served a substantial meal. This was another of my many underestimations. I was in for a big surprise.

As I stood in line, holding a large steel cup, waiting for my share, I looked in the hot-box as the cook stirred its contents. I could see barley, celery, carrot and lots of onion. I hated onion.

Then something else started to rise in the broth, breaking the surface as if it was the head of a diver gasping for air. I jumped back; it was hideous! It was a head, a boiled sheep's head!

'What a culinary delight! A fucking sheep's head! How fucking nutritious,' I said quietly to myself as I received an unwanted cupful.

My cup was overflowing with boiled sheep head remnants. This was my weakest moment. I didn't know how I was going to stomach what looked back at me: an eye. Beside that delightful morsel floated half a tongue, and a chunk of cheek flesh.

Before this, I believed I could handle anything that the instructors dished out, and had so far proved it to myself. But this was stretching it.

Those who still remained had to satisfy the instructors that they could operate efficiently with the standards they set. An SAS operator would be required to be able to live off the land, ensuring survival within an enemy environment. They didn't want fussy eaters and this test was sure to give results.

It was the SAS selection course. I could go home at any time I chose.

It was fucking disgusting. How could they expect us to function in the remaining challenges after this meal?

I was about to protest against the sickening slop, when Tony took the lead. He ate some and then spat it out.

'This is shit. I'm not eating this shit,' he protested in the deepest Irish accent that I had heard from him to date.

'Is there something wrong, Ranger Ridy?' the instructor questioned Tony.

'Yes sir, there is. This is shit and I'm not eating it!'

'If you were behind enemy lines, would you eat it then?'

'I guess so, sir, but we are not behind enemy lines.'

Troy looked at me with a hard stare, warning me not to go down the same road as Tony. I nodded with understanding and reluctantly started on my soup, watching the event unfold. I had a rubbery piece of sheep tongue bouncing around my mouth as the conversation continued.

'I will ask you again, will you eat this meal that has been prepared for you?' the instructor said.

Troy's face screwed up as though Tony had just committed a cardinal sin and was unaware of the consequences. The instructor went on.

'At this point, Ranger Ridy, I'm obligated to counsel you over this matter, as per the directive from the senior instructor. Please follow me and we will have a quiet chat.'

I took this opportunity to reflect on how close I had come to ending up in the same mess as Tony. I sat behind a tree to eat my meal. Instructors were everywhere. There were at least ten of them, ensuring that we ate this meal and didn't throw it away.

I devised a plan. I ate as quickly as my stomach would tolerate. I had broth, onion and the sheep's eye, which kept looking at me, still in my steel cup. While the instructors stood over me, I allowed the onion to slip out of my mouth and under my shirt. It slid down my chest to rest in my lap.

I continued to drink the broth slowly and carry out my subterfuge whenever a piece of onion touched my lips, its exit from my mouth being hidden due to the size of my cup. I did this in full view of the instructors, who were there to ensure we ate all of the contents of our cups.

The broth was finished, with only the eye still to be consumed. I picked it up, showing the instructors that this morsel was saved till last. I dropped it into my mouth like I would a succulent oyster. I bit down hard on it; a fluid foreign to my tastebuds filled my mouth.

The experience was not pleasant. I wanted to clean my teeth, urgently. I would have to wait until the challenge was done to enjoy that luxury, though, as my teeth-cleaning gear had been taken from me earlier, in case I thought to use the toothpaste as food. That's exactly what I wanted to do now.

The instructors finally removed themselves from their position of vigilance. I started digging a hole in the ground between my legs. I flicked the onion that was sitting on my waist down my pants and into the hole.

The whole operation lasted sixty seconds. I stood up, but unfortunately the hole I dug left a telltale sign. The moisture from the onion was rising to the surface. Quick-thinking, I pissed next to the hole, but not on it. On inspection, it would only look like I had pissed.

There wasn't any benefit for me in consuming that meal: I was now feeling extremely nauseated, with stomach pains. It was a challenge they set for me and I had met it, utilising a little subterfuge to remain in the selection process. I never told anyone about my cheating.

I moved to stand in the middle of the road to await our next challenge. I didn't want to sit anymore. Each time I did I became faint. My feet were starting to complain to my brain that they deserved a rest, but I had to go on. I just hoped the next activity would start soon, so I could distract my brain a little longer and complete the course.

I was so exhausted that I wasn't operating as a whole individual. To endure these tasks, I had to figuratively split my body in three: the brain was responsible for alleviating the pain; the body was to do the work and help the brain not receive pain signals; and the heart was what was going to get me through when the brain and the body failed to do their job.

Tony was putting his gear into the Land Rover I was standing next to.

'Did you pull the pin, mate?' I asked.

He didn't answer me.

I got my answer when the vehicle drove off down the road with him in it.

'Gather round, rangers, I need to talk to you,' the instructor said civilly.

'Ranger Ridy would not partake of the meal that you just ate. Men, this is not fucking Sunday school. I have a responsibility to the regiment to mould the best reinforcements I can. I take this responsibility very seriously. I need men who are willing to give one hundred per cent when it is asked of them.

'The meal you have just eaten proved that you could follow unpleasant orders and not argue. We train this hard to save lives. I won't send reinforcements to the regiment who can't follow unpleasant orders. Some of you will end up passing and eventually you will be given a job in an SAS patrol. The men leading those patrols are my friends. I promise you, gentlemen, I will only let the best join my regiment. Ranger Roberts, it's your turn to lead the push.'

He finished his speech.

Chapter Thirteen

The trailer push

The speech did wonders for me: now I truly understood that I could be one of the best. Enthusiastically I followed the instructor to be briefed for the next challenge.

'Ranger Roberts, I have left this challenge for you. It's going to take some engineering skills and a lot of ingenuity. I'm sure you're up to the task. Follow me and I will give you twenty minutes to come up with a solution.'

He didn't speak to me until the twenty minutes lapsed. I was looking at a Land Rover trailer. It was missing one wheel. In the trailer were two poles and thirty metres of rope. I measured it while I pondered the problem.

I had a solution: I would get the lads to put their packs in the trailer, on the side the wheel was fitted, to act as a counterbalance. We would lash the poles under the trailer with their ends jutting out on the side without a wheel. By lifting the poles and pushing, the trailer could be moved forward. Also, I would have to provide protection.

I had one question to ask the instructor when he returned.

'Have you got a solution yet, Ranger Roberts?'

'Yes sir.'

I explained my solution.

'Sounds good,' he replied.

'Sir, I have one question.'

'What is it, Ranger?'

'Sir, the team is now five men. Can I have only one man act as protection?'

'No, you must have front and rear protection,' he rapidly answered. 'All right Ranger, let's see if it works. I will get your men for you.'

He left me staring at the trailer that was missing a wheel. I didn't believe that three men could push it.

This problem wasn't going to be solved easily, and a lot of brute strength would be required. The brute strength had been sapped out of us a long time ago.

The lads came around the corner to recognise their next challenge. Their faces told the story: another challenge that would drain their remaining physical strength. This job was for the heart and they all knew it.

I explained the plan. Their faces lightened, and the counterbalance idea lifted their spirits. We quickly went to work. It didn't take long to achieve the desired configuration. The poles lashed to the underside of the trailer were lifted and the trailer slowly became level.

It took a lot of strength, but the trailer was moving. I had neglected to ask the instructor how far we had to move it. I quickly did this.

'That's for me to decide. If the solution you have come up with is the right one, I will stop you five kilometres past that point. It's up to you, Ranger Roberts. Get the correct method of tackling this problem and your men will stop earlier,' he informed me.

I was stopping the boys every kilometre to rest and change protection. We had travelled four kilometres, but the strain was taking its toll. The lads were pushing beyond exhaustion; they probably had only one kilometre left in them.

With three men lifting this trailer up and pushing to go forward, the effort was extremely taxing. I started to realise that this system was not the right one.

I looked at the trailer, trying to get the latent clue that eluded me. A battle of indecision raged in my brain-box. The question was simple, but the choice was monstrous. If I was wrong, I was going to torture men who were already at breaking point. A hard decision had to be made.

I had another technique that I had to try. If this technique was successful, we would only have to push five more kilometres. If it failed, we could still be pushing next week. Something else encouraged me to try this technique; it was what the instructor had said.

'When you get the right technique, I will stop you five kilometres from that point.'

This instructor could watch us torture ourselves for weeks if he had to. However, if a technique worked that didn't bust our balls, it would obviously be the correct technique. There was an easier way and I believed I knew it.

I stopped the team and explained my new idea. They quickly rearranged the trailer. We now had a pole across the top of the trailer, lashed down by rope. The pole extended over the side where the wheel was fitted.

The packs were removed from the tray of the trailer and put onto the pole. Now we had five packs, weighing approximately two hundred and fifty kilograms, hanging on the pole on the outside of the trailer. As the last pack went onto the pole, the missing wheel side began to rise. We had discovered the trailer's fulcrum, or point of balance.

We all looked at the trailer in amazement, as it levelled itself. The three-man pushing team, myself included, took up our positions. We pushed the trailer, now exerting our strength on the pole that held our packs. No lifting was required.

We used the same strength as we had previously to gain momentum. This action led to a pleasant surprise. The trailer moved comfortably forward without much effort. I smiled at Nathan, who had one finger on the pole, showing the team how simple this task had become.

The next five kilometres were easily achieved. We had lost a lot of time busting our balls doing the first four kilometres. The sun had set when the instructor informed us that we had completed the challenge.

'Tonight, men, you will have a good sleep, and start again at 0500 hours.'

He moved off to have a meal. I hoped my nose was upwind of his cooking. As we settled with our heads on our packs, a group conversation began.

'I'm hungry. It has been three and a half days since I have had a decent feed,' I griped.

'Paul, if you could eat anything in the world, what would it be?' Troy asked.

'Lobster. I love lobster.'

The rest of the team, and even Ben, agreed that lobster would have to also be on top of their list of preferred food.

'Okay, lads, if you pass this course, when we get to Perth, I will buy you all a lobster dinner. I know a great seafood restaurant,' Troy invited us.

As the lads drifted off to sleep, I too was sedated by the thought of sitting down in a comfortable restaurant eating lobster. Troy had guaranteed a big effort out of the lads with this enticing invitation. Clever of him. Tomorrow he would be placed in charge of the final challenge. My fork picked up a succulent piece of lobster. It tingled my tastebuds.

I slept comfortably.

Chapter Fourteen

In the bag

'Well done, maggots, but it's not over yet. The bus will take you to your next destination to commence the next phase of the selection cycle. From this point you will continue to be under assessment and can be removed from the cycle at any time. Trust me, maggots, if you thought the selection course was hard, prepare yourself, for the worst is yet to come. We have a tradition that the successful rangers get the opportunity to see the sites that we hope you have grown to hate just one more time. We call it the "memories of pain". Enjoy!'

With his last comment, he quickly alighted from the vehicle. The bus driver turned the key, and the engine started. The drive up the hill towards the gym exposed two thoughts: the first, it was refreshing to be driven up it and not driven by abuse; the second, a reminder of the first morning when I had to attack this hill by myself, having to catch the rest of the group.

The memory quickly faded when the gym that we had spent hours in appeared. Opposite the gym was the line of pipes that we had become extremely efficient in balancing on the top of.

The logs lay to the right of the entrance to the airfield. We were just about to enter the driveway of the airfield when suddenly a blue van flashed in front of us, screeching to a stop. The bus driver, slamming the brakes on, propelled me forward clumsily.

As I frantically gripped the seats to slow my momentum, I saw a metal bar smash the windscreen. We came to a standstill and an explosion of glass peppered me. Windows to the sides and rear of the bus were smashed simultaneously. A hand holding the metal bar was raking the excess glass from the frame. The sound was frightening. I was totally confused.

Metal canisters flew through the air. As they landed, they emitted white plumes of smoke. The canister at my feet spun as the smoke rose from the floor, contacting my skin. The sweaty exposed flesh was the first part of me to experience the burning sensation that was the telltale sign that we were being exposed to CS gas.

'Tear gas!' I screamed.

Dumb move. The gas forced its burning elements deep into my lungs. I coughed uncontrollably; teardrops streamed down my face. I turned to try to create distance between me and the canister that was spewing its unpleasantness. I had moved two feet when another canister landed at my feet. This one was different and had a fuse lit in its end.

I had no time to avoid it. I jumped. Now mid-air, the canister exploded underneath me and deafened me. It was a flashbang. Numerous canisters exploded within seconds; the bus shook and the magnesium flares that fired on contact with air were sprayed in all directions, blinding me.

I was almost incapacitated, not being able to breathe or see. A black figure wearing a gasmask flicked himself through the smashed window. His feet landed flat in the centre aisle. Still having amazing dexterity, he was able to coat-hanger me. An edge of the back of the seat jammed my ribs, and the final inches to the floor were quickly covered as a boot pressed me down. A weapon barrel contacted my forehead and I stopped struggling.

A cotton bag was placed on my head, plastic ties bound my hands and I was quickly ejected from the bus to leave the sounds of broken glass underfoot, and to recognise the familiar sound of gravel from the airfield.

It was only minutes since Troy warned me about this dreaded experience, known to the educated as 'going in the bag'.

The next push I got was not expected. It was the pain of a boot in my back. It flung me chest-first into the tray on the back of a truck, and winded me. I tried to protect myself, rolling onto my side. I tried to raise myself, only to receive another boot in my ribs. This stopped any more thoughts of self-preservation.

A thorough body search was carried out, while I lay on the ground nursing my new injuries. I spat the dirt from my mouth, my eyes blurred and irritated from the effects of the CS gas. With lack of sight, my hearing became my premier sense.

No one had said a word. There was just a purposeful shuffle of boots, and then the finger clicking started.

One click meant stand up.

Two clicks meant sit down.

Three clicks meant move.

Our education to this new communication was severe. Until all prisoners had learned it, we were physically put into the required position. Until all prisoners were obedient and moved into the correct position by themselves, we were left in the sitting position. They had control and they knew it.

I heard our equipment being loaded onto a truck, but there was still no word from our captors.

One click, quick stand up. Because we all stood up with such speed, we bumped into each other. Standing up straight with your hands handcuffed behind your back is not easy, and the situation created a domino effect, all of us falling to the ground, struggling like stranded walruses. We tried to regain our upright position to appease our captors. It must have been a funny sight.

One of the captors, being human, released a muffled giggle. A clear outburst of laughter would have displayed a serious lack of professionalism. The mirth was quick to subside.

We were being loaded onto the truck. We heard three clicks and started to move. The Snatch team objective was to transport us to the Interrogation team.

I heard two of my mates, in succession, groan as they hit the steel floor of the truck. I wasn't looking forward to my turn. I felt four hands on my shoulders and arms, and one each on my knees. Three clicks, they started to raise me.

Suddenly a tug of war with my body began. It seemed the bloke hanging onto my right leg wanted to pull it out of the socket. I was glad he was the victor, even though my face hit the dirt first, with my body slumping after it.

My pants were being pulled down to my ankles. My dick suffered rough treatment from the gravel texture of the road. I started to raise myself to get out of this painful and uncomfortable position, only to feel a boot in the middle of my back, which stopped that idea. What were they looking for?

They had just done a thorough search of us, three minutes prior. Then I realised after the second search ceased that they had found what they were looking for. It was my personal knife, tied onto my waist.

It was a habit that I had adopted, as a pocket knife was extremely handy throughout the selection course. Usually I would carry it in the front pocket of my pants, attached to a cord, so it would never be left behind. With my quick exit from the shower, I must've slipped the knife into my waistband unawares. The knife was hanging halfway down my leg.

My captors had not seen the cord on my first search, but to their credit one of them later saw the cord around my waist and wanted to make sure that there wasn't anything lethal connected to it. There was, and now I was due for more rough treatment. My captors thought I was going to use it as an escape device.

I finally felt the pain I had dreaded two minutes earlier, after a short whispered conversation between my captors, which was probably about why I had gone through a thorough search without this lethal item being found.

My sore face and body finally made contact with the steel floor. I was flung onto a bench seat initially, and then roughly repositioned away from the rest of the prisoners. I collected this information by tripping over their feet.

The captor who dragged me onto the truck wasn't about to miss out on his turn. He seemed to enjoy the fact that he was the final one to give me a lasting impression of this day. That they were all pissed off was easy to assess, not only due to the rough handling I was experiencing but also because their operation had almost developed a flaw: my hidden knife.

Little did they know that the extra treatment I received allowed Peter to concoct his plan. This was to create more embarrassment for this Snatch team.

Time was slowly ticking by. The rough treatment we were still receiving meant that at this stage no one had spilled. The bagging was quick and efficient. The searches were thorough and deliberate. It was going to be difficult to escape now.

While they expected me to be the difficult one, they should have suspected another. Peter's plan went into first gear when he yelled out, 'Say nothing.'

Peter believed escape was possible. He had chewed a hole in his bag that was small enough to see out of. With his newfound vision, he could see the guards' locations and that they were getting comfortable right next to him.

If Peter's plan was to succeed, he would require some space away from the guards. His shouted comment was enough to earn him a rough relocation next to me.

Peter and I had discussed a plan. We would do our best to cover the other one's escape attempt. With him sitting next to me, I knew my chance had gone and that he was relying on my assistance.

Both of us were trained in morse code, and Peter started to tap a message on the small of my back with a combination of short jabs and long presses: 'Hole in bag. See.'

This was done with the guard closest to us being totally unaware of our activities. I acknowledged the message by shaking Peter's arm.

A strong smell of gun oil and cordite, mixed, came from the weapon barrel that belonged to the guard.

Peter knew there were two guards down the back, and the one who was paying far too much attention to me would not be a threat to him. He continued with his plan. In our training, we had learned that the best chance of survival is to escape early, and this was his intention. Prior to capture he had secured a knife under his armpit with tape. It had been there since the mass exodus of rangers from the selection course, only removed when he had a shower.

With string secured to his knife and upper arm, and me shielding his movements, he rubbed the tape away. It must have been a painful experience. The tape and his armpit hairs were as one. The knife unrolled, as he had planned, straight down his sleeve to his hand. He cut partially through the plastic cuffs, but the blade sliced his hand.

I sensed he was holding in a scream that had engulfed his lungs; his body trembled next to mine. Adjusting to this situation, he rested the blade on the plastic, allowing the bumps and swerves of the truck to assist in the cutting action. The knife finally achieved its task.

Now with the knife in his hand, he ripped his bag off and lunged across the truck with the knife thrust forward. I heard him slice the canvas cover. With a foot on top of the back of the bench seat, he exited the truck.

The truck stopped. I heard a scream and I was sure it was Peter. The sound resonated, and it seemed like there was echo in his voice. He was releasing pain. I was hoping that the shrill cry related to the injury he had caused himself earlier and not to a new injury caused by jumping from the truck at full speed.

The guard sitting next to me brushed past my leg swiftly. I heard him land on the gravel as his boots made contact with the road, and there was a distinctive sound of a patter building to a full sprint.

With the third guard committed to the chase, and the other two already engaged in bringing Peter down, the rest of us were alone. Twenty seconds passed with no word, then whispers started.

'Where are they?'

'They've gone.'

Escape was the first thing most of us thought about. Rapid conversations began between the other prisoners. It was hard to discern who was speaking. The chief question was how to get their bags off their heads so they could see where they were going.

'Let's get off the truck,' Troy said. His was the first voice I recognised.

He continued, frantically, 'Assist each other to remove the bags. Put your head behind each other's backs and bend down until you feel your mates' hands. Grab each other's bags. Do it quick; do it now!'

Troy, obviously now able to see, must have noticed I hadn't moved from my position: he yelled, 'C'mon Paul, they've gone!'

I struggled to the back, but kept tripping over equipment and rolling. I must have have been halfway through this obstacle course when Troy said, 'They're coming back. Peter didn't get away! They've got him. We're off, mate. Good luck. They're still two hundred metres away and running.'

'Cheers, mate!' Their farewells were said simultaneously.

I heard another shuffling of boots and they were off.

I kept trying to reach the back of the truck, and just as I had my foot searching for the edge of the back I felt an almighty shove that threw me back to the middle of the truck.

'Fuck it. Shut it and get back to where they left me, and I might not get a beating,' I said quietly.

The struggle back under my own steam gave me more bumps and bruises than I would have received if I had been flung there. When I finally reached my seat, the guard standing over me pinched the flesh above my right collarbone. I heard someone else whimper. It was Peter, sitting next to the guard who now sat between us.

It lifted my spirit immediately to know that some of the other boys were being defiant. I was feeling sore and a little bit dizzy. My head had hit the equipment on the truck floor.

I wanted to be defiant as well, but I was also wary of receiving additional punishment. In my determination to make contact with Peter, I designed a coughing system.

Two coughs, pause, three quick coughs.

It only took two goes before someone else knew and understood, and then the third time all of the team remaining in the truck were doing it in unison.

It annoyed our guard that we were coughing to rhythm and in unison, and we soon got a clip around the ears, each, for our show of defiance. But it was great to feel that we were still together.

It was about twenty-five minutes before the rest of the team was recaptured. I heard everybody received a touch-up for attempting to escape. One of the guards complained that he had a broken nose.

The changeover couldn't come quickly enough for the Snatch team, whose whole responsibility was to capture us and escort us to the interrogators, covertly. To explain to their commanders how recruits could escape from trained professionals would be very embarrassing for all involved in the snatch.

The handover to the interrogators finally happened. The language was foreign, which confused me. Our guards had handed us over and we were immediately split up and herded away in different directions.

My mates were brushed past me on the left and right side of my body, which added to my confusion. I heard groans that indicated that someone had suffered a boot up the arse.

I was being pushed down a flight of steps. I could smell the grass; dew was releasing the fresh essence of it. The smell was rising with me, and then above me. I panicked slightly.

I was totally disorientated, but then realised I was going underground and was relieved. I kept going down, and then I was left alone.

I was starting to hate my sense of hearing. People were screaming in foreign languages, yet all operators at this stage were remaining silent, even though they were suffering flushing, a slight rough-up, and hosing down with cold water. There were a few groans and whimpers, due to being freezing cold and now wet, but no English was heard.

I decided to use my coughing system as a security blanket. I wanted to know if any of our hut members were nearby. I coughed the code: two coughs followed by three coughs. There was no reply so I tried again, louder this time. There was still no reply.

I felt a lot emptier and lonelier when I didn't get a reply, even though there were other prisoners suffering next to me. Then someone brushed against me. I gave my cough code. It was returned, and immediately I felt relieved to know that one of my mates was going through the same torment as myself.

The coughing system was comforting but I used it too much. It became a double-edged weapon. It was a good communication system for us, but our captors also started using it to try to identify us as a team. They managed to trick us into believing that they were fellow hut members.

The guards placed their mouths to both of my ears and coughed my code simultaneously. I knew my system had been compromised. My one comfort had been stripped from me. I hardened to this realisation and concentrated on ensuring that these pricks would not get any information from me.

I knew that if I withheld all information for seventy-two hours, any details would be useless to them. The SAS squadron headquarters would have gone into deniable condition. Everything that was pertinent to a successful operation would have been changed.

Patrols would have been extracted and reinserted in new locations and issued new codes. This time period was a golden rule among the operators: don't say anything for seventy-two hours; don't sign anything for seventy-two hours; just survive.

Time became an unknown. I had my freedom taken away, and my senses dulled. I had been restrained for a long period of time. My sense of touch was limited. I had a bag over my head. I had my vision reduced to only shadows.

If someone approached me, their body would darken the light in my bag. My heart would race. Maybe it was only a passing guard, or a poor sod going for his turn in interrogation, but maybe it was my turn.

The light in my bag got darker. My turn. I was ripped around in the opposite direction and pushed into a room, where for the first time since capture the bag on my head was removed. I glimpsed an officer dressed in foreign uniform controlling proceedings, and a picture of what was supposed to be the dictator of this unknown country, who had snatched us.

There was a blinding light from the flash of a polaroid camera, and I tried to focus my eyes to see what this officer wanted. He was ranting in his foreign tongue and was pointing to a pen and a piece of paper, as well as a set of purple prison pyjamas.

I knew what he wanted: he wanted me to sign for these clothes and I refused. Yet he kept insisting. I kept silent and shook my head.

He became irate and came out from behind his desk. There was a quick jab in my ribs, and I found my face being pushed into a piece of paper. He continued his ranting. Aggression wasn't working on me; the more aggressive he became the more I was determined to remain silent. I was getting pissed off with this little foreign-speaking prick. He punched me in the face. My nose began to bleed so I decided to snot all over his special piece of paper.

We finally understood each other. I didn't want to sign anything. As I was going backwards out the door, I saw how irate he was with me for destroying his piece of paper. He had probably spent a considerable amount of time gluing two sheets together, the top one being a simple issue form for the clothing, but the one underneath probably being a statement explaining how I had confessed to war crimes against this country and its people.

My training had taught me that a piece of tangible evidence like that could create a whole lot of embarrassment for my government. Additionally, an individual could be signing his own death warrant with one such stupid mistake. Another golden rule was never to sign anything. The decision not to sign left me naked for the next seventy-two hours.

Chapter Fifteen

Seventy-two hours

I was standing naked with the bag back over my head, at the same spot I was in prior to my entry into the office of the little irate Asian officer. I heard a woman's voice. Instinctively, I tried to cover my manhood, a ridiculous move when your hands are behind your back, handcuffed with plastic ties.

I smelt her perfume. I was then swung around in the opposite direction to which I had been facing. I could still smell her perfume. She was following me. She must have had a full-frontal view, and was now watching my arse wiggle down a long corridor.

Fuck me, where are we? I thought to myself.

I must have gone at least seventy-five metres that I believed to be underground. I was shoved into an extremely dark room and travelled a good three metres, landing hard and twisting my ankle.

The pain literally sat me on my arse. I wanted to investigate the dark room, but each time I tried to move the pain in my ankle made me decide I should stop and rest. In this lonely, isolated and wet environment I tried to maintain some dignity in case the lights went on. I tried to find a comfortable sitting position in order to show that they hadn't broken my spirit.

A torch shone in my face, and within the blink of an eye I was propelled backwards, sliding on my back with my balls and thighs stinging from the enormous force of water.

As the water hit the bag on my head, I must've had my mouth open. This caused the wet cloth to fill my mouth and windpipe. I couldn't breathe. I tried desperately to get the cloth out of my mouth using my tongue. It felt like it had almost reached my lungs. The jet of water had hit my face full on. Pain wasn't an issue; I was suffocating!

The pricks were softening me up with a large fire hose. I bounced around the dark room scared for my life as a result of the pressure being directly applied to me.

The woman tried to humiliate me with comments like, 'What could you do with that little dick?'

At this stage, that intimidation technique was ridiculous. A full burst of a fire hose onto your groin tends to make your dick try to crawl inside.

Fuck the humiliation, fuck the pain, I couldn't breathe!

The fire hose stopped. It must've been about two and a half minutes of water pressure torment. Throughout this period I was unable to breathe, and my vision turned to a pale shade of grey. The next likely bodily function would have been me losing consciousness.

I believe I was in the grey when the water finally stopped. Weak, beyond movement, I could see only another shade of grey as a torch shone on me. I vaguely remember the guard saying, 'He's fucking swallowed his bag'.

He reached down and pulled the wet pillowcase off my head and out of my windpipe.

The first breath of air hurt like hell, and the second had to be forced into my lungs. Gasping and gagging, I tried to get as much precious air as possible into them. Lying in the foetal position, I enjoyed the simple act of breathing that most take for granted.

I was left alone. Loneliness was a blessing.

They returned with Miss Perfume. She was the one who placed a dry bag on my head. One click of the fingers, ha! I couldn't stand if I tried. I was enjoying breathing too much. In any case, the oxygen hadn't re-entered my muscles, so I was still limp and lifeless. Just let me breathe, I thought.

I felt a female hand, soft and gentle. I tried to raise myself, but my arms collapsed beneath me. I wasn't going anywhere. I realised that if I couldn't stand for her, those other pricks weren't going to get me up.

Two guards forcefully raised me, grabbed me under the shoulders and started dragging me. I felt no pain this time; I was just numb. My toes were being dragged in the same fashion that you see in anti-Nazi movies, where the poor soul has had his feet belted and is being dragged back to his cell. My toes were ripping against the concrete and I knew this should be painful. The pain came later.

The bag was now loose, and I looked down at my toes. Not a single toe had missed out on some sort of damage. I was dumped at an entrance to the hall and my bag was removed. I crawled against the wall, assumed the foetal position, and once again enjoyed breathing.

The sounds of torture filled my ears. Men were being flushed in toilets.

Their heads would be raised as a guard forced a piece of paper under their noses, I assumed. With a foreign accent, the guards continually repeated the words, 'Sign it, sign it, sign it! Dry, dry, dry. No sign, wet! No sign, wet!'

As soon as prisoners were dry they either had a bucket of freezing water dumped onto their naked bodies or they were dragged to the pressure hose room.

Escape came to my mind, but the realisation that I was carrying too many injuries to do this successfully hurt. I would require at least three days of rest before I could move with any speed. Escape was not an option at this time.

My mind had decided that our capture had been the real thing: I was now the property of a foreign country. They would continue the physical torture to soften me up and then move on to psychological torture. Name, rank and serial number is all I would give to these pricks.

At this point, something within me was switched on that was extremely instinctual. I felt myself falling into a dark void. This was not from the physical effects of the torment and torture that I had experienced. This was some form of protection mechanism within me that now ruled my mental state.

The form of escapism was simple: it was a dark void that beckoned my consciousness. All feelings and emotions were released and trapped within this void. I had become the ultimate soldier; I felt nothing and I had no desire to feel. I was a killing machine.

Rest now, kill later.

I repeated the words in my mind as the dark void comforted me.

Left alone to enjoy breathing, with still no response from my limbs, I was so weak that I must have fallen asleep. This seems hard to imagine among all the hollering and groaning from my mates at the hands of the guards of whichever country had taken our freedom. My hatred grew for these guards, and bile rested in my mouth. At the first opportunity I got, I was going to spray this murky wet filth into a guard's face.

Rest now, kill later. Rest now, kill later. Rest now, kill later.

The dialogue volume and consistency slowly faded as I slipped into my comfort zone, the dark void.

The next thing I remember, I was in a surgery. Lying on a table, I was still handcuffed but these ones were steel. My toes were being bandaged and as I focused, there was a pretty face in front of me. Her beauty and perfume hit me simultaneously.

It was Miss Perfume. I was completely naked except for two bandaged feet.

She was doing a complete examination of all my bruises and cuts. I was a fine mess, with a sprained ankle, a cut above one eye, a large red welt in my rib area, and more than likely a fractured rib. Bruises covered my body and my toes were severely damaged.

The initial torment/torture was only the beginning. Even the kindness that was being shown to me by Miss Perfume did not allow my mind to eliminate the falsities that it had accepted as truth.

Miss Perfume, very diligent and professional as she attended to my wounds, didn't say a word, and I was far too weak to make a pass at her, so I closed my eyes and fell asleep.

I awoke this time alone in the surgery. Lucid, I surveyed my surroundings. Confirmation hit me when I realised that I couldn't be in Australia. The same photo of the dictator hung on the wall. The medical journals and reference books were titled in a foreign language. Incense reeked through the office. There was absolutely no indication in this surgery that allowed me to think I was in an English-speaking country.

The office door flew open. A man wearing spectacles and a white coat, with a stethoscope hanging around his neck, stepped into the surgery. Miss Perfume followed him. He said something in his foreign tongue. Miss Perfume jumped to grab some paperwork.

The doctor shoved a clipboard under my nose, indicating that I had to sign for the treatment that I had just received. I refused by shaking my head, yet he insisted and this little battle of wills was to last about five minutes.

I finally snapped and yelled 'Fuck off!', the international language for 'No'. I also took the opportunity to release the bile phlegm ball from my mouth onto his clipboard. The doctor looked at me with disgust in his eyes. He left the room. Immediately, two guards entered wearing balaclavas. They quickly put my bag back on and withdrew me from the room.

They had won this little battle. I had fucked up. When I was silent I was stronger. Now they knew that if I was pushed enough I had the potential to snap verbally.

The interrogators had achieved their objective. Every one of us had uttered a word. I didn't know if my rest had helped me to withhold longer than my mates, or whether I cared. I was, however, the last to break and the last to be moved to the holding area.

Finally, I was taken up the stairs and smelt the dewy grass. It was very dark and very cold. The guards put me into an upside-down 'L' position, with my upper body bent at the waist and my legs straight. Hearing a vehicle reversing towards me, panic rose within. 'Jesus, they're going to run over me!' I thought.

The vehicle stopped just before impact with my thighs. Someone hoisted me up. My head and upper body were wedged between the tray of the ute and the tarp that was correctly fitted. I had my legs lifted and the tray was shut behind me.

We bounced along a road for about fifteen minutes and I tried to memorise the direction we had travelled by the feel of the turns. If I got a chance to escape, I hoped to not be too confused about my escape route.

That all changed and by the time we got to our destination, I was totally confused and disorientated. Now all that stored information was useless to me. I let it slip from my mind so as not to confuse my next attempt.

My mind was relieved but empty. I tried to think of something pleasant: rest now and get fit, then kill.

In the holding area, the guards gave me a rubber mat to sit on. It was the first time my arse had felt comfort in I don't know how many hours. I started to relax. My hatred towards the interrogators and guards intensified. I had been seated for approximately twenty minutes, when a guard made an announcement.

'Prisoner number thirteen has given us all patrol identities and patrol attachments, as well as the location your men have been operating in against our people.'

It was psychological torment for the poor sod that wore number thirteen on the bag on their head. As I started to feel the warmth of the mat under my arse, the guard continued.

'The last prisoner has given us enough information for all of you to be accused of war crimes against our country.'

'Prisoner thirteen's name is Paul Roberts.'

I was shattered! I knew I had remained silent and had only had one outburst. This lie made me so angry I started to repeat the same words I had said in the false surgery in a soft whisper, 'Fuck off, fuck off, fuck off!'

I said this at increasing volume until the guards came over and kicked me and told me to shut up. I raised the volume again. 'Fuck off, fuck off, fuck off!'

I was ripped out of the building, yelling, 'Fuck off, fuck off!'

I was hoping the boys would recognise my voice and know that I wouldn't betray them.

This defence found me placed in a wire cage. I had to sit with my knees pressed into my chest. The back of my head was uncomfortably squashed into the top of the cage. This incarceration was the most uncomfortable period of my life.

The cage was a wire dog kennel used to freight dogs on aircraft. I spent my first night freezing cold in the open air, and bloody uncomfortable. The guards poked and prodded me throughout the night to ensure I didn't get any sleep.

The morning couldn't come soon enough, the only true indication of time. The other prisoners had been through twelve hours of sleep deprivation and time alteration. I was forced to intermittently witness the effective techniques used to plague my mates. The guards would remove my bag to ensure that I endured the psychological ploy, reminding the lads and myself that I was the reason for their torment.

The method was extremely simple. They would let the boys fall asleep, then wake them up just as they had dozed off, telling them they'd had four hours' sleep, and exercise them.

Suggestions are a really good tool when used on individuals who are fatigued.

The boys were roused, out the door, past my position near the entrance to the building. I heard and smelled them as they passed my cage. The guards were taking them on another exercise run.

One guard noticed that I was still in the cage, so he opened the lock and dragged me out. He was shuffling me towards the holding area when he stopped and another guard dribbled something to him in a foreign language. The other guard took control of me and walked me a short distance.

Freezing cold throughout the night, I enjoyed physically shivering from the cold and in my cramped condition. It seemed to warm my flesh. I wasn't, however, enjoying walking with all these areas of flesh exposed to the cold air.

The guard turned on a tap. I heard water pouring into a bucket, then the tap being turned off. The next sensation I experienced was freezing water cascading over my naked body. I wouldn't be dry again for the duration of my incarceration.

Trying to avoid any more damage to my feet, my movement was considerably slow. The guard moved me inside the building. I started to use my senses more effectively this time.

There was no light coming into the building. The doors had rollers on them, and the guard panted from the exertion it required to move the doors. I took the opportunity to assess the material from which the doors were made. I risked leaning against the doors, hoping that I wouldn't fall flat on my face.

A large metal clang resonated from the impact of my shoulder against the door. The attentive guard righted me from my leaning, stationary position rather briskly. Enough information had been collected to assume that these doors belonged to an aircraft hangar. The need for more information led me to start counting my paces as I was dragged through the doorway.

I was on a large concrete floor space and my feet chilled with each pace. My spirits sank. It was going to be extremely difficult to escape past the guards and the two hundred-kilogram doors.

The guard halted me from the slow forward momentum we had achieved. He pushed my foot with his until I felt a texture other than concrete. My mat! I almost yelled those words out loud with excitement from the warmth that my foot was experiencing. I quickly lowered my body, in case this luxury was stripped away. It had been fifty-two paces from the doorway to my mat. The dark grey shade indicated to me that the guard still stood in front and above me.

He moved, and the colour under my bag lightened. I sensed a bright clear light. I assessed that this building housed a lot of fluorescent lights, further confirmation that the holding area was an aircraft hangar. I became disheartened.

Reality and the concept of time eluded me while I was confined with handcuffs, and the bag over my head. Time passed uncomfortably.

I heard the patter of bare feet running on the concrete. Heavily sucking air, the procession passed me. Around and around they went. I don't know how long the guards kept screaming at them.

'Round again!' A foreign accent.

The boys, in pain, kept grunting, encouraging each other to keep going. The guards must have really pushed these men, extremely fit and hardened individuals, to their limit again. Men were tripping over from fatigue, their mates encouraging them to get up and continue.

This was an awesome feat, considering the only time they could've possibly known that someone had fallen would be when an individual tripped over the person who had fallen.

The encouragement that the lads were giving to each other caused the guards to raise the volume of their commands. The lads retaliated by raising their volume. The holding area echoed with voices. The guards resigned themselves to the fact that their prisoners had won this little battle of wills.

'Prisoners to their mats,' that hideous foreign-accented voice bellowed.

'We'll see how much talking you do to the interrogators. Prisoner one, you will be first.'

The guards ripped our mate up from his mat. We heard a grunt as he left, the shuffling of his bare feet diminishing into the distance.

'Don't say a thing,' cried one prisoner, and more voices chorused the cry.

'Don't say a thing,' all prisoners screamed.

Then the violence started. There was a smart slap across my head, hard enough for me to experience the sensation known as seeing stars. That didn't stop me.

'Tell them nothing,' I screamed.

There was another hard hit to my head, and I felt blood pooling in my inner ear. Still, that didn't stop me. I was violently grabbed by four hands, and my sore feet couldn't keep up with the speed at which they moved me. Once again, they suffered damage. I was taken outside the building and the tap was turned on.

The bag was removed so I could visually experience the torture. The guards connected a smaller pressure hose, smaller than the one that almost killed me. This hose still had enough pressure to sting my bare flesh. It forced me against a wall, my legs crossed over trying to cover my genitals.

I turned my arse, which suffered the torrent. I don't know how long I had been doused; I was starting to go numb. I knew that from this point on I wouldn't be getting too mouthy.

I was taken back to my mat, shivering from the cold. The pain in my feet and my busted rib caused me to pass out. When I awoke, my hands were cuffed to my front. Another prisoner was being dragged out for his dose of interrogation.

The procession of prisoners continued, destination unknown.

When would be my turn?

How long had I been passed out?

No one would be forthcoming with the answers to my silent questions. Hours and hours of being made to stand up, perfectly still, was the new torment that I now endured. A technique that rapidly fatigued me, a quick jab into my injured rib, would always result in me mustering the perfect attention position. Fear was always the motivator to ensure I adhered to the guard's directive. Tedious and painful, torment was now torture, and my hatred grew for the demented guards.

Night and day, the only difference was the temperature. The hangar was constantly illuminated with massive rows of fluorescent lights, giving the illusion that daylight persisted beyond its normal cycle. Trips to be drenched would present opportunities to assess the time, either day or night. Intelligence collated two cold spells (nights) and two hot spells (days). I assumed that it must have been about forty-eight hours since capture. These pricks had made me stand upright for two days. Someone was definitely going to die.

A smile reached my lips as I imagined how much enjoyment I was going to have, sending these malicious bastards to an early grave. I had another insight: I only had to hold out for twenty-four hours. One more cold spell and one more hot spell, and I could make my attempt at killing and escaping.

My body must have momentarily relaxed at this thought. A sudden jolt to my rib area quickly brought the familiar grey cloud over me once again. I could no longer muster the attention position, and I went limp and headed for the concrete floor.

Upon regaining consciousness, I heard a tarp being pulled over me. I yelped in pain as its texture and weight grazed my toes. The air was chilled and the grey shade under my bag was now darker. Lying on a stretcher, my shoulders were wedged between the two poles.

After being driven for about fifteen minutes, feeling the turns and depositing the information in my memory, the tarp lifted and someone assisted me off the back of a vehicle. The height of the drop proved it was a truck.

Fear rose in me to an uncontrollable level, fear of the unexpected.

Two guards, one either side of me, supported my walking. The moisture once again rose to my nose.

Panic, panic!

I recalled my near-death episode. The guards tightened their grip and forced me down the same stairs as before.

I knew what would happen next: interrogation. Tell them nothing! I repeated this to myself. Hold out for seventy-two hours.

The first trip to the interrogators, my bag was removed. My eyes took time to focus, finally clearing to reveal the image of Miss Perfume. She was sitting behind a desk and said something to me in a foreign tongue. I looked like I didn't understand, yet she continued ranting. She read some sort of statement that I was meant to sign. Not this game again!

She walked around her desk and stood in front of me and presented the statement written in her foreign language.

I knew what this seductive witch was up to; she would use her sex appeal. These people were good; they wanted to break us slowly. Her objective would be to get me to refuse to sign, which they expected of me. They wanted me to complain that the statement was in another language and that I couldn't understand it.

If they achieved this breakthrough, she would soften up and ask if I needed to contact the Red Cross, and offer me food. The same demeanour she had displayed in the surgery would be shown to her prisoners.

She didn't expect what she got from me. It was another one of those statements I didn't want to sign, so once again I spat on it and she was disgusted. But that was nothing to what she was about to receive. With my hands handcuffed at the front of my body due to my fractured rib, I grasped my dick firmly and commenced to wank furiously.

She quickly called the guards and I was roughly removed from her perfume. At my last glimpse of her she was smiling. I thought it strange that this witch smiled at me.

I experienced another rough ejection from this room, up the stairway to smell the dew, and I was thrown into the truck. The truck took a completely different route. I was frustrated that the guards were so diligent.

They moved me into the holding area to experience another nightmare that would haunt my future. John Lennon's song 'Imagine' was played over and over. As soon as the song finished they played it again.

The guards physically raised us off our precious mats to dance to this song. I smiled, though my body ached in pain. Imagine all those hardened men, dancing to the song 'Imagine', naked, with their dicks swinging in the breeze. Hour after hour they forced us to dance. It wasn't funny anymore.

Again, they roughly lifted me off my mat and took me out-side for the ritual hosing down. Familiarity became normal. As soon as I was dry, I expected to get wet. The torture we suffered became uncommonly comfortable. Trying to rationalise this concept allowed me to understand that I wasn't dead. Anything else was tolerable.

Tossed into the truck, the usual ritual, I was finally left standing outside a door to await my second interrogation. The interrogator ordered the guards to bring me into his office.

'Remove the bag,' he commanded.

My bag was quickly removed. The guards left the interroga-tor and me alone in the room. The man had a small body. Red blood vessels spotted his cheeks. He started to rant and rave in a foreign tongue. I shook my head, trying to get him to understand that I didn't understand what he wanted from me. This infuriated him and he became violent.

He used open-handed slaps to get me to react verbally. I enjoyed this treatment, as we were equal. It frustrated him as much as it intimidated and frustrated me.

His face went red and the blood vessels seemed to almost burst. This gave me a degree of satisfaction and enjoyment. As for the head slapping, I got to a stage of expecting it and threw my head hard against his palm, which I hoped would hurt his hand.

It seemed like I suffered this torment for three hours, but still I uttered nothing.

Finally I managed to hurt him. My ears were ringing and my head throbbed, but I did it. He left the office holding his hand. The ritual began again. I was ripped out of the chair, my bag put back on, and my handcuffs checked.

I was pushed and bumped into obstacles on the way back to the holding area. I was far too dry, so instinctively walked in the direction the guards had been taking me for my constant hosing down.

I stood there shivering, waiting to be pushed towards the hangar. In a kind gesture, someone popped a small piece of Mars Bar into my mouth. Even this act of kindness, I suspected, was a ploy for information.

More interrogation followed. Sitting at the desk the guards had left me at, my bag removed, I stared at another large photo of these people's dictator. Voices could be heard down a hallway. Some poor sod was suffering thumps to his body, groaning every time he received the blows.

Two men entered the room, talking to each other in clear plain English. I immediately assessed this interrogation technique to be the typical 'Mick and Jeff' style that the cops use very effectively. One is an arsehole and the other is nice. The nice one is continually offering their prisoner things to soften him up. Mine offered me food and I was hungry. I had only eaten one bowl of rice in two days. I nodded yes and he left to get me some. The other demanded, 'What's your hut identity?'

I remained silent. I put up with his ranting and raving and kicking over my chair, another cop trick. You can't get charged with assault for kicking a chair, right? No matter that the prisoners have no chance of protecting themselves. My hands were still cuffed in front of me. Hitting the floor with a fractured rib was extremely jarring.

The other interrogator finally returned. He had a chicken leg on a plate for me. He walked up to me and put it in my mouth. As I raised my hands, the arsehole who hated chairs ripped it out of my mouth, almost taking half my teeth. My mouth began to bleed and I became angry.

My hands moved like lightning and I grabbed his hand, his fatty fingers and my chicken leg. I began munching on the leg. I must have bitten his finger because he moved with a yelp of pain. He looked at me as though I had become some form of sick animal. The guards quickly removed me from the room, back to the holding area to endure anything and everything that pleased our guards.

The individual interrogations stopped. Our captors shifted tactics to group interrogation. My hatred towards my captors intensified. I was extremely frustrated that I didn't have the strength to attack and kill them.

This new form of manipulation was based on the information they had extracted from the poor sods that had failed to keep their mouths shut.

In the holding area, the enemy stated correct details of hut members and their names. The ones who couldn't remain silent would be shot, for they would be of no further use. Their heads would be cut off and displayed in local villages as heads that belonged to war criminals.

The last twelve hours within the seventy-two-hour period were known throughout the world by Special Forces operators as the twelve hours of hell. If you could maintain silence, you would save lives.

At the end of the twelve hours of hell, the enemy would shoot you dead, if you were lucky, or you would be packed up and sent to a prisoner of war camp. I looked forward to being killed. The pain was becoming unbearable.

The twelve hours of hell teaches you not to trust anyone, not even yourself. You are too fatigued and are easily manipulated into making the wrong mental assumptions.

Initially, they moved us from the holding area to the main interrogation centre. They placed me next to another naked prisoner; our arms brushed against each other. The guards removed our bags. When my eyes finally focused I saw my selection course instructor 'Pommy', the one who made my first day sheer hell. I had seen so many instructors I had almost forgotten him.

He had no handcuffs on, so I didn't know if I could trust him. The next thing the guards did to him eased my misgivings. He copped a solid hit to his sternum, doubling him over, and they quickly cuffed his hands in front of him. Our bags were placed roughly back on our heads. I felt a strange comfort having another prisoner suffering next to me.

They had twelve hours left to break us to confirm that the dead men hadn't told lies.

The guards lined all our other mates up and made them brush past us so that we could feel their clothing and warmth. This was to isolate us, and that was exactly the effect it had on me.

Why were we the only two left naked?

Next came a run with a bag over our heads, which was a shuffle for me. The run was through a paddock full of grass and cow shit. I tried to get as much on my feet as possible so I could upset these pricks by stinking out the hangar.

Pommy and I, being very fit, were forced to keep going for about an hour in an attempt to exhaust us. However, an hour's run, even full of injuries, was easy for us.

'Talk now!' the guard bellowed.

Pommy said nothing. I said, 'Fuck off!'

Pommy giggled and copped a back-handed clip for his trouble. They ran us another twenty minutes down a steep incline. We still had bags on our heads and tried glimpsing at our feet to see where we were going. We came to a drain system that had a racing torrent, charging at about chest depth.

'In,' the guards simply said, in that annoying foreign accent. 'In and up, in and up, in and up!'

Sure, anything to get some peace, I thought.

I hit the water and the pressure was strong. My toes stung and I yelped. The guards laughed. I tried to do what they demanded, struggling like an uncoordinated salmon. I felt Pommy move alongside me and grip my arm to help me up the torrent.

'C'mon, Paul, we can do this,' he encouraged.

I was shocked. He had never used my first name until now. I decided to ask him his. If today we died, I wanted to know the man's name that perished with me.

'It's Dave,' he offered. 'C'mon, Paul, keep pushing. Don't give them any reason to drop you. Think of it this way, imagine how ridiculous we look,' he encouraged.

I laughed, and kept laughing.

Expecting to die shortly, laughing at this situation seemed sane, however ludicrous.

When we got back to the hangar, in the back of a ute by ourselves, with the tarp over the top of us, I said to Dave, 'Is that four hours of hell gone?', expecting that in eight hours' time I would no longer feel pain.

'Yeah, mate, hang in there,' he replied.

More hours followed of the dreaded 'Imagine' mixed with foreign music. We were both then dragged away and made to pull each other's arms by means of rope over a high beam in order to torture the other into talking. The bags were removed so we could watch the experience and feel the individual's pain.

We jacked up and refused. The way the bloke hit us, I figured he must have been a kickboxing champion. He was wearing a balaclava and giving both of us a working over at the same time.

I don't remember much after that, except that I was in a foreign country, captured, and that I had to escape and kill.

Then the bag was raised.

'Well done. You've passed the exercise, but you are an aggressive prick,' Dave said.

I snapped out of it. Wherever I had been, I never wished to return.

My mind finally accepted that this was a training exercise. No one was going to kill me and I could drop the hatred I had towards my interrogators. I realised something else: I was the only guy still there from my selection cycle. I asked, 'Where are the boys?'

'You've been asleep for six hours,' Dave said.

That explained his fresh clothes and the fact that he had showered.

'The commanding officer snuck them into the regiment barracks earlier this morning. You passed out at hour eleven of the twelve-hour hell. The doctor advised everybody concerned to let you recover and sleep, and to let you wake on your own steam. 'How ya feeling?'

'Like shit. I thought they were the bad guys,' I said. 'When we were in that water drain and you said to me, keep going mate, don't give them a reason to drop you, I thought that you meant if I quit they would kill me.'

He laughed uncontrollably. Upon composure, he explained his comment.

'Paul, I meant that if you gave up, they would drop you from the course.' He laughed again.

Everybody in the hangar laughed. At least I had gotten the holding area right, I thought.

'Your mates have had their handcuffs off for twenty-four hours now; the selectors just couldn't trust you,' Dave replied.

'They were smarter not to,' I replied.

I started to focus on the area in which I sat. My rubber mat was still under my clothed arse. Clothes ... I must've been dressed when I passed out. The mat had become my most precious item during the interrogation.

I needed a piss and began hobbling to the only open door at the end of the empty hangar. The only furniture in the hangar was a table, a couple of chairs and the tape recorder responsible for some future mental scars. I felt like smashing it, but I needed a piss more.

Reading material including novels, crosswords and of course the mandatory porn lay on the table. I finally reached the open door, the only entrance in or out, as someone called out, 'Where ya going, Ranger?'

As I turned to reply, my fractured rib dug into my insides. I bent over to alleviate the pressure. I was suddenly feeling nauseous. Miss Perfume moved to assist me.

'I'm going for a fucking piss!'

I apologised to Miss Perfume for my bad mouth. She replied, 'What you've been through in the last three days, I can't blame you. It's this way, Ranger.'

She had such a sweet voice and this was the first time I had heard her speak English with an Australian accent.

This woman was starting to look like an angel, and I put this down to my being horny. I hadn't seen a woman for four weeks. During my interrogation, she only spoke dribble to me. In my mind she was an enemy.

I was wary of her most of all, because I knew I could handle aggression and clam up, but to a soft, friendly, seductive approach, I was vulnerable. I knew that, but I couldn't let them know that weakness.

I was so wrong. It was training, it was an exercise, and they were Australians interrogating me. I finally started to do my piss and the pain was excruciating. I was pissing blood. I decided to sit. This relaxing position gave me the opportunity to collect my thoughts.

Miss Perfume waited outside the door ready to assist me. Seventy hours ago she was dressing my feet. How could I have been so wrong?

My mind tried to adjust to what had just happened. I now had to reorder it and take the enemy out, replacing them with Australians. The hatred I had built against these individuals had to be redirected. I had been quite prepared, if I got fit enough, to make an escape attempt and kill as many of these people as I could. I probably would have died in the process, but I hadn't been prepared to put up with that shit any longer.

How could I have been so wrong? It was training, an exercise. This was a prerequisite I had to pass in order to join these elite soldiers.

I remembered the wanking stunt I had performed in front of Miss Perfume. I made a mental note to apologise to her. I flushed the toilet and raised myself painfully and went to apologise. She was extremely sympathetic and started to explain to me that no one was certain within the interrogation team whether I could be broken.

She told me that those of us who lasted the longest and went through the last twelve hours were the only ones who passed. The group had been cut down from twenty-one men to thirteen. The thirteen left had passed because, as she said, 'You had the right stuff.'

Throughout this conversation she referred to me as 'Ranger'. She must have been an officer. I asked her for her rank and her job. She replied, 'I'm a captain in intelligence with nursing skills.'

This explained why she was so young, but so highly ranked.

I took a punt and asked her, 'Are we getting R&R tonight, ma'am?'

'Yes, Ranger.'

'Are you doing anything?'

'No, Ranger.'

'Would you be seen with me for a drink?'

'That sounds fine, Ranger. I'm sure any girl would have a drink with a soldier who wears a sandy beret.'

I hadn't been given mine yet, but I wasn't telling her that. We had to do the patrol course and parachute course before being awarded that honour.

She assisted me to my mat and left by the correct protocol.

Dave approached and said, 'The commanding officer is sending his car to get the rest of us.'

I slept all the way back to our barracks. The commanding officer met us at the gate. There were salutes from all of us. He returned his and said, 'Well done, Ranger, have a shower and take the rest of the day off. Your mates are at the pub waiting for you.'

I didn't expect to see Miss Perfume again, she being a captain and me a ranger, but I saw her at the bar, chatting to my mates, who she had been torturing for the last three days. She appeared to be relaxing.

Our eyes met and as I approached her the song 'Imagine' started playing on the jukebox. I froze in my tracks and started shaking. I turned around to get some open space and fresh air. She came up behind me and touched me. I felt pain. It was not from her; rather it was my own mental scars.

She knew I was uncomfortable and asked, 'Should we leave?'

'Yes,' I said.

I then noticed the twelve men who had successfully completed the course doing the same. Ben was puking over the balcony.

'Have you got a car?' I asked.

'Yes.'

'Let's go to Kings Park.'

I needed open space.

* * *

We sat looking at the view. The Perth city lights mesmerised us. We stared into the view for hours. I didn't talk much, neither did she. We kissed at the war memorial; we both knew what would eventuate.

We said nothing as we strolled back to the car, arm in arm. She drove the car directly back to the SAS regiment barracks.

She was staying in the officers' accommodation and sneaked me in. This was a move which, had we been caught, would have been bad for both of our careers.

We didn't care. The door shut, and she turned the light off. I quickly turned it back on. We made love like two animals, ripping at each other's clothes, kissing passionately, vibrantly and rigorously, and trying new positions. As the sweat built up something else built up: for her, all the tension she had held inside from putting us through those three days; for me, the aggression and the anger from being a victim.

We both achieved some outlet in this lovemaking. As we orgasmed together, we let all our tension and the rest of the shit leave us. She began to cry and I stroked her, holding her. Then I made love to her, softly and more sensitively this time. We were healing each other, or so I thought.

At some stage I must have fallen asleep, to wake in the middle of the night. I needed a hasty exit.

I awoke screaming, 'Fuck off, fuck off, fuck off!'

Chapter Sixteen

The infiltration

It was my second year of operational duties. The next task I was involved in was to be an internal operation, totally within the Australian borders.

The sergeant in command of this operation was Barry Johnson, who was assisted by his permanent patrol second-in-charge (2IC) Phil Barnes. This duo was notorious for being given sticky assignments. They had just returned from overseas, where they had required a hot extraction. The commanding officer directed that they were to rest from combat activity and perform an internal task.

I felt honoured to have the opportunity to learn new skills from these men. Barry wore a telltale knife scar on his cheek. He would tell you if asked about its origin that it happened during training; however, the other sergeants knew the truth. I suspected I would never know. With dark hair and an ethnic, possibly Greek, ancestry, he was a solid man with features similar to a heavyweight wrestler. He was an awesome sight.

His loyal offsider Phil had completed selection with Barry. He had refused his own command of a patrol, so as to remain

Barry's 2IC. Phil's features were the opposite of Barry's: he had a long, lanky body that was muscular, similar in structure to that of an Olympian long-distance jumper. His legs were like tree trunks. If asked why he remained Barry's 2IC, his answer was, 'To keep him alive.'

I felt safe working with these men, and the loyalty they showed each other was commendable. I was looking forward to the job.

The job started with the usual situation of a warning order given by the commanding officer. The job was a cache job, live. This would require us to carry a lot of equipment, so Phil, realising this, grabbed me, and we started getting the stores together. Our patrol commander Barry would be getting his orders from the commanding officer; he would need a couple of hours to work out the plan of how the job would be done.

He said to Phil and myself, 'You blokes be back by 1100 hours for orders. Nathan and Troy, get your personal equipment ready.'

Nathan and I had been in same patrol team since we had completed the selection cycle and the freefall course, our choice of insertion skill. The choice by Command to put us together in this newly formed patrol pleased us, as now Troy was joining us. Three members from Hut 10 would be together again.

This was Troy's first operation with a freefall patrol. He had completed his freefall course at the same time as us, but the Signals squadron would not release him. As soon as a position on a patrol became available he jumped into the world of the SAS operator. His excitement was well-justified and well-earned. This was to be his first internal operation.

By 1100 hours, all necessary equipment had been arranged and signed for. After orders, there would be patrol tasks that required attention. Once these were complete, all the members, with their own self-discipline, would be checking their own personal equipment required for the job.

Additionally, all weapons would be 'zeroed'. To zero a weapon, an operator fires down-range, landing rounds in a group on the target. The operator adjusts the group to his eye by manipulating the fore and rear sight of the weapon until he gets his group in the centre of the forehead.

At the end of the orders there would be a test fire of all the weapons. Everybody knew that they had to get their rounds on target prior to infiltration of an area. If for some strange situation a member didn't get his rounds on target, he would be excluded from the mission.

There was a time limit for the test fire. This enabled everybody on the job and the commander to know that all weapons were operating and that all members could hit the target with the efficiency that was required within the profession.

The job was a simple task, one that we had done before on many occasions. The cache was 'live', meaning we had to carry food, weapons, ammunition, grenades, claymores and water, plus all the equipment to make the cache.

The cache was to be left there; the location would be given to Special Forces Command by secure means. It wasn't our job to know what it was for, just that we had to cache the equipment and keep the location secret.

It was a simple mission: dig a hole and put the equipment in it, then cover the hole back up. The execution was always difficult. As operators, we would normally be carrying sixty kilos each, independently. This mission required us to carry additional materials for the cache, which meant fifteen kilos each extra: an enormous weight, with water being the heaviest item.

For this patrol, we had to carry in water individually to last us for a week. This was about fourteen litres per man, on top of the water for the cache, which also had to be carried in a twenty-litre plastic jerry can.

To freefall a normal load was difficult, as it was hard to remain stable during freefall. Now we had to fly with the heaviest load that had been asked of me since I had joined this freefall troop.

I had the privilege of strapping the twenty-litre jerry container to my chest, with my equipment — a shovel to dig with, my loaded pack, webbing and my weapon — on my side.

I looked absolutely ridiculous standing in front of a mirror, jumping up and down, doing my own deniability test.

The deniability test is done by all operators. Prior to boarding our means of transport to the drop-off, our commander would ask us each individually to jump up and down. If a noise was heard during this test, it was always embarrassing for the operator. Self-discipline dictated that this eventuality didn't arise.

If a noise were heard within my equipment, I would quickly find the source and wrap some cloth around the item, and proceed through the drill again. I was not enjoying the test of deniability, for every time I jumped up the bloody shovel strapped to my side was digging into my flesh.

We sat around as a group and discussed the best way to strap this equipment on and still be able to freefall safely.

I was apprehensive to say the least. The shovel and the water jerry were where the problem lay. During freefall, the more stable you are, the better you fly. Having a jerry strapped to my chest and a shovel head under my armpit, I knew I wasn't symmetrical, which meant one thing: a definite bumpy ride.

With the deniability tests completed, it was now time to apply the dreaded camouflage cream, which wouldn't be removed until the job was finished, after the debrief. I was ready to do my job again.

The transport would be a truck with its tarp down, and it wouldn't be opened until we were backed up to the aircraft, which was to be used for our insertion. There wouldn't be any mucking about: the equipment would be loaded and as soon as all patrol members were on board, the aircraft would taxi to its runway.

We would still be sorting out our gear and getting it secure. Everyone would take a seat and get comfortable, then regulate their breathing after the hasty activity on the tarmac. Once recovered, we would sit silently until we reached a thousand feet, and just concentrate on the job.

A thousand feet would be the signal to throw regulations out the window; it would be a mad scramble for the best spot, which was usually on top of the pallets. Due to the size of these pallets, a man could stretch out full-length and get some valuable sleep, the professional soldier's most valued friend.

It was twenty minutes from TOT (time over target), and the RAAF crew member woke me from a deep sleep. I was usually the one who was stirred first. I had put this down to my appearance; having a baby-face meant I had a more approachable aspect.

There was a standard regiment joke about us lads with young appearances, which was, 'Make sure you take your balaclava on every job you do. We don't want the bad guys falling over and laughing.'

It was a definite struggle to put all the equipment on. The webbing went on first. The shovel handle was passed through my webbing waist belt, running down the side of my left leg. The shovel head was tucked under my left armpit, cushioned by rags strapped onto it, the only protection between flesh and metal. The handle was strapped to my side using three-inch-wide gaffer tape. With two separate wrappings, one across my upper chest, and one above my webbing belt, it felt secure.

The parachute went on next. I swung it onto my back, bending forward to get the weight as high as possible. All straps were tightened this way: leg straps first, shoulder straps next. The effect would always be that upon rising I was slightly hunched, due to the straps being so tight; uncomfortable now, but symmetrical in flight. I looked down at my feet. The item that would ensure that I didn't fly symmetrical was next to be secured: the twenty-litre water jerry.

Two snap hooks would be attached to my webbing, high on my shoulder straps, one on each side. The jerry would be attached by two snap hooks on either side of its handle, securing it in place. I connected the hooks and felt the weight. I clumsily struggled to get down on my knees, with the jerry resting upright, balanced on an aircraft seat. A crew member was walking past, and all I could do to get his attention in this contorted position was to reach out and grab his lower leg.

'What's up, mate?' he inquired.

'Could you grab this roll of tape and wrap it around the jerry and my lower back under the parachute? Just keep wrapping tightly until I tell you to stop.' I passed him the tape and he began.

'Stop, that will do — thanks, mate,' I offered.

'You look like a pregnant turtle,' he laughed, as he moved towards the cockpit.

The jerry felt secure and snug against my chest. If I did look like a pregnant turtle, I seriously hoped that this pregnancy would not be aborted through flight.

I connected the pack via snap hooks that secured it to the parachute shoulder straps. The jerry now sat on top of the pack, which was upside-down and in front of my legs. The pack shoulder straps now became leg straps, and I stepped through them, tightening them up snugly around my upper thighs. The weight and my body position demanded that I rest my pack on the aircraft seat in order to affix the next item.

This was the rifle, always affixed on the right-hand side of the body. The butt was level with my shoulder and the body of the weapon was flush against my body. The barrel went over my hip and rested on my upper right thigh, which was the best position for it not to entangle parachute lines. The chest strap of the parachute webbing secured the rifle strap.

The rifle was always last on and first off, in case I had to protect myself. As this job was internal, it was highly unlikely that we would use our weapons, but it was not impossible. We always trained and prepared for the worst situation.

Five minutes from target I was finally ready. I did two jumps up and down to see if I could hear any noises, collapsed onto the strapping seat and continued perspiring.

One of the RAAF crew members gave us cups of water so we wouldn't be dehydrated when we left the aircraft. The red light came on, which meant sixty seconds before target. My legs were starting to tingle and were going numb.

I needed assistance from the crew member to stand up and move to the open ramp. I would be in the second group to go; Barry would lead the patrol by freefalling by himself. The other two groups would be two-man drag-outs, a technique we'd developed to ensure that there wasn't too much separation during freefall.

The difference with civilian freefall was that it only required a parachute, whereas we had so much equipment that when we hit the air we were unsymmetrical, and this created a very bumpy ride. Also, it was always done at night, with only a cylume light stick taped to our helmets to identify us in freefall.

At the thirty-second call we were all on our feet, being assisted by the RAAF crew members to the open ramp. The outside air made our camouflage uniforms flap around our bodies. Barry had the heels of his feet flush on the edge of the ramp. A RAAF crew man was holding his pack so he wouldn't exit before the green light.

The green light came on, and we yelled above the noise of the engines of the Hercules aircraft.

'Go go go!'

Barry was swallowed into the lonely blackness of the night. His plunge swiftly became uncontrolled because a strap securing his pack was loose. He slid and tumbled out of our view.

A quick visual inspection of Troy's equipment was all I had time to accomplish. The check was reciprocated and we dived from the aircraft into the unknown.

The unsymmetrical equipment quickly forced us into an unstable flying process. As I followed Troy from the aircraft, clinging to his arms, my legs should have been trailing, our heads together. On this occasion, I couldn't get my legs up and we clashed together head to head, toe to toe, our bodies vertical. We dropped to earth like pins falling to the carpet.

The shovel, although padded, caused a deep gash near my armpit, but far worse was that we were now spinning, twisting and tumbling through the night. My side became warm from the blood. My heart became chilled.

Don't concentrate on what you can't fix, I thought!

Instinct and training dictated survival. We had to slow the spin speed or we would lose consciousness. Immediately, trying to attain a humanly tolerable speed, I dropped the leg opposite to the direction of the rotation. Troy did the same. It worked; we were slowing.

The incident had cost us in altitude and location. All members of our patrol wore cylume light sticks on their helmets. Upon searching, however, I couldn't see light in any direction.

Slowly spinning to the right, we finally adjusted to a stable flying position. Comfortable for about three seconds, smiles appeared on our contorted faces. They disappeared suddenly, though, as we entered a rapid left-hand spin.

Our altitude was now five thousand two hundred. The designated break height was four thousand feet. With my brain screaming for stability, I let go of Troy.

The last thing we needed was one of us freefalling through an open parachute. The golden rule was to know the position of the other patrol members. Since I only knew the position of Troy, maintaining visual contact with him was essential.

By the time I stabilised he had tumbled nearly three hundred feet below me. His cylume light stick was shrinking rapidly. As I watched, he threw his body into the delta position.

His head was down, arms by his sides and legs straight. He was still trying to get stable. As he slid beneath me, our situation became extremely dangerous. I took evasive action and tried to slide away. He seemed to be magnetically attached to me and followed my every move. He had no idea of what was happening above him. From my position, I could see the difficulty he was having getting stable.

His dump height was three thousand five hundred feet. After three tries he reached his ripcord.

'Jesus, he's going to pop his canopy!'

We were still at four thousand feet. As the canopy flashed off his back, I couldn't help but gasp.

'Shit, I'm too close!'

As it ballooned, my face got whipped. Fortune favoured me though, as there was enough air in the canopy to bounce me off.

It was as though I'd bounced onto a trampoline incorrectly and had fallen, flailing, off its side.

Fortunately I hadn't collected any suspension lines. If we'd become entangled, certain death for us both would have been the result. I raced past him, at about five metres' distance.

'Shit!' he yelled.

Plummeting past I wore a relieved smile.

At two thousand five hundred feet I pulled my ripcord. My canopy opened beautifully. I looked around three hundred and sixty degrees, trying to spot anyone. I could see Troy, his second cylume light stick hanging, swaying gently beneath him. Since I was the senior patrol member at the lowest altitude, I was required to lead the team to the designated target. This contingency plan was spelled out in our orders.

Troy would be concentrating on my second cylume stick. We had designed this system such that we could follow the light of the soldier below. I reached down to my leg, broke the elastic band and let the cylume light stick drop. It was attached to my leg by a two-metre cord.

Since we had dumped at different altitudes, the canopies of the patrol members would create a stack above me. As I gazed silently into the nothingness before me, I knew my next responsibility.

Get everybody down safely.

The wind direction was all-important; I knew my canopy and myself were driving with the wind. I was now looking for a safe place for the team to land, as well as praying that the upper winds were at the same direction as the ground winds.

The team was good at canopy control. We were jumping with round canopies. During mandatory rehearsals, we landed within twenty-five metres of each other. This was a huge feat, considering that the canopy responses were slow, and when you hit the ground with a wind speed higher than eight knots, which was the majority of times, you would be landing backwards.

The jerry strapped to my chest was obscuring my vision; I was at a thousand feet and trying to focus through the blackness, when a helmet came floating past me. The air seemed to be filling its empty cavity and resisting gravity, but nothing resists gravity, and it continued falling past.

'Fuck, someone's having a rough ride.'

I was at five hundred feet and still couldn't see the target. It was pitch-black: there were no lights, no fires and no torch flashes. The RAAFies had fucked up again and put us out in the wrong spot.

At two hundred feet the blackness lightened and there was the ground, the most inhospitable ground that you could wish not to land on: all rock, jagged rocks, and boulders. This landing was going to hurt!

At two hundred feet, I was too low to do any major adjustments. I was lucky; I was bringing the team into wind.

'But the ground,' I said to myself. 'If no one breaks a leg on this jump, I'll be very, very surprised.'

I hit the ground hard and did the best para roll that I could, washing off the momentum of the impact.

That bloody jerry, literally now! For my own blood was dripping out of my shirt. The jerry striking a boulder brought me to a full stop and winded me. I twisted around to see if Troy was following in the same path that I had taken. He was. Good, this would give the lads at a higher height a chance to land together.

Barry didn't cross my mind. I knew of and respected his experience and I knew he would find us. All four of us had landed safely, with only one minor mishap; Troy had sustained an ankle injury, a sprain. He knew as well as us that there wouldn't be any assistance until we were well clear of the drop zone.

He would have to put up with the pain, knowing Barry would move us at least five kilometres from the drop zone before we stopped and rested. There, anyone injured would be given first aid, some serious painkillers and strapping.

My cut was manageable and I would have to wait the same period as Troy before having the medic dress the wound.

'Where's the boss?' I asked Phil.

'Fucked if I know,' was his reply, quietly whispered. 'What happened?'

Just as I was about to explain the boss's untidy exit, we heard that familiar sound of air passing through the vents in a canopy. Barry was off line to our right and the problem was that a rocky knoll was between him and us. Phil came up with a brilliant idea just in time. If it had been any later, Barry would have set himself up to land on the other side of this knoll.

Because Barry could not see any cylume lights to follow, Phil kept throwing his cylume light stick into the air. Barry focused on the green cylume light stick that was being thrown into the dark space above us. He began to make his next move towards us.

He just cleared the knoll by feet; he was also concerned about how low he was, because as he came over the lip of the knoll he had his knees up to his ears. We could almost hear his sigh of relief, as he extended his feet and prepared for the mandatory backward roll.

He had vomit all down his front. Troy asked him if he was all right and he whispered, 'Rough ride, but better out than in.'

The drop zone was now secure. We would be carrying all our equipment plus a thirty-kilogram parachute away with us. The bag that would be used to carry the parachute was tucked under our leg straps. We travelled approximately five kilometres from the drop zone, stopped and buried the parachutes. Once this was done, we all sat quietly and regulated our breathing. Then we listened.

When in visual range of our landing spot we were always edgy and concerned that if we were seen there could be a follow-up. If we got through the night without bumping into anybody or anything, day two would be a whole lot more relaxed. But we were always diligent and professional about our own security.

If no one was following us up and there was no enemy activity, injuries would now be attended to. Then we would move at a serious pace towards the designated cache location. As free-fallers, we would usually walk at least twenty kilometres towards the target in case anyone saw our landings. Twenty kilometres, even in the desert, will usually get you over the next horizon.

Chapter Seventeen

The installation

During the first stop my job as patrol signaller, much to the joy of Troy, who had carried a radio set his whole career, was to get the location of where we were from Barry, who at this stage would have had to do a resection to get our true location.

'Fucking RAAFies,' he said, as he passed me the true grid reference.

'Won't be long, Boss,' I said, as I quickly coded the grid reference and tapped on the morse key back to SAS headquarters.

The grid reference indicated that we had landed ten kilometres away from the correct drop zone. Thanks to the RAAFies we had an extra ten kilometres' walking on top of the usual twenty. We had walked about five kilometres, so simple mathematics told me that we would have to do twenty-five kilometres in one night.

We would complete this distance during the night, be absolutely shagged and end up sleeping in temperatures ranging from forty degrees to fifty degrees Celsius, but because of the exhaustion we would all sleep soundly when it was our turn.

One of us would be awake in case of enemy activity. There would be an additional patrol task to ensure that the sleepers moved into the shade, as the earth rotated through the sun's orbit from east to west. Being absolutely exhausted, it's easy to sleep in the sun and then become dehydrated, which would then make us useless.

The next evening would be a 'box' reconnaissance of the area where the cache was to be put. All sides of this area would be checked to ensure our orders weren't compromised and that we weren't walking into a trap. On this job, everything seemed ridgy-didge. We stopped for twenty-four hours and rested, with the two blokes on observation post changing every four hours. Day three, at night, was when we would be putting in the cache. Everything was going according to plan.

* * *

By day four, the cache was in its secret location and this was reported back to squadron headquarters by code. Squadron Headquarters (SHQ) would immediately send the location to Special Forces Command. Our job was done.

Prior to infill, Barry, along with the RAAFies, had discussed our means of exit and transportation. There was no joy from the RAAFies, as they had a task on the night we required exfiltration (exfil). The next option was the army.

This option was to be a Pilatus Porter, a very small plane that could hold a patrol very uncomfortably. These planes could land on a five-cent piece. We had experienced pilots, and the army pilots of these aircraft were especially good. They didn't have much choice!

It was up to Barry to designate the landing route. This could range from outback roads to desert pads, and beaches. Barry decided that we would use a beach due west of the cache location.

We had ninety-five kilometres to walk to the exfil. This would be achieved over the next three nights, and the fourth night we would be in the exfil location, or so we thought.

The next stage of this operation would be to walk at least forty kilometres, to ensure that Barry had some time and space so we could patrol the beach to make sure it wasn't compromised. We would cover as much distance as we could while fresh.

We set off that night and Phil asked me how much water I had. I replied two bottles. He proceeded to ask everybody the same question and then returned to me.

'Barry wants you to code a message for the water resupply during the walk tonight.'

'Will do,' I whispered.

There was nothing unusual about this request. I would code the message when we stopped for our ten-minute rest, which we did every hour.

Phil also added, 'Ask for the technique you came up with, the one that we rehearsed at base before we infiled.'

I felt proud that I had instigated this new technique and that it was going to be used for this operation. It was a great idea, even if I say so myself. We had rehearsed it a dozen times without one failure. Prior to the operation we had an aircraft designated to us so we could practise our jumping skills and this newly introduced technique, constructed by me.

The concept was discussed among us. This was always encouraged, because each of us was quite capable of intelligent input. We were assessed and trained to be capable of applying solutions to practical situations. Individuals wouldn't have passed selection without displaying these abilities. It didn't matter what year you did selection, every patrol member was expected to offer input.

So, during rehearsals, all members of the patrol were asked to initiate new ideas, but the commander would always make the final decision. The concept I had designed involved a fire hose, the length of twenty metres. Once Barry gave me the go-ahead to try the system, it was a quick trip to the nearest fire station, and a request to see if they had any spare hoses lying around. They were extremely helpful, and it wasn't a problem to give us a serviceable length of fire hose.

We returned to the landing ground, and acquired two clamps for each end of the hoses. The test would be to see if we could drop the hose from a moving aircraft, the reason being that a helicopter hovering or landing would definitely compromise our mission and location. Due to this, a low-flying aircraft was our only option.

It was pleasing to see the hose bounce along the ground and land safely when we did the first test. Barry, the pilots and I wanted to increase the height to see if the technique would still work. It did, so after twelve drops we knew exactly the height we could use, this being two hundred feet.

This height would clear all hills and knolls on approach. The drop-off operation rehearsal absolutely assured us of its success, and confirmed in our minds that the water resupply would go according to plan.

The hose filled with water and the clamps secured to the end wouldn't be touched until our aircrew loaded it in for our necessary water resupply. It was planned for the pilots to do the water resupply twenty-four hours after the cache was in.

* * *

The walk that evening was tremendous. We had covered about twenty-five kilometres when something happened. In the middle of the desert were two ventilation towers in the centre of a huge compound, with twelve-foot high fencing and razor wire lining the top. The huge ventilation towers were as big as three houses put together — an awesome sight.

Barry approached me and gave me the exact grid reference for this location. So now, in addition to the request for the water resupply, I would be encoding an installation report and the grid reference to the location to report our findings to headquarters.

As we started to move off, a vehicle approached us. We slowly moved lower to the ground and remained perfectly still. We were right out in the open and about thirty metres from the fence. The vehicle was driving along a tar road, which was about twenty metres inside the fence.

The vehicle slowed and took a sharp left turn; it travelled a short distance, then stopped. There was a gate they were checking; we were just outside the gleam of the vehicle head-lights.

If they were professional about what they were doing, we would have been busted. But as we had travelled a large distance, I'm sure the security patrol believed that this location was impenetrable. The slack attitude of the guards also allowed us to identify that their accents were American, and that they were referring to other people who also belonged to the installation.

Be wary of what you say. This night, five individuals heard a story while the guards checked the gates. An annoying American accent, loud and brash, explained to his mate that a woman by the name of Robyn was enjoying a lot of sexual experiences during her twelve-month posting.

It was a simple comment.

'Have you fucked Robyn yet?'

'Last night,' the reply.

'Mother-fucker! She will have fucked all twenty of us by the time her twelve months are up!'

This simple statement was to give me even more information to encode in the installation report. The guards had given us the number of personnel located at this installation. Furthermore, it wasn't an Australian installation — it was American.

The vehicle moved off and so did we, but we were once again reaching that exhaustion stage as the sun broke the horizon. I was quickly getting my radio set organised. All the others would be providing protection for me, as I sent this detailed information to SHQ, who would send it to Special Forces Command, who would pass it on to the Commander of the Army.

This is where it gets dodgy and we knew it. The next place this information would end up would be Parliament House. Once our politicians knew, fuck anything could happen and usually did!

At this juncture, though we didn't know it, someone, some group that had more influence than the regiment, decided that what we had reported seeing that evening meant we all automatically became expendable. Being totally oblivious of the decision taken in the halls of power, we collectively couldn't give a flying toss about the installation; all we were interested in was our water resupply.

All members had begun the walk with at least two bottles. Being extremely disciplined in our water consumption, each member had ensured he would still have some water left at the time of resupply. On average, we each had close to a quarter of a bottle left.

Chapter Eighteen

Responsible deniability

It was always mandatory to still have some water prior to a resupply, just in case it fucked up. This time we knew that the water resupply wouldn't fail; with a dozen successful attempts behind us, we knew water was on the way. It was about midday when we heard the familiar drone of the aircraft designated for the water resupply.

We had communication with the crew via a UHF radio. They identified our location, once we had given them the code that had been arranged before we left. We saw the ramp down on the De Havilland Caribou and two crew men assisting the water hose off the ramp.

The hose hit the air and hit the ground. It didn't bounce on the ground as it had done during rehearsals. At the first impact, it coiled like a snake dropped from a great height: its last nervous reaction that signified it was dead. The water hose lay on the ground lifeless. Water poured out the ends of the hose. The desert floor quickly drank our precious nectar.

If we weren't real men, at this sight we would have cried and released the same amount of water that disappeared in front of our eyes. We were devastated, and rude gestures were thrown back to the aircrew. They turned their back on us. The aircraft climbed and then disappeared over the horizon.

On inspection, the hose had not split or perforated; water was only coming out of the ends. We all raced to save what precious water was left in the hose.

The wing nuts that were used to secure the clamps to the ends had been loosened; someone was fucking with us. We managed to get ten bottles of water from the hose.

'Fuck the army!' This statement was bellowed in a chorus from all of us, except for Barry.

Barry just seemed to take it in his stride and was trying to calm us down. We were still in an operational environment, and he wanted us to maintain our professionalism. Phil approached Barry and questioned him.

'Well, what the fuck are we gonna do now?'

'Calm down and follow me,' was his reply to this direct question from his 2IC.

This was the first time a discussion was held without all members involved. Phil and Barry discussed our situation among themselves.

Troy spoke first.

'Have you blokes heard of a book called *Nineteen Eighty-Four* by George Orwell?'

'Yeah, one of my favourites,' I answered.

'Do you know there's a United Nations treaty numbered Nine One Nine Eight Four regarding Australia's boundaries?'

'No, I didn't. What's it state?'

'Well, it's a political treaty that has been signed by our prime ministers since the late sixties. It states that that the Asian continent can use Australia for rural settlement of Asians who are displaced.

'Australia is Asia. In the new millennium there will be three world powers and currencies to match; hence the introduction of the euro in Europe. The three world powers are Europe, the Americas and Asia. Due to our geographical location, you can guarantee that your future family members will have Indonesian as their primary language and be forced into the Muslim religion.'

'That's pretty full-on, Troy — fucking unbelievable to be more exact,' Nathan joined the conversation.

'Okay then, if it's so fucking unbelievable, what do you think when you watch the news after a secret brief?' Troy directed his question to Nathan.

'Okay, I admit the Australian public is very naive and apathetic. Sure it's a giggle to go home and watch the news. It always gives misleading information and purposely favours the western world or western propaganda, when the brief has told us the complete opposite,' Nathan finished.

'Welcome to the world of Big Brother. This treaty states that Australia will be required to settle displaced Asians, hence our immigration policy leaning towards Asians more than any other race.

'The scary part of the treaty is that if the white Australian doesn't like this situation and he decides to defend himself, his family and his land, then under the UN treaty 91984 he will be charged as a criminal and will be charged with murder, even if he acts in self-defence against a foreign invader.

'The first nine in the treaty identification number dictates the year of the start of this process; together with the last four figures this scares the shit out of me — it seems to be a practical joke by the drafter.'

We all sat in silence pondering what Troy had just told us.

I remember sitting in a classroom trying to understand this world that George Orwell was writing about. It shocked me that this fictional world was imagined in a man's mind; however, in my mind this world of *Nineteen Eighty-Four* was real.

I decided in that classroom that by 1984 I would be strong enough and fit enough, and would have obtained enough skills, to be able to protect my friends, family and myself. I joined the army. Now those figures plagued me again.

Troy went on. 'Look at it this way. If what we saw last night at the installation was part of the UN treaty that I have just explained, then our water resupply fucking up would have merit.'

I wanted to know more. 'Do you think we have found ourselves in a responsible deniability situation?' I asked Troy.

'What's that?' Nathan inquired.

'It's when something happens that has to be covered up to keep the public unaware of the real situation. The usual comment from those involved is "It didn't happen. We weren't there,"' I answered him.

Had we, as Special Forces operators, found ourselves in a very untidy responsible deniability position, but this time as the victims? Had the powers in charge decided that with what we had seen, it would be better to leave us in the desert than to have to face us asking for explanations about this vital secret information?

The official story would be that an SAS patrol had died in the desert, which was ridiculous, because we were highly trained in survival ability, we constantly had to live off the land, and could even find water in extremely arid spots.

The decision would be made in the halls of power that what we reported would never be known. Ridiculous maybe, but our reality was shaping into a conspiracy beyond our control.

Troy, at least, was convinced. 'In my opinion, it's inevitable that Australia will become part of Asia, especially the top half, which is referred to by those who know as the Brisbane Line.'

'What's the Brisbane Line?' Nathan inquired.

I answered for Troy.

'It's an imaginary line known by the Indonesians and our politicians to stretch from Brisbane city, across Australia to Carnarvon on the west coast of Australia.'

'Ah, you're both wankers,' Nathan abused us.

'Get fucked,' Troy returned.

Both men were being thrust into this very untidy situation. Both were trying to grip some sense of reality they could accept as truth, one in total denial and the other in conspiracy mode. I didn't know which concept was the healthiest. The abuse from each of them was rising in volume.

Being the senior member of this group, I took responsibility for calming Nathan and Troy. Once this was achieved, I began to set up our radio. I was trying to occupy my mind with something else instead of the memory of watching that first impact, and seeing our precious water seeping into the hot desert's red sandy floor.

I placed the men in protective positions by the time Barry and Phil had finished their private conversation and communication had been set up following the correct tactical protocol.

I finished the set-up and moved to my radio set to await my instructions from Barry. This would be to send the failed water-resupply code and the location where we would require the second attempt. I looked over to where they were hunched over a map, trying to locate a water-resupply spot. They returned and instructed me to establish communications. I wrote down the new grid reference they gave me and added it to the coded message.

This was when everything turned to shit and I was to endure a new nickname, 'No comms Paul'.

I kept trying to establish comms all through the day at the insistence of Barry, but had no luck. When the sun finally set, Barry called us all together and said, 'We're going to head back to the cache site, dig it up and recover the twenty-litre jerry full of water.'

We would be walking all night again. We were still fifty-five kilometres short of the ocean and we now had to go back forty kilometres to our original start point, though our route would be longer this time, because we were going to avoid that Yank installation like the plague.

So we travelled that evening about forty-three kilometres with only two water bottles each. When we finally arrived at the cache site it was about 0900 hours.

Barry asked me to set up comms, as the boys slowly dug up the cache. Barry was very experienced in handling his troops, who were fatigued and exhausted. He had each man do ten shovel loads, and then rested them.

After trying every type of antenna, I knew I had done my best. It was now about three hours since I'd started calling SHQ. I tried one more solution. The last call was clear: No-Code, a definite no-no that broke all the rules in the book.

The message I sent was, 'We need water now! Patrol location: live cache site.'

Still no answer.

The conspiracy was growing. Barry was pissed off and grabbed my pack, which carried the radio. We were sharing it between the five of us. The others had dropped their packs forty-three kilometres back where the water resupply had failed.

Barry had been a qualified patrol signaller prior to being given command of his own patrol. He returned about an hour later, after having had tried every antenna known to man, and threw the pack down.

'No fucking joy,' he lamented.

I looked around. All the patrol members' faces dropped. The first signs of lack of water could be seen on my mates: cracked lips and bleeding. We were all sucking the blood from our lips to ensure no precious fluids escaped our bodies.

After relieving the cache of the jerry of water, we each had six bottles. Barry put the water discipline rules in place. There was no drinking unless ordered and it was to be only a green army bottle capful.

Hopefully, this discipline would allow us to reach our destination, which was about ninety kilometres away. We were headed for a group of dams we had found on our maps, just five kilometres short of our designated pick-up point. The maps were twenty years old and we were all praying that these dams would be full of water.

We started late afternoon; it would be 'fuck the rules' from now on. We would move day and night. By the time we reached the other packs we had drunk two bottles each, and there were four to go before we reached the dam site.

By the time we got there we would be twenty-four hours late for pick-up, but it was okay. We had a loss of comms procedure which dictated our nominated time of pick-up. If we were not there, the same designated aircraft would try to pick us up exactly twenty-four hours later. We would be on time for the second pick-up.

We arrived at the dams with no water left. We were all hoping that five kilometres away from the coastline would be enough for the dams not to be brackish.

I spotted the dams first. There were four in a row. My legs had a sudden burst of energy, and I ran to the lip of the first dam. My heart sank. Sure, there was water there, but it was black and silty and had dead animals in it. I sank to my knees and just looked at this depressing sight.

Then I heard one of the boys.

'Let's check the next one.'

When I finally looked up, the rest of the patrol was standing around the last dam. As I reached them, Nathan had climbed down the side of the dam, and was spitting the water out. His comment lowered all our spirits.

'It's fucking salty!'

That was the last straw. It started with Barry dropping his pack and proceeding to give it a kicking. He violently lost the plot. We all released the built-up aggression by yelling, 'Fuck the army!'

We looked to the sky, asking why. Our feet were rooted by this stage. Even the plaster dressings were not protecting the damage done during the walk to the dams. Everyone of us was limping and the weight we'd lost was phenomenal. Our bodies were now eating the muscles away. We were in poor shape and we knew it.

It was about 1600 hours and we still had to travel the last five kilometres to the beach to get our designated aircraft to land and pick us up at 2400 hours. Everyone's lips were swollen, cracked and bleeding again: the same situation we had been in back at the cache site.

Those last five kilometres capped off the whole ordeal. It took us three hours to travel that small distance. We were carrying equipment that now weighed between forty and fifty kilograms with no food at all and no water. It was slow.

When Barry flopped, we all did the same. By the time we got to the beach, we were resting every hundred metres. We found the hardest part of the beach by driving our heels into the sand. An impression more than one centimetre would bog the plane for sure. The length of the landing ground had to be one hundred metres long. We had the desired length and hardness.

Going into survival routine, we fastened anything clear plastic to live tree limbs to collect water. There were only tea-trees, which were very spindly and sparse with leaves. It was a technique which would only work when the sun was up.

I wondered why Barry had ordered this action. Weren't we going to get off this shore at midnight? I knew that in a survival situation it was always better to do things now, not later. Later, you might be too weak to manage a simple task such as this. Barry, the most coherent, applied this principle.

I was told to set the radio up and establish comms with SHQ, giving the code that we were waiting exfil. I followed orders. So for the next three hours I kept tapping on the morse key. I was away from the group because the high ground was above us, which would achieve better comms. Because we were on the ocean, the radio waves would travel more easily to Swanbourne, Perth, the home of the SAS regiment.

I was directed to go to the emergency frequency and contact Perth and also Canberra, which would be manning the frequency twenty-four hours. The only reason they would not answer was that they were ordered not to, increasing the blanket of silence that we were trying to get through.

Barry approached me at 2330 hours and checked the set for serviceability. Everything was working at our end. When 0100 hours arrived, there was still no plane. At 0200 hours Barry told me to pack up and get some sleep. After packing the set up, I collapsed on the spot and slept for a solid four hours.

The morning arrived. Troy had been extremely sick and was vomiting throughout the night, precious fluid and blood from some lining he had ripped inside himself.

I knew we had to get comms or Troy was going to be the first one to die. I grabbed the radio set and noticed that Phil and Nathan were not there. I asked where they were. Barry produced his map and showed me a black square, a homestead on the map. It was about fifteen kilometres away from us.

The boys had left a couple of hours ago. Hopefully they would find water. Barry then directed me to put the set down and just rest.

'Save your strength,' he ordered.

I was absolutely shagged and was operating on what little adrenalin and endorphins I had left in my body. It was about 1600 hours when they returned. By this stage, the remaining three of us couldn't move, or more to the point, didn't have the energy. Our tongues had swollen and filled our mouth cavities, a very unusual experience that I don't want ever again.

The boys who had gone looking for water had found some. Probably equivalent to ten litres, the water was found in a life raft container, usually attached to an HMAS patrol boat. Someone a long time ago must have found it on the beach and had used it to collect water off the drain of the homestead, which had been abandoned years before.

The desert had taken over the homestead, but because this half container remained in the shade, it had stored the precious water that saved our lives, for the time being. Troy required water immediately.

The three of us that had remained behind had swollen tongues and couldn't move. Phil and Nathan doused their neck scrims, usually used for camouflage, in the water and administered it into us, past our swollen tongues. We were gagging from the introduction of water into our systems again.

I again slept for a couple of hours and woke to find Phil squeezing water into my mouth. The swelling of my tongue was subsiding, and I could feel the fluid passing into my stomach. I ached all over from being too dehydrated, but I was alive.

I fell asleep again, or passed out, I'm not too sure, to awake the next morning rehydrated. They had been administering fluid to me throughout the night. After everyone recovered, we had five more bottles to survive on. If we didn't get picked up soon, we would all die.

It was 2100 hours that night and we heard an aircraft approaching us. We listened for the sound. Freefallers could identify most aircraft by getting to know the distinguishing sound of a particular aircraft. This one was ours. We moved gingerly, with our feet ripped to bits. We lit the fires for the aircraft to identify its landing ground.

The Pilatus Porter plane landed safely and picked us up. There was ice-water on board. Even with cracked lips stinging like hell, we all slowly sucked on a piece of ice. Then the aircraft lifted and we were leaving that desolate place, where we had almost perished.

There was an officer on board. This person had a personal relationship with Nathan, which was very unusual. They had gone to school together and had been best mates. I assumed his conscience couldn't live with the fact that one day he would face Nathan's family, knowing the truth, having played a part in events that had created a deniable situation that killed their son. Thank fuck for human emotions.

I was awoken when we landed on another advance landing ground, onto a dirt road. The officer took Barry and Phil off the aircraft. With the officer and our patrol commander and 2IC gone, we took off again.

Our next stop was at the regiment barracks at Swanbourne. Finally a familiar place, but the face at the door was unusual. It was a regimental sergeant major (RSM). He said to us, 'Have a rough trip boys?' No one answered him.

He continued, 'The commanding officer has put you blokes on stand-down (short leave). Get your feet fixed and get some rest. Come in next week for your next order.'

The RSM was gone. No one was going to question him as to why we had been left in the desert without any water.

I was never to work with any member of that patrol again.

Nathan and Troy still lived in the barracks. The RSM told me that the duty driver would drop me off at my home. When I got home I dumped my gear and stripped off and headed to my shower.

I must have passed out in the shower for I found myself on the floor with the water running very cold. My skin had shrivelled like a prune so I must have been there for some time. I tried to stand to fight the pain in my feet, but then thought it was a better idea to sit back on my arse. I reached up and turned the taps off and dragged myself to bed. I was to stay in bed for seventy-two hours, waking up every now and again only to be too exhausted to move and suddenly falling asleep again.

After my long sleep and rest, I decided to eat everything in the fridge and then repair my feet. The gash in my side had become septic and required treatment and a dressing. I had pressure sores from losing so much weight, so I treated these as well and dressed them.

Nathan called and told me the truth about how the officer he knew came to be on that aircraft. He must've been fighting between his emotions and the professionalism he owed to regiment. He threw away his career in the regiment that night. His next delightful posting, due to these actions, was to the Australian High Commission in Papua New Guinea, probably the worst posting they could send him to.

This officer involved had disobeyed orders and had cocked a 9 mm Browning pistol in front of the face of our designated pilot while he slept. The pilot was then led to his aircraft at gunpoint. Unbeknown to us, he had had a loaded weapon trained on him during the whole flight.

My selection course instructor 'Pommy', Sergeant Dave Sherrick, turned up on the sixth day of my stand-down. He had my next warning order in his hands. As I opened the door he said, 'You lucky prick. They gave you a guerrilla warfare specialist's course. You are to fly to Sydney in three days' time.'

'What about my patrol?' I asked.

He explained that our patrol had been disbanded. The newer members were posted to other war role squadrons, and Phil and Barry were doing build-up training for their next tour with the Counter Terrorist Team.

He never asked me what happened, and nor should he have. What happened to us would remain only in the minds of those involved. If you chose to, it was far better to let it slip away, for you always had something else to concentrate on that would require one hundred per cent concentration.

My next distraction would be to study the theory of guerrilla warfare. I had three days to absorb this new information. I would be expected to know and understand all the theory behind it when arriving at the location of the course. Sergeant Dave was about to leave and said, 'Paul, remember the old saying: you weren't there, it didn't happen. Get on with the job and forget what has been placed in your mind.'

I did just that and prepared myself for the next stage of my career.

* * *

Forget what had been placed in my mind ... if only I could, I wouldn't be sweating in this dark empty roof space. The pain from the cramps I was suffering after perching on the beams for hours was miniscule compared to the pain in my head. A fractured ankle saved my life on the night of the Blackhawk disaster; now, as it cramped up, I knew where my mind was going to take me. Pain in my ankle was one of the triggers that spiralled me back to the nightmares that controlled me. I shook with fear of the inevitable. Sweat off my face cascaded onto my scarred hands. I breathed deeply in some vain attempt to remain in the now. With no choice, I was back there.

Chapter Nineteen

The aftermath

There is no light to my front; but I can distinguish the outline of the Blackhawks. There are four in total and they seem to be off target to the right as I look at them. The lead helicopter is making dramatic moves to get to the drop site. Blackhawk II *and* Blackhawk III *seem to be racing each other to the same drop site.*

I'm in a room which is designed to observe the outdoor training exercises so that individuals can later be critiqued on better ways of conducting counter-terrorist assaults. The benefit is that the troops learn how best to stay alive and kill their targets more proficiently. The glass window in this room is always hot to touch. I'm resting on a set of crutches due to an accident early in the training day when I broke my ankle. My seat on the helicopter has been taken by a younger soldier.

'Fuck, they've collided,' I always yell.

No one is in the room with me to hear the devastation in my voice.

Night becomes day as one of the Blackhawks bursts into flames. The screams from my mates are clearly audible through the plate glass window. I grab the chair I have been sitting on and throw it through the window. I want to help. The aggression building up inside could explain this unusual behaviour. I feel closer to my dying mates now that the window is removed.

As the glass and the chair fall away from my view, I see the Blackhawk on fire invert and plough into the ground upside down. I squeeze hard onto the wooden window frame, completely oblivious to the shards of glass that are now embedded in my hands.

'No, fuck no!'

The survivors' echoes pierce the night.

The reverberating screams traverse the room.

The physical pain does not register or resonate over the emotional pain I am experiencing. The other damaged Blackhawk lands hard on its skids. The burning remains of the first Blackhawk illuminate the rescuers who have reached the upright helicopter.

Men are pulling bodies out of the wreck. As they go to grab their mates, they find that only bits can be extracted from the wrecks. I turn away; I can't do any more than what is already being done.

I sit on the floor with my back against the wall. The screams slice through the dark night, overpowering the sound of metal as it crackles and buckles. Voices of the rescuers match the screams of our mates. I look down to my hands. There is still no pain. I decide that I am in shock.

Then I'm deposited inside a doomed helicopters before the crash, watching my mates' final moments.

All the operators are standing, kneeling and hanging onto the rope, ready to drop as soon as the first operator leaves the Blackhawk. All the others will be on top of him.

A flash of light. I see five strikes occur, each strike hitting metal and flesh. Obviously the flesh loses the battle. The first strike hits the fuel tanks and fuel is pouring in on them. It then ignites and the screams are deafening.

I'm suddenly flung back to the empty room where I witnessed the disaster.

I see Troy trying to rescue someone. The light of the fire gives me a visual image. Troy is tugging at an injured mate. He falls backwards, pulling out what he has been struggling with, to realise he has only the head and upper body of Nathan lying across his chest. Troy is violently ill. I sit down numb, no pain, and no tears, totally bewildered as to why I can't express any emotion at this graphic loss.

I'm standing above the line of body bags.

No, no not that memory!

Relieved, I found myself at our local pub the night after the memorial ceremony for the men who died in the Blackhawk disaster. Corporal Nathan Walters and Sergeant Peter Chauci would not be sitting next to me.

Today, I was sitting quietly at the bar with the men who were injured and could walk, and the men who were now dealing with the memories of being involved with the rescue. Troy wasn't present; he had left to get some serious therapy and have his burns attended to on the other side of the country.

The bartender didn't try to make small talk; he had seen this scene before and knew that his favourite customers wanted to drink until they were drunk. He also ensured that nobody disturbed us. We always drank to forget.

Dave Sherrick and his covert team entered the bar. None of them enquired what had happened on the last exercise. They joined us at the bar, ordered their drinks and drank in silence. I looked at the five men who had just joined us. Ben Jones was among them. I raised my bandaged, upright thumb towards my chest, stopping midway, and instead of completing the gesture, I used my palms to pick up my glass of beer. These men had all recently resigned from the regiment. Superb timing. I needed to distract myself from my morbid thoughts; I decided to size up the new covert team that Ben had been assigned to.

Dave Sherrick, their boss, hadn't changed much since my first meeting with him on the selection course, when he ensured that I suffered for being late to my first morning parade. He wore short-cropped hair that was black, pitch-black. I was sure that he would've had speckles of grey in his hair. He must've dyed it. That would explain the shine that was coming off it. He was wearing a T-shirt that exposed more tattoos than he had when I first meet him. In his mid-thirties now, he was as fit as an Olympic athlete.

Peter Ingram was Dave's 2IC. I hadn't worked with him before, but I sure had gotten pissed with him many times. He was a good man to have in a brawl. He and I were incorrigible when together. If there was a fight to start or finish, we would be the ones involved.

He was of average height and broad-shouldered. His blond hair had grown past his shoulders. Two earrings, one in each ear, gave him the appearance he needed to carry out covert operations.

Frank McMahon sat with them at the bar. Frank was tall and lanky, definitely the youngest in the team. He also had baby features and would obviously suffer the same ridicule that I had on occasion. His hair was still short; he had only completed his resignation period less than a month ago. He wore one earring and on his arms there were freshly inked tattoos which I hadn't seen before.

Phil Fields was introduced to me after I completed the selection course. We were at the Gatwick club, the other ranks boozer. Dave Sherrick made the introduction.

'Paul, I would like to introduce Phil Psycho Fields to you.'

I held out my hand to shake his. He didn't even look at me, but said, 'If Dave introduces you to me, I think you're all right.'

He spoke over the top of my head. Rude prick, I thought.

That situation was years ago and miles away. I was flung back to reliving the horrific memory that I was trying to drown out. Ben pointed his thumb up against his chest and smiled. The five of them stood together and moved towards the door.

Dave whispered into my ear, 'I will contact you in a few days.'

I nodded my head. Ben murmured, 'Thank fuck you are alive. I was seriously worried about you. This gig we have got is a ripper. Looking forward to working with you.'

I nodded my head again. They were out the door and gone.

I continued to get a skinful, and tried to forget what I had seen. It was going to be a long night. I asked the bartender to grab me a carton of heavies and order me a taxi.

The cab pulled up out the front and some of the lads wanted to share it with me. One of the lads grabbed my carton and placed into the cab.

Our driver looked at my bandaged hands and my plastered leg, and the crutches I was finally getting used to. We started to drive off and the cabbie asked if any of us were involved in the worst military peacetime accident. This is how the media portrayed the Blackhawk disaster. No one answered him.

'Who's first?' I asked the lads in the back.

'We're all getting off at the same spot. Do you want to join us, Paul?'

'No thanks, lads, I think I will just go home.'

'Well, we live just around the corner from you. If you want some company, drop over.'

'Thanks.'

That's all I said, not wanting to commit to the invitation I had just received. The cab stopped and dropped the back seat occupants off at a house just around the corner from mine. In the short distance to my place the cabbie said to me, 'Mate, I'm really sorry about your mates.' I didn't answer him.

I wished he had kept that last comment to himself. I had almost sedated myself enough to clear the horror from my mind. It annoyed me more as I had to ask him to help me with the carton of beer. As I opened the door and was using my good leg to shift the carton across the floor, the phone rang. I let it ring until the answering machine got it.

It was a female caller.

'Paul? Paul, c'mon Paul, if you are there, pick up. I have been really worried about you. You know my voice, it's Liz.' She hung up.

I knew who it was. She was correct to assume I would recognise her voice. Liz was the sister of Tony Ridy, who failed the culinary delight challenge on the selection course. I was grateful that they didn't look alike, apart from the alluring presence of freckles. They were possibly different stock, but I never asked her.

After failing, Tony had decided to take a discharge from the army and join the National Safety Council, as did some other SAS operators. The individuals who were in charge of the National Safety Council ripped the funds off. It collapsed, and some SAS members returned with their tails between their legs. Some couldn't face that embarrassment and just disappeared. Tony, Liz's brother, was one of the latter. It was rumoured that he and some other ex-SAS operators hired themselves out as mercenaries.

I'm sure that at times Liz only maintained my friendship to ensure she had a link with the regiment, in the hope that some information might filter down about Tony and the other rogue SAS members. My relationship with her was purely selfish. I got what I could, when I could. We had sex on many occasions.

I could take her out for the evening and dump her for another woman who was coming on strong, if I believed the other woman would have sex with me. On occasions, Liz would do the same to me. This flippancy didn't affect our friendship. She seemed to understand that my professional life didn't leave room for a relationship.

The phone rang again. I didn't know how long it had been since I'd heard Liz's voice on the answering machine. I bounced to my feet to realise that my fractured foot didn't want to feel the pressure of the floor. I staggered towards the phone, knocking over the dozen empty stubbies that were placed at arm's-length from my chair.

I instinctively thought that the phone call was coming from the regiment. I looked at my hands that were still bandaged and my fractured ankle and it forced me into reality. The regiment doesn't need someone busted up like me, I thought.

I continued to plough a path to the phone. I lifted the receiver. I was out of breath.

'Hello.'

'Hello Paul, it's Liz.'

'Hi Liz, just let me catch my breath. Be a mate and don't mention the Blackhawk disaster.'

I removed the phone from my ear and started to suck deep breaths of oxygen. Within twenty seconds I had composed myself enough to hold a conversation. I spoke into the phone again.

'Hey Liz, how are you doing?'

'Better than you by the sounds of it. Are you pissed?'

'Yep.'

'Do you want some company?'

'I'm not much company, Liz.'

'Can I make that decision?'

'Well, Liz, I guess you have seen me worse.'

'Paul, I think a visit will do you good.'

'Liz, all I want at the moment is to pass out drinking, but I must have a pretty solid tolerance because it's not working. I only have a dozen stubbies left to do the job.'

'Paul, I'll go to the bottle shop and get another carton.'

'Now you're talking, girl. Do that and get your pretty arse over here.'

'I'll see you soon.' She hung up the phone.

I looked at the chaos I had caused as I tried to get to the phone. After smelling my armpits I decided to have a quick shower. The rushing water might sober me up enough to tidy the mess I had created. I removed the bandages from my hands and covered my plaster with a plastic bag. I had sweated even more now, with this challenge complete. I definitely needed a shower.

As the water ran over my body, I visualised Liz's body in front of me. Her brown hair, wet from the water … Her strong back facing me, as I ran my soapy hands over her shoulders down to the small of her back … I held my hands on her hips, then clasped them around her narrow waist to rest them above her belly-button, allowing me to pull her towards me, to feel pressure from her arse cheeks against my dick …

I dropped the soap onto the plastic bag plaster. It had enough weight to disturb my fantasy. I quickly regained my thoughts of the delicious Liz. She turned her little body to pull me down to kiss her. I returned her kiss, falling passionately into the moment. Her pert, solid, upright breasts hardly lost their shape as she pressed them into my chest. I reached down to feel her breasts; the nipples were already hard and poked between my fingers as I caressed them. As she faced me, I lowered my hand to locate that little bit of flesh that gives the owner so much pleasure ...

The front doorbell rang. I was snapped back to reality, sporting an erection. The escape had been just that; the horror returned. All sexual desire eluded me and my erection dropped. The subject of my fantasy was at the door, but now I couldn't indulge because I was in mourning, or what I conceived to be mourning.

'Liz, hi,' I said, giving her a welcome kiss.

'It's great to see you. I thought you were ...' she paused, probably remembering that I'd told her I didn't want to discuss the accident.

'What have you been up to?' I restarted the conversation.

'You know, a bit of this and a bit of that. Yourself?'

A pause.

'I'm sorry, Paul, I keep on tripping over the subject that you don't want to talk about. Please forgive me. I was extremely concerned about you. Considering this is the only subject of discussion within Perth and Australia, I'm sorry again. Pass me a beer and I will shut up,' she babbled.

I looked at her and she looked back at me. I felt like crying at that moment, except that the last time in my life I shed tears was at the age of twelve. Something or somebody or some time had hardened me enough to never shed tears again.

I continued to drink as fast as I could. To alleviate uncomfortable moments, I turned the TV on. Liz sat on the couch with me. She snuggled in close so I could smell her perfume, and feel her body warmth. Her head rested against my shoulder, as the side of her upper torso pressed into my ribs. Her firm breast tickled my ribcage. Still no sexual urges arose from within me. I drank another beer.

'Paul, can I stay tonight?'

Liz was the first to speak in over two hours. Her request was common and my usual answer would have been, sure! This time I added a condition.

'Sure, mate, but you will have to sleep on the couch. I'm not going to have a comfortable sleep with this ankle. I will probably be tossing and turning all night. I'm off to bed now, to try and get some sleep. See you in the morning.'

'Goodnight, Paul, and thanks for letting me stay here. I'm so relieved that you are alive.'

'Thanks, Liz.'

I put myself in her shoes for a moment. Here she knows most of the blokes who perished and wouldn't have heard a single detail of who had died and who was alive.

I reminded myself to fill in the blanks for her tomorrow. I went to bed.

Sometime into the night I was awoken to feel my ankle being raised up onto a pillow. I opened my eyes to see Liz, naked, making my ankle comfortable. My mind flashed back to the horror night. Liz noticed my distress, and whispered into my ear, 'Paul, let me take the pain away.'

She slipped her hand down the upper part of my body. She started caressing and rubbing me. The attention she was giving me diverted any more thoughts that plagued me. I started to relax and enjoy the sensations.

Liz straddled me and slipped me inside her. After she lowered onto my full length, she slowly raised and lowered herself repeatedly. She stopped and looked down at me and asked me a question. 'When are you going to quit and stop trying to kill yourself?'

'I have quit.'

This answer drove her into a frenzy. She rode me like a cantering stallion. The energy she was expending was phenomenal. She began to shake and became rigid simultaneously, as she experienced her orgasms.

She fell forward with her head and breasts onto my chest, and hugged me like she had never done before. I returned this moment of intimacy and held her close. Tears dropped onto my chest. I raised her head so we looked into each other's eyes. I asked her what was wrong.

'I just am so relieved that you weren't one of the ones killed. I love you.'

I didn't return the endearment. She had awoken the horror demon again. I didn't blame her for it. It was just that I couldn't control these dark memories. I waited for her to fall asleep, as I tossed into the awareness of the night when fifteen of my mates left this existence. The flash as the Blackhawk caught alight was where it always began.

Once the visualisation had appeared within my memory recesses, it couldn't be stopped from completing the whole horrific journey.

As she slept, I got up and took a sixpack of beer out of the fridge. I sat on the couch, placed my beer at my feet and turned the TV on. I ritually changed channels during the ads, to keep my mind from entering the dark world that I desperately wanted to avoid.

After my fifth beer I must've fallen asleep. I woke when I felt my last bottle being gently released from my hand. Liz lay on the couch with me. She pulled my sutured hands around her to hold her. My hands felt the material of one of my T-shirts, which she was now wearing. I felt comfortable holding her and fell peacefully asleep. I awoke to find myself stretched out on my own queen bed. It was midday. Liz was gone.

I rang the duty officer at the regiment to ask when we would be required to come in. He must've been reciting the same details to all the members who decided to stay home and contact the regiment by phone. He answered my question.

'All One Squadron members are not to come to the regiment until Sunday. You are to park your vehicles at the married quarters and enter the back of the regiment. You are to move to One Squadron building. You are not to talk to the media. Presently, there is a media circus at the guard box. You are not to tell anyone about these movement orders. Paul, speak to you later, I have got other calls coming in.'

'Thanks, sir. See you Sunday.'

The only personal part of that conversation was his good-bye. I felt alone. Sunday was three days away. I cracked another beer. The day rolled on. The only break from the monotony was opening the front door to allow Liz in.

'Have you eaten any food today, Paul?'

'Yeah, steak and eggs in a can.'

'Let me fix you something.'

'I'm not guaranteeing that I will eat anything.'

I was becoming boring and predictable. I didn't enjoy this situation. Liz turned up every night to resupply me with beer. I wouldn't eat much, but she always cooked me something different each night. The only change to my dull and boring routine. She would sleep on the couch after she'd poured me into bed after another session of hitting the piss.

Sunday finally arrived. I hopped into our SHQ. I hadn't shaven since the horror night. I didn't look like the highly trained professional that I was, nor could I care.

The squadron sergeant major (SSM) opened the address, 'Men, we are to remain silent where the media is concerned until the inquiry is finished. You are all to see Dr Bornin, who is the military psychiatrist assigned to getting you all back to work. The inquiry will be a lengthy one and you will all be asked to give evidence. Are there any questions?'

Beside me I heard a comment: 'Sounds like a witch hunt to me.'

My hand shot straight up into the air.

'Yes, Paul.'

Within the counter-terrorist group, your professionalism granted you first-name status with all operators, no matter what their rank. I had come a long way from that first year of selection, when nobody told me their name.

'Bill, I have two questions. First, do you believe that the hierarchy is looking for scapegoats within this squadron? Second, will the inquiry be told of the general's refusal when we requested that some of the Blackhawks and crews be posted to regiment so they could train with us and ensure that their flying skills matched the special operational needs?'

'Paul, to answer your first question: listen up, our own honesty will get us through this. The hierarchy will be looking to make someone responsible. They are getting a lot of flak from the media. The second question is up to the individuals who were there at the time when the regiment requested the posting of the Blackhawks and crews. Yes, the generals did refuse that common-sense solution that may have averted the accident.

'Are there any more questions?'

The SSM addressed me in a sterner voice. 'Paul, you will be the first to see the shrink. You will have a shave and report to my office as soon as you are finished.'

'Yes sir.'

I addressed him with the formality that he deserved, especially after he had directed me to do something. Anything less would have been disrespectful. I respected him immensely for who he was and what he had achieved. I did as he asked and fronted to his office. I knocked on his door and a female voice said, 'Come in.'

I waited silently to be asked to sit down. The woman was in civilian clothes and aged about forty, with dark hair speckled with light grey. She had a full body, and her dark-brown blouse was buttoned up to the top of her neck. She had distinctive lines around her eyes as she looked at me over the rim of her glasses, and shook my hand gently, due to my hands being bandaged. She said, 'Take a seat please. I'm Dr Bornin. What is your name?'

'Paul Roberts.'

She shuffled through the files on top of her desk and found one with my name on it. She opened the file and read the contents before addressing me again.

'Paul, how are you doing?'

Sitting before previous psych boards I would get the treating psychiatrists to talk about themselves and walk out of there without them learning anything about me. It was an old trick that the senior operators taught me. The treating psychiatrist was usually in awe at having an SAS lad in front of them. Throughout the day they would have to listen to clients. When one of us was the client, getting them to talk about themselves was easy.

A simple glance at a family photo, or a picture on the wall, gave enough distraction for questions to gravitate to their personal life. They usually felt quite refreshed to have the conversation directed to themself. A competent assessment was guaranteed. This time, though, I decided to be blatantly honest. I was getting out anyway.

'I'm not doing too well. I haven't been getting any sleep. I'm drinking far too much and I'm isolating myself, apart from one friend who has been dropping over in the evening. My hands have twenty sutures in them and I have a fractured ankle.'

The last part of my answer was completely irrelevant to her as a psychiatrist, but I said it so she would realise that I wouldn't be holding any information back. She asked another question.

'How do you feel about your friends dying?'

'I'm pissed off,' I replied rapidly.

'That's normal. Do you believe that this mourning period will pass?'

'No. This is the first time I have mourned loss of life. Usually, there is just an unfortunate accident and someone dies. There is no big memorial service, just an auction.'

'An auction?'

'Yes, an auction. We buy the dead man's equipment for ridiculous prices and give the money to his widow and family. At the last auction, I paid five hundred and five dollars for the guy's bush hat.

'That's the usual way we mourn. You have to understand that when someone dies, it's not good to linger on the fact that they are dead. It doesn't change our situation; soon we still have to do the same task that the person who perished was doing. It's better to forget what's been placed in your mind and feel fortunate that it wasn't you this time.'

She sat amazed opposite me, her mouth slightly opened. This reaction reminded me of how the rest of the army thought the SAS were nutters. She broke the stunned silence that she inadvertently found herself in.

'How do you feel about being fortunate this time?'

'Guilty.'

'What do you mean by guilty?'

'Just that I feel guilty. That morning I fractured my ankle doing rehearsals. That twist of fate ensured that I wasn't in the

Blackhawk that burst into flames, nosediving into the ground. I should be dead.'

'Are you glad you are not dead?'

'I dunno. I'm confused.'

'Last question. do you want to remain in the Counter Terrorist Squadron?'

'No, I have resigned.'

'Thank you, Paul. I hope everything goes well for you.'

I rose and accepted her gentle handshake. I left the SSM's office to almost limp on top of a line of men waiting their turn to see the shrink. My crutches got me to where I had parked the car. My mobile phone rang.

'Paul Roberts speaking,' I answered.

'Paul, it's Dave Sherrick. What are you doing?'

'Heading home. I've just been to see the shrink.'

'She told you that you are sick beyond repair.'

'How did you guess?'

We both laughed.

'Paul, are you still interested in giving me a hand?'

'I'm not much use to you at the moment. It will take at least four weeks before I'm operational again.'

'Yeah, I guessed that. You know me; I'm a stickler for prior planning and preparation. Four weeks will be cool. I still want to have you on board. It's pretty exciting stuff. Call you in a week … Bye now.'

'Bye, mate.'

What was I going to do for a week? I was sick of drinking piss. I decided I needed a training routine, but what? I couldn't run. I couldn't ride a bike. My hands still needed four days before the stitches came out. Swimming was out, until they removed the plaster. What could I do?

I would walk with my crutches as far as I could, increasing the distance each day. The west coast offered plenty of walking paths right next to the ocean.

This resolution lifted my spirits. I would be fit for the task that Dave and his team were doing. The trip to the psychiatrist had relieved me considerably. Just having the opportunity to tell somebody how I felt gave me a push back into reality. I went shopping to cook dinner for Liz. I bought flowers for her and reminded myself to apologise for being such an ungrateful prick.

* * *

The doorbell rang; it was Liz. I opened the door and she was greeted by the aroma of spaghetti marinara. She was struggling to hold a carton of piss under her arm. I relieved her of this cumbersome burden. I placed it down on the floor, just inside the door. I grabbed her around the waist and gave her one of my infrequent sincere hugs. I looked into her eyes and lightly kissed her lips. I broke our embrace and returned to the kitchen to continue with my culinary surprise. I said, 'The flowers are yours too. How's your day been?'

She stood in the doorway, astonished.

'C'mon, Liz, is this all that much of a surprise?'

'Yes it is. Thanks for the flowers. I don't recognise you.'

'Thanks. I will take that as a compliment. Sit down and I will pour you a wine. I need to say something to you.'

'What about? What changed you?'

'I will answer your first question. I want to thank you for being there for me. I couldn't have handled these past few days by myself. What changed me? Today I saw a shrink and, for first time in my career, I didn't hide how I was feeling. I was totally honest and it felt great. Now I'm back with the living, I want to tell you something that I should've told you years ago: I love you, Liz.'

I stunned her like I stunned the psychiatrist; she sat there with her mouth slightly opened. A tear ran down her cheek. I kissed it away and then told her my intentions.

'I'm definitely leaving the regiment. I want to buy a camp-ervan and travel around Australia until we find some place nice to settle down. I want to leave the regiment behind and start a new life where I don't have to bullshit my way through every-thing. Liz, I want you by my side — if that's what you want?'

She sat there even more stunned. Her eyes were wells for her tears. They overflowed and ran down her cheeks.

'Yes, yes, yes.' Her volume increased with each yes.

'Oh Paul, I have waited years for you to ask me to be with you.'

'Good, that's settled. It's official: you are my girl and I'm proud as punch!'

My embrace of her was never again to be anything but sincere. We held each other until the water cooking the spaghetti boiled over, and I raced to the stove to ensure this spe-cial meal wasn't spoiled.

'Liz, I don't want to keep any secrets from you. Dave Sher-rick has asked me to give him a hand on a gig that is going down in Perth. I told him I would assist him. When it's fin-ished, we are out of here. The army owes me long-service leave, so when my ankle heals and I have finished doing what Dave needs, we're gone. Sound good?'

'Yes, Paul, I'm so happy.'

We enjoyed our meal together and then moved to the bed-room. She removed her clothes and I looked at her, realising for the first time that I was a very lucky man. We made love passionately and when we had spent our energy, I fell asleep in her embrace.

I awoke to the smell of breakfast as Liz busied herself in the kitchen. For the first time since the accident, I had almost gone a whole twenty-four-hour period without a flashback.

We had breakfast looking at the ocean from the position my unit offered. I asked Liz to move in until we packed up and left the SAS regiment for good. I finally felt relaxed about my decision to leave the death-wish life behind.

I started training and my fitness level rose again. My hands healed, and the scars weren't that noticeable. The plaster was removed after being on for three weeks. The doctor told me it was the extra walking I did that speeded their recovery. I rang Dave to offer my services for my last gig.

'Dave, this Paul Roberts. I got the plaster off. I'm for the gig.'

'Good, mate. I will drop over to your place and give you the details. Hey, I hear that you have hooked up with Liz. Smartest thing you have ever done, dopey. I've got to go. Speak to you soon.'

'Cheers, Dave.'

With my plaster off, I decided to go for a slow jog. After a short five-kilometre run, I quickly showered to await Liz's arrival. The phone rang.

'Paul, it's Liz. I have to work tonight and won't be home until late.'

'Cool, Liz. See you then.'

This was a convenient situation. Dave and I would be able to discuss what he required of me on the last gig of my secret-squirrel career.

Dave arrived at 7 pm. I got him a beer and he sat quietly enjoying it. After the second beer, he demanded to know the details of Liz and myself and our union. The third relaxed him enough to explain what he and his team had been doing over the last month. I'm sure he deleted all the details that were not relevant to my involvement from this point. He pulled out some newspaper front pages from under his jacket and tossed them towards me.

'Read the paper lately?'

'No, you were the one who taught me to only take notice of the secret briefs. The papers write what they are told to write.'

'That's right. I did tell you that. Just read the headlines and I will fill in the gaps.'

The newspaper headline read brazenly: 'Military-style armed robberies in broad daylight. Armed robberies happening all over Perth. Kidnappings and home invasions.' I looked at him for an explanation.

'The team has been getting orders, addresses and photos of the targets. We have been selected because we are professional. We have been rehearsing every job we have done down to the finest detail,' Dave stated proudly.

I didn't expect anything less from Dave's team. Dave continued, 'The cops don't have a clue. The team is in and out before they arrive. Surveillance cameras are either smashed or their lenses are sprayed with paint. There is no evidence that we were there, except for very shaken individuals who report that the robbers wore black clothing and balaclavas and didn't speak a word. We shove weapons into their faces and move them into the location of the safes and make them open them. The police are given figures of the amounts stolen: a lot less than what was actually there as the money stolen is dirty drug money. We are coming to the end of the operation: all known drug money has been stolen from the drug cartel. The principals we have kidnapped and placed in a safe house. They have been gagged, handcuffed and fed probably once a day for four days. They have not had a word spoken to them.' He paused.

I wondered why he was explaining to me what was common practice in how to handle prisoners. He seemed to be enjoying his ex-regiment career. I wondered whom he referred to when he said: we are getting orders.

I assessed the way the prisoners were being treated. Male or female would have received the same treatment, and equal. These men were professional and to them these prisoners would've been just drug lords. None of them would hesitate to send these scum to the stairway to heaven if ordered.

At this stage, the team only knew that they were busting a drug ring and stealing dirty money. They expected the final orders of the operation to be: waste them and remove all evidence of the hits. The last part I assumed. The rest of my assessment would have been extremely accurate.

'Paul, have you worked out who we are working for?'

'No Dave, I was assessing what you have done with your prisoners.'

'I don't have to ask. I'm sure you are right. The state government is our employer.'

'Beautiful, Dave, you are sanctioned as well. When do I start?'

'Tonight, and you will earn five grand for your trouble.'

That was half the amount I was getting for my superannuation after ten years of contributions. The irony was that the federal government super netted me ten grand after ten years, and in one night's work I was to earn five thousand dollars from a state government.

'Sure, I'm in. What do we have to do?'

'Due to the kidnappings, one of my team has to remain to watch the prisoners. There are four more jobs to do. Phil and

Ben will do two; I want you to be my backup on the other two jobs.

'The first phase is that we will meet a suit (politician). We are to do two pick-ups of packages during the night at designated spots. We will be approached by an individual who will give us the code that will ID them as the pick-up agent. Easy enough tasks.'

'Sounds clear. What time do we leave?'

'Now. I've just got to make a call to the safe house. Can I use your phone?'

'Of course.'

After a quick phone call he said, 'It's on! Let's make some real money.'

We both jogged lightly to his car; my ankle was holding up and not giving me any pain. He threw his car keys at me and said, 'You're driving.'

As the senior operator, it wasn't unusual that he asked me to drive. He reached into his glove box and placed a Browning 9 mm pistol into my lap. He said, 'It's got a full magazine and a round up the spout.'

I didn't check it, as I trusted him.

'Drive to the Fremantle jetty. That's the first pick-up.'

We drove in silence to arrive at the designated pick-up. Dave got out of the car.

I could see the exchange happen, with my pistol pointing at the suit and waiting to cover Dave if he gave me a signal that he was in trouble. He returned to the car and tossed a bag in the back.

'Perry Lakes next, Paul. Approach from the southern end.'

We arrived and I parked the car to point my pistol at the suit handing over a bag of the same type as the one that sat in the back of the car. Dave threw the bag in the back and said, 'It's time to get paid, but first I want to stop at a landline.'

I drove a short distance to locate a landline. Dave got out and made a phone call.

He returned hastily to the car, and said, 'There's no answer at the safe house.'

Dave reached into the bag and opened the package inside. What he said next scared the shit out of me.

'It's fucking powder.'

Then he tasted it.

'It's fucking speed. I think we've got twenty kilos of the shit. This is supposed to be cash. Everything is turning to shit!'

As he rubbed his head thinking of what to do next, I started the car and headed towards my place. We had twenty kilograms of amphetamines. I was shitting myself.

They were trying to fit us with this shit. We wouldn't see daylight for a long time. Dave finally spoke.

'We've got to get rid of this shit.'

The pay-off location was about ten kilometres away, in the direction that I was driving from our last location. We discussed what we would do. The plan was to locate the pay-off vehicle, cut it off at its front so it couldn't move, and dump all twenty kilos in the car. I was to take a low position and keep my pistol on the person doing the pay-off. When we had dumped the speed we would get back to the safe house to interrogate the prisoners, and also to see if the lonely operator survived the night.

The pay-off was a woman. I screeched in front of her car. She must have pissed herself as I trained my weapon onto her forehead. Dave ordered her, 'Open the door bitch.'

If she didn't comply in the time that she did, in one more second I would have drilled her. We thought as a last option that a dead politician with twenty kilos of speed in her car would create enough of a fracas for us to have the opportunity to disappear into oblivion.

She moved quickly enough. All twenty kilos of speed was delivered onto the passenger seat and we quickly moved off. The safe house was our next destination.

The code was given as we approached the building: four flashes of the headlights. The response would be two flashes of torchlight. The signal was returned.

Dave was in the back seat ready to fire if the safe house was compromised. The safe-house keeper drew his weapon as I neared the front. He was expecting to see two men in the car and if I wasn't quick enough to identify myself, I'd have an extra two holes in my head. Dave quickly showed himself. I yelled out my name. He slowly lowered his weapon.

We approached him and asked him about the prisoners. I let them go as ordered by Dave. They would be walking around the northern suburbs of Perth still bagged, gagged and hand-cuffed. The phone rang at the safe house, and there was a short exchange.

'Everything's turned to shit. Meet us at Buckingham Palace.'

This code designated an already organised place, one kilometre past Memorial Rock at Kings Park, in the bush. We all approached on foot. On the journey to Kings Park we told the safe-house keeper what had happened. We finally married up with the other two and asked them how their operation went. The answer was, 'Without a hitch.'

They had shorter distances to travel to their pick-ups and the two of them had no idea that they were carrying speed. They had followed orders to the letter and didn't realise that we were being set up to take a fall for the sanctioned activities. Dave ordered them to dump it in the Swan River.

As the one still waiting to finalise my discharge date with the regiment, I was the safest. Ben had also walked out of the operation at the right moment. He was involved in the first robbery but he'd decided that his family was more important than excitement.

They wouldn't accuse me, a serving member of the SAS regiment, of running drugs. The boys decided not to contact each other. Every man for himself. They returned to their normal lives, or so they thought.

The next couple of weeks were the hairiest of my life.

Frank was a family man like Ben. Phil told me his last breathing details.

'Paul, Frank was picked up driving his vehicle and was arrested on sight. After only one night in the watch-house, he was supposed to have committed suicide with a garbage bag over his head. What a load of shit!'

I agreed that none of us would commit suicide by suffocation. We were specialists in small-arms fire, and stealing a weapon off a cop would be ridiculously easy. A bullet to the forehead would be more likely. This situation was getting out of control. Phil had more information for me. He said, 'Peter was found at his place and had supposedly shot himself with three rounds to the heart. Mate, I'm out of here. I'm getting out of the country. I just dropped in to say goodbye.'

He'd also dropped in to steal my passport, but he didn't inform me of that. When he left, I looked for it, in case I was also to find that skipping the country was the only option left. I turned the house upside down looking for it. It took me hours before I faced the fact that Phil had stolen my passport. Desperate men will do desperate things.

How could he use it? We didn't look at all alike, I thought.

Phil did a runner. He never got out of the country. They put surveillance on his ex-SAS mates' locations and almost caught him on Magnetic Island, Queensland. At the time he was labelled Australia's number-one criminal, and all those involved in the hunt for him had orders to shoot on sight.

He finally turned himself in, in Perth, and is serving the longest sentence they could give him: three lifetimes. These days, he would be detained in solitary confinement with the key thrown away. We were trained in escape and evasion techniques, and for him to escape with the label of number-one criminal would be embarrassing for the authorities in charge of his incarceration.

My phone rang; it was Dave.

'Meet me on our beach in half an hour.'

I didn't say anything; I hung up the phone.

I knew exactly where he wanted to meet. 'Beach' meant 'car park' and 'thirty minutes' meant 'thirty kilometres' away from where I lived. We had used this meeting spot before.

As soon as I hung up the phone I told Liz about the shit we were in. We both got into my car and drove to the meeting spot. While I was driving, I took stock of the fact that Dave and Ben and I, and possibly Liz, had yet to suffer what the others had gone through.

My first question to Dave was, 'What's going to happen?'

He looked at Liz before answering me.

'Believe me, Liz, I thought this was all aboveboard. I'm glad Paul has filled you in. You kids are going to have to get out of town.'

'Dave, I know you wouldn't get mixed up in this if you didn't believe you were doing some good. What's happened?'

'Ben's in the clear, but unfortunately the idiots doing the arrests believe Paul and you were involved from the start. I have taken an option that will eventually put you in the clear, but it's going to take time. We are up against Federal Police now. They are investigating the whole shitfight.'

'What option are you taking, Dave?'

'The Federal Police have offered me a deal if I give evidence against those involved in this fiasco. I have agreed to their conditions, as long as you walk as well. They have agreed that you walk, but can't guarantee what the state cops are going to do. There has been a bulletin sent to every cop station in Australia, describing who we are and giving orders that we are to be arrested on sight.'

'This is one almighty fuck-up, Dave,' I said.

'I know, mate. Just get out of Western Australia as soon as you can. Good luck; maybe we will have a beer one day.'

That was the last time I saw Dave. That afternoon I bought a campervan, and at midnight I turned the key in the van and drove east across the Nullarbor Plain.

There was no sign that we were being followed.

The fiasco caught up with me at my mother's house when I was raided by the New South Wales Police. I feared for our lives. Liz and I still told no one of the sanctioned operation that had gone sour.

Chapter Twenty

The raid

Liz and I arrived at my mother's house the day before Anzac Day. The regiment sent my boxes of gear by the usual channels. A civilian freight company transported all ten boxes. I emptied the boxes to organise the contents, so they could be categorised prior to a garage sale.

The sale would be over the Anzac Day weekend. I thought it quite appropriate, considering the main items I was selling were my unneeded army equipment and clothing. I was joining the civilian world.

I advertised the garage sale with signs on the highway. I rang the local fire brigades and told them they could grab some cheap items. I also tried contacting the local cadets, which in my time had operated through the local high school. This had changed, and the community now ran it. There was a pertinent reason for contacting the cadets.

While sorting out the items, I found I had an inert claymore mine, its cable, firing devices and about a dozen military pamphlets on everyday soldiering skills. Being sentimental, I would donate these items to the local cadets as training items.

An inert claymore mine is just that: inert. It carries no explosives.

When I finally contacted a cadet, I asked him some questions that only a cadet would know the answers to, to identify him as a cadet. He said he was a corporal in the local cadets. I asked him, 'What's a CUO?'

'A cadet under officer,' he answered confidently.

He was correct. I then asked him when his next parade would be. Next Friday, he told me. I felt quite assured that he was a cadet and made it clear to him that he should give these items to his officer in charge.

I didn't think any more of the exchange and felt comfortable that these harmless items were going to be used correctly as training items. I moved back to the garage sale to continue selling my army gear.

On my return, a childhood mate turned up with some lads from the local Army Reserve unit. Then a firefighting truck arrived. Men were racing to the gear to secure the items they wanted. It wasn't long before I was running out of gear to sell. The last items to go were my packs. I was feeling generous and told the men there to make an offer.

'Five dollars,' one said.

'Ten dollars,' another said.

I now had an auction on my hands. The packs were sold at a fraction of what I had bought them for. All items were now sold. The money would be used to finance our journey in our campervan. I offered the weekend warriors a beer each. We sat down and enjoyed a relaxing chat.

The afternoon turned into evening. After watching the 8.30 movie I went to bed. I woke later to hear my mother's door being banged on. I instinctively grabbed my tracksuit pants so I could assist her with what I thought to be a home invasion.

I pulled the curtain back to see what was happening. Five men wearing black, with weapons, were on the concrete landing. I ran to the rear of the campervan. As I turned the handle on the door, I heard a command.

'Police, open up!'

A very nervous bark and loud banging on the door continued. I obeyed the command to open the van door. Three police officers were outside pointing weapons at me. My professional training kicked in. In an instant I assessed their position and their weapon readiness. My mind was working with clarity, and absorbed the details of the incident.

One cop with the rank of sergeant was below me and to my right. The fat sergeant cop didn't have his safety off. Two more cops to my left were young and definitely too inexperienced to be holding weapons.

My mind already had me running into the bush. The body just had to follow the brain's instructions. Two seconds into the raid, my mind had me injure one cop; the other two cops would be responsible for inflicting injuries on their mates.

In that fraction of time, I could collapse the fat cop's larynx. I would slip behind him with the training and speed with which I'd been wired. This would allow the simple brain of the front cop on the left to react, firing his weapon. His round would go into the sergeant's body.

He may not have had to suffer the anguish of shooting a fellow cop because he would probably be dead. The third cop was so nervous, he didn't have a clear line of fire. If he shot on reaction, his round would end up in his mate's back, that of the second cop.

Liz and my family's safety came to mind. Jesus, this was out of control!

Calm everybody down, I said to myself, which I did.

'Relax, men, I'm not carrying,' I said clearly and concisely.

I recognised the uniform of the Tactical Response Group (TRG). They were lined up on the concrete landing, an extremely dangerous position in which to congregate without knowing that other locations could be manned with a weapon pointing at them.

This put the group of five men into an enfilade position, like shooting ducks at a sideshow shooting gallery. If I was armed, by myself and threatened this way, I would have started at the back, and regulated my breathing between shots. Three would have extra holes in their heads. The domino effect of three dead cops falling onto the two in front would have trapped them against the house wall and front door.

The front two would have fallen to the ground, which was concrete. As a professional, I would have shot into the concrete, in quick succession, expecting ricochets to do some damage.

My next response would've been to cut the distance down between these attackers and myself. I had a vehicle between the front porch and myself. I had protection; they had none. It would've only been a few more seconds and these TRG heroes would've been dead dumb heroes.

What they should have done before the assault was find out the location of their target. As no surveillance had been carried out, the TRG had not established my whereabouts and as a consequence had raided my mother's house.

Do surveillance, for the protection of yourself first, then for the operators around you, and never ever put yourself or any of your mates in an enfilade position in relation to your target.

I was snapped out of my critique. The fat sergeant cop, with adrenalin pumping through his large body, pushed me up against the car and frisked me. I only had a pair of tracksuit pants on and was freezing.

I asked the fat cop if I could get a jumper. He looked at the older looking cop with the TRG black uniform on. He nodded his head.

I moved into the van. There were police everywhere, looking in cupboards and under the mattress. Liz was complaining about the male officers not leaving while she got dressed. I pulled a jumper over my head and left the van. The male cops followed. As soon as my foot hit the ground, I was pushed against the bonnet of the car.

A pair of steel cuffs was applied.

I was moved to the garage to sit on my army trunk, as the search continued.

Cops were in the roof of the house, under the house, and in the gardens. The cops that I couldn't observe were turning the inside of the house upside down.

The TRG cops walked past me, carrying their Uzi sub-machine guns at full arm's-length down by the side of their legs. They moved to the closest vehicle, secured their weapons, and continued searching. I had no idea what they were searching for. Liz and I assumed that the size of the raid was related to the Perth fiasco. This was big.

The TRG specialised vehicle was in front of five police cars. Civilian vehicles numbered five also. I started to do a head count of the personnel that were there. Over twenty: a couple of female cops, numerous male cops, the TRG numbering five, and two people wearing civilian clothing, one male and one female. I noticed that the female had an armband with the letters 'MP'. She introduced herself.

'My name is Sergeant Ryder. I'm detached to the 5th Military Police Company. This man is Captain Wright of the Army Ordinance, whose specialty is bomb disposal.' She indicated the man in civilian clothing.

'I don't have any bombs,' I stated.

A TRG member came to the front of the garage with a blanket. He laid it at the feet of Sergeant Ryder. The TRG member called out the items that they believed belonged to the army.

'One green army torch, a compass, cylume light sticks, hexamine tablets, various articles of camouflage clothing, and a prismatic compass.'

Every item there I owned. The TRG officer made another comment. 'What a miserable haul!'

I giggled.

'Shut up,' Sergeant Ryder commanded.

She didn't know what I was giggling about. I was relieved that they thought I was a thief. The Perth fiasco wasn't the reason for the raid, and I relaxed, knowing that I probably wouldn't face the same demise as my mates in Perth. However, there was more to this raid that I was still unaware of.

Sergeant Ryder looked at me with disgust. She tried to prove that she was in charge and in control. In the SAS, MPs didn't scare us. We fucked them up every opportunity we got, and got away with it because of who we were. The MPs wore red berets, and as soon as one of us saw one, it would be a challenge among us to see who would come up with the best practical joke. Somebody was always apologising for our behaviour, but not us; we couldn't give a shit about the redheads' authority. They were our toys and we always played around with them. So when she told me to shut up, I automatically slipped back to the old days and thought, what a disrespectful bitch! I'm SAS. I could kill in a second.

With this thought, my eyes must have taken on their psycho killer look. She looked over my shoulder and her eyes showed fear. Then her nipples became erect. I looked directly towards her breasts, and asked her, 'Are you enjoying this?'

The younger cops around her noticed her erect nipples, and nudged each other to make sure that no one missed out on the sight. I didn't see her again after my last comment.

I had a conversation with the cop standing over me. I tried to explain that I owned each of the items at my feet. I believed that the camouflage clothing items were the ones they suspected were stolen from the army. I stated, 'In the regiment, each building has a storeroom where the lads store unneeded equipment. I thought, wrongly, that all these boxes contained army greens and course notes from when I was in the battalion.

'We wore cams (camouflage clothing) and also overalls. Operators did not wear greens. In fact, the webbing that the Australian soldiers wear today was designed by trial and error by the SAS operators. These items are very valuable items, especially worldwide among soldiers who work in jungle and bush environments. I own everything there.'

The cop said nothing.

I was moved into the house. I could hear the cops trying to explain to Sergeant Ryder in another room that they didn't have enough evidence to make a charge stick.

My mother, by this stage, was suffering a mild angina attack and was hyperventilating. I turned to the cop holding her.

'Are you pleased with yourself?' I asked him.

His reply was, 'Hang in there, mate, we're just trying to convince the MP that it's been a botched operation.'

I shook my head. 'If she thinks that she's got an SAS lad on the line, she will have me fizzed [charged].'

My mother was resting in the care of Liz. The cops were so relaxed with me, I asked if I could go outside and have a smoke. My mother didn't allow smoking inside her house, I explained to the young cop looking after me. He removed the cuffs and said, 'Okay, I could do with one myself.'

I had a short interchange with two TRG cops. One was going to Swanbourne next month to do team-leader training. He asked me all sorts of questions, which I ignored.

'The *Secrets Act* lads ... Wait till you get there, then your eyes will be opened,' I encouraged them.

They respected this answer. They left me, and returned to their vehicle. I was alone with one cop, no handcuffs, and having a smoke. A thought came to me: do a runner.

My mother lived right next to the bush. It was my bush. I had played all types of bush activities I could think of in this area, and if I did a runner they would never find me. I knew every creek-line, every hill and a lot of kilometres, which I had explored as a kid.

Another young cop approached me and said, 'You're right, she won't let you go. I'm arresting you for goods in custody.'

He didn't even read me my rights. Instead, he apologised. 'I'm sorry, mate, you were right. This bitch is some control freak.'

'I told you,' was my reply.

So after twenty or more people trampled on my mum's lawn, searching the house inside and out, they were now all gone, all of them slipping out the back to avoid confronting me again. One cop was left to escort me to the police station. So I, the dangerous out-of-control criminal, was asked politely to move to the young officer's vehicle.

In the hours it took for the police to finally let the MP have her way, I had built a bit of a rapport with this young cop. Probably he had dreamed about being in the SAS once in his life, and saw that he didn't have the right stuff. So being in the presence of an ex-SAS man, he was showing a lot of respect and asked me to ride in the front with him. I obliged. I was such a danger to the community that I was riding with one cop.

'This won't take long. We will make it as quick as possible,' he explained.

The processing began with fingerprinting and mug shots. I must be the only criminal in Australia who has had his mug shot taken with a beanie cap on. It was cold and no one asked me to remove it so I left it on.

I was finally interviewed and told that the items I was being charged for were the items that I had given to the young boy who I had identified as a cadet: army pamphlets and the inert claymore mine. None of these items were in my custody, the first anomaly of that evening. More would be exposed.

The army explosive specialist must have told the police that the mine was live, another anomaly. This would account for the TRG being involved in the raid.

What an incompetent fool that officer was. He must have picked up the inert mine and, finding that it weighed the same as a real one, automatically assumed that it had explosives in it. The weight belonged to steel plates glued in to simulate the mine's correct weight. What a dickhead!

He even apologised to me.

'Too late now, dickhead!' was my reply.

I was getting sick of all the apologies. The people involved in the raid were being too nice to me, clearly feeling that the army personnel were being harsh towards me, but I worried that their sympathy could backfire on me. I didn't want to be there any longer than I had to. If outside agencies that were committed to hushing up the Perth fiasco found me in police custody, I would definitely perish. The situation was serious.

I gave a full statement and got out of there quickly.

I really didn't want a black mark against my new name, recently changed to start a new life. If the authorities wanted to bury me in the sand and take the opportunity to kick some in my face, then having my name and photo in the system made me extremely vulnerable. However, it wasn't myself I feared for. I had a plan that would temporarily ensure the safety of Liz and my family. I was ready to place myself into a situation with an unknown outcome.

That morning I contacted my mother's solicitor. After a short conversation about the arrest, the excessive force the police used, and how they'd charged me with goods in custody when I'd given them away, he told me to phone the Commissioner for Police of New South Wales and ask him to explain his officers' actions, and also why they activated the TRG. He told me that if I didn't get any answers from the commissioner's office I was to contact the media. I should inform the commissioner that this is what I would be doing. I was to give the commissioner the opportunity to drop the charges against me, before embarrassing his force in the media for all of Australia to see.

I agreed to what he said and thanked him for his wise advice. The media was part of my plan. It was no good hiding under a rock when they knew where I was. So instead I got in their faces. It was not a clever idea going up against the establishment, but I was determined to keep a clean record.

Being told to contact the commissioner, well, that was beautiful. The commissioner would create a safety net that I could never design. When he was involved, nothing could touch us. He would be well aware that my solicitor and others would know I was contacting him. Inadvertently, he was about to become a huge shield between them and us. If anything sinister happened to us, he would be involved in the investigation; his career could be hurt. I felt safe that he would not jeopardise his career for a small fish like me. That's what I thought.

The commissioner refused to speak to me. I told his receptionist of my intentions and hung up the phone.

'I will have your job, you rude prick,' I vowed.

I rang my appointed solicitor, and told him that the commissioner would not speak to me. He told me that he'd had contact with the commissioner, and had informed him that we would be fighting the charges and the media would be involved.

'Contact the media, Paul,' he said.

I felt safe; the commissioner was now involved. I immediately rang *A Current Affair*.

Chapter Twenty-One

Court

I was on the north coast of New South Wales, when the pre-arranged contact with my solicitor finally resulted in a court date. He told me that the police had retained a Queen's Counsel and had advised me to retain a criminal barrister. The costs were going to be extraordinary. My legal team consisted of one solicitor, one assistant solicitor, and a barrister, all for one charge of goods in custody.

They were trying to break the defendant in the good old establishment way; they would make me pay a huge amount of money to establish my innocence. The barrister cost me $3250 a day, my solicitor $800 a day, and his assistant was $450 a day. A simple thought came to my mind: these people were demanding enormous sums of money and had never placed their lives on the line for their income.

The major problem that arose was the communication between my solicitor and the New South Wales Police Commissioner. I had embarrassed them by utilising the media, and as a result the public had been reminded again that the police force displayed incompetence.

On my first appearance in an Australian court, I was confronted with another charge. This was another trick the cops used to prolong the experience.

Well, for some reason things turned around my way. The usual magistrate for the court was sick. This was an absolute blessing because the magistrate to hear my case presided in a Sydney court. It wasn't going to be easy for the cops to lie to this magistrate; he wouldn't be having drinks with them after the proceedings, when they could pat each other on the back after convicting another innocent Australian.

Another surprising event arose. The prosecution's star witness, the female sergeant MP, was not to appear at any of my court proceedings because she had suffered a mild heart attack. It's funny how karma catches up with you, I thought.

Then, although the New South Wales Police Commissioner had threatened it, there was no Queen's Counsel to prosecute me. Having this new-found knowledge, I reflected about what went down in Perth less than six months ago.

Two things could have happened at this point, the first being that I wasn't meant to get through these proceedings and would be killed by some obscure accident, or the authorities would cover everything up.

My barrister informed me that we would fight the charge that they had just given me, which was possession of stolen goods. I had statements from senior SAS operators reflecting my honesty and integrity, and the fact that the items the MP was so sure were stolen were rightly my possessions.

The paperwork that the regiment sent instantly cleared me of this trumped-up charge. The police prosecutor complained to the magistrate that they didn't get any assistance from the army. The magistrate's answer was, 'The man is innocent.'

The magistrate closed proceedings for that day and I was happy with the result. They knew they wouldn't be able to prosecute, because the stolen goods charge had been trumped up. The day cost me $4500 and I still had to face the original charge of goods in custody.

The New South Wales Police learned that day that my operational level far exceeded their authority. Here I was with knowledge of corrupt activities. They were facing a blanket of silence that could only result from a powerful group deciding that my particular case required responsible deniability.

So after day one I knew to keep my mouth shut about the Perth incident, because the power group had already decided at this time that I was untouchable in relation to it. That was a relief, but I still had to contend with the New South Wales Police Force.

The next unusual situation, which by this stage of my life was becoming normal, was that surveillance was placed on me. At this time, certain individuals broke and entered into my unit and the places I had stayed at in the last twelve months.

I believe that some group was trying to establish how my barrister and myself were going to fight the case. I reported all break-ins to the state police. Nothing was stolen; just covert entry and photos taken of the papers they were interested in, I assumed.

Day two of the court case finally arrived, another day in the same courtroom.

I found out that the search warrant was thrown out because it took the raid party too long to get organised, and the warrant wasn't for four to six rogue ex-SAS men as the police stated to the media, or for myself. The warrant they had that night was for my brother, in his name, for not paying child support.

This was a civil matter, so the warrant had to be served before midnight. To this day, I still have not seen a warrant for my arrest with my name on it. The argument for the warrant was ludicrous because no warrant existed, but for some reason they argued back and forth about it.

The cops lost all evidence relating to what was found in the van. Half a day was wasted over this, the same old trick again, designed to wear me down so I couldn't financially support myself to prove my innocence.

The magistrate adjourned court for lunch, and I went outside for a smoke. When finished, I moved into the waiting room. One of the cops brushed past me and whispered, 'You're dead.'

In a loud voice I resounded, 'I'm not afraid to die. Are you?'

He walked away swiftly. I had embarrassed him in front of lawyers, my barrister and other witnesses, and the accused waiting for other trials which wouldn't be happening today.

Now I was really pissed off.

I asked my barrister if I could look at his copies of the police statements. The expression on his face finally changed from the shocked look he carried after witnessing my retaliation to the public death threat. He passed me twenty different statements. His expression matched my own: defiant.

The cops were sweating; they had something to hide. I believed the answer was somewhere in among these pages. I moved inside the courtroom and laid the statements out on the large desk that I had spent the morning sitting behind, listening to cops lying about the whole incident.

I started to look for patterns that would incriminate my accusers. I was looking for something blatantly obvious, evidence of a conspiracy, and there it was! All the police statements were printed by the same printer! Wherever there was the letter 't', the printout on paper looked like the letter 'l'.

The twenty statements in front of me all had the same anomaly. The large number of police officers involved would not all work out of the same building and use the same printer, and there was only one feasible reason that all statements would display the same printer malfunction. They must have met to discuss how to defend their conduct during the raid. The powers in charge must have decided that all statements would be typed by the same typist. I had evidence that the New South Wales Police Force had conspired against a civilian. What democracy?

As my barrister sat down next to me, I showed him what I had found in the statements. My barrister was surprised that I found this anomaly. His defiant look returned.

'Now we are going to have some fun, but expect them to lie through their teeth. They always do. Let's stick with the plan,' he stated.

The plan was to attack the ordinance officer on his knowledge of explosives.

My knowledge of explosives was extensive. I had reached the level of Special Forces Instructor, specialist in explosives. So after a short interchange with my barrister I told him I would slip him notes on how to make this witness less credible than myself.

The barrister and I communicated with short notes that impressed the magistrate; he could openly see that I was giving my barrister the knowledge he required to cross-examine the witness. We made this officer look like a complete idiot who in fact had only a minimal knowledge of explosives. He was an administrator, not an operator.

The police were asked to swear their oaths individually. The barrister started to cross-examine them. After a short question-and-answer exchange, he directed his attack on their credibility. The statements were his hammer. Some police were caught completely off guard; a long pause sealed their demise. Others attempted to answer the accusations only to be tripped up and proved as liars.

The magistrate was pleased with my barrister and attacked the police on their integrity. He didn't like cops either.

By the end of day two, the magistrate didn't believe the police evidence and rebuked them for lying in his court. I felt good; things were going my way. I smiled at the cops who had just lied in an Australian court. Relieved, I headed home.

When I arrived home, the staircase to our unit was no obstacle as the jubilation welled up inside me at the prospect of seeing and holding Liz. Two feet from our door I heard a deafening, shrill cry. Liz screamed.

Protection mode kicked in. I slammed my foot against the door next to the handle. The door lock snapped easily; however, the top hinge of the door split from its original position and embedded the top of the door in the plaster wall to the right. The door stuck in this position and denied me access.

'Quick Paul, I've got him.'

I could see Liz leaning over the balcony hanging onto a man's shirt. I shoulder-charged the door to find that the top of it moved only inches, still restricted by the baton, as the door embedded further into the plaster wall.

'Quick Paul, I can't hold on to him. He's getting away.'

I slammed my shoulder into the door again: it splintered, but the scar in the plaster only lengthened.

'Paul hurry! I'm slipping!' A desperate cry.

'Give fucking way,' I screamed at the barrier.

Repeatedly kicking the door, I finally gained access to our unit. I flew towards the balcony, watching with horror as Liz's feet left the surface of the balcony floor.

'Let go, Liz! Let go!'

My eyes were concentrating on Liz's slim waist. Her upper body was completely over the balcony, hanging onto the man, who she was determined not to let go of. Her feet were still rising off the balcony floor and her waist was the highest point.

Grab her waist, grab her waist, I kept saying to myself as I covered the distance of the room. My foot landed on the edge of the doorway that separated the unit and balcony. Two metres to go!

It happened so fast.

With my next stride I would be close enough to save Liz from this peril. Her small delicate feet were now at a right angle to the balcony. I reached out. They shot past my first lunge; I missed by six inches. Gravity was now dictating her descent speed.

I lunged again to watch the bottom of the soles of her feet miss my final attempt by one inch.

I flipped my body over the balcony in a desperate attempt to break her fall from this fifteen-foot height. She screamed before impact. A loud audible snap followed the scream. With the horror of the sound I closed my eyes.

A second later I hit the ground. An instinctive professional para roll saved me from any injuries. As my momentum slowed out and I came out of the roll, my eyes opened to scope for the man who had caused this disaster.

He was ten feet away and moving with the speed that only adrenalin can provide. Liz was lying on her side; blood was pooling around her head.

'Liz, you okay?' I asked calmly.

There was no answer. The sound of the sickening snap entered my head.

Still sitting, I lowered my hand onto her shoulder and with downward pressure slowly rolled her petite body towards me. Her head moved first to a position that is impossible for a human being to achieve.

The snap was her neck breaking.

This sight immediately made me sick. I continued the forced body roll of my beautiful Liz. Grotesque was an understatement.

Liz's beautiful, classic facial features were no more. She had fallen face-first, and the bones that had sculpted her goddess appearance stuck out awkwardly, piercing the pristine flesh of her face.

Seated on the ground, I puked between my legs.

Liz was dead.

There was no need to check for a pulse. I held her lifeless body in my arms, and gave her the hug I had so desired to give her on my return. Anger overwhelmed me.

I looked in the direction in which the assailant had fled and spotted him one hundred metres away from us.

'I'm going to fucking kill you!' I screamed the vow.

He heard me, for his pace increased miraculously.

I started rocking, holding Liz in my arms, and a guttural growl rose from within.

'No, no, no!' The intensity increased.

'Why? Why? Why?' The volume increased with the intensity. I howled, I cried, I howled, I cried, I howled until there was no oxygen to assist me with this release. Finally, I sat quietly sobbing, still holding my Liz.

A soft wind brushed my ear. I smelt her; not her perfume but her unmistakable essence that only she possessed.

'Liz?' I asked in a soft whisper. 'Liz, is that you? I love you,' I said, pleading for this personification of energy to answer me.

The answer came within my head, as clear as having a conversation with her.

'I love you too, I always will. I will always be with you.' The last word faded as the wind that carried it disappeared.

Liz's energy was no more on this plane.

I felt alone. I held her body tighter to mine and wept.

The police arrived.

Everybody knew Liz and the two officers in attendance first were our friends. The lady copper, Joan, had recently been socialising with us, dancing at one of the nightclubs. The initial shock of seeing Liz in my arms dead created a long pause, but to her credit, her professional training kicked in and she politely made a request to me.

'Paul, I need you to let go of Liz, please.'

It was easy. Liz had gone.

'Paul, what happened?'

'Another break-in. This time the fucker pulled Liz off the balcony. He bolted down the road.'

She passed this vital information to her police station via her radio.

'Hey, Steve, don't let anyone hurt her.' I said to the other cop on the scene.

My comment sounded ridiculous; I was losing it. But Steve showed no indication of this. He looked at me with tears in his eyes and spittle on the sides of his mouth from where he had suppressed the rising vomit.

'Sure, mate. I'll keep her safe,' he reassured me.

'Paul, do you have anywhere safe to go?' Joan inquired.

'I'm going bush.'

'We will need a statement.'

'Not from me. Ask everybody, they saw it,' I said indicating the residents who were congregating on their balconies. The police were already taking statements from the witnesses.

With that understanding, I bolted up the hill and ran into the bush at the easiest access, and kept running. I finally stopped when I was two ridge-lines away from the site where my heart was broken. I collapsed and cried until I fell asleep.

Two days I remained in the bush and felt nothing. I was numb.

I returned to our unit to find a note left on the door.

'Liz's funeral at 4 pm today. I hope you are all right. Love Joan.'

It was midday; I had four hours to get ready. Liz's parents must be in town. I couldn't face them yet. I had a shower and drove to the graveyard. On the way, I thought of how Liz and I could be close friends with the police in this state, but how another state's police could possibly be responsible for Liz's death.

'Friends in one state, foes in another state. Fuck the foes!' I exclaimed.

I stood at the hole in the ground that Liz was to be buried in, still numb. The procession finally arrived. Liz was lowered into the ground. I was oblivious to everything and everybody around me. Liz was buried.

Liz's father's hand gripped my arm tight, releasing me from my stupor.

'Follow me, son,' he said as he led me to a lonely spot. He then said, 'Kill the fucker!' He didn't look at me, he just said it.

Liz's dad was well aware of my background. He was proud of the fact that one day his daughter would marry and have children with a man who had served with the SAS. The fucker had taken that opportunity away. I looked at the ground and stated two simple words.

'First chance.'

We hugged.

'You'll always be my son,' he complimented me.

'Thanks, Dad.' I returned the compliment.

He left.

I went to the pub. There I stayed every day for five months. The publicans looked after me, the barmaids looked after me, everybody looked after me. I couldn't appreciate their kindness, for I was too inward-focused and numb. One month before my next court date I packed my pack and went bush to dry out.

After detoxing, I found myself again. For the next three weeks I spent my waking and sleeping hours remembering the enjoyment that Liz and I had experienced together. I felt refreshed and restored and strengthened to continue the battle against the injustice I faced. I held a firm belief that Liz would be there to support me through this ordeal.

Day three arrived and it was my turn in the witness box. To the amazement of everyone in that courtroom, except for the police, we weren't fighting the raid on myself carried out by the Tactical Response Group.

No, this trial had done too much damage. The powers in charge had decided that changing the name of this elite special squad would cover their arses in court. The TRG was now to be known as the State Protection Group.

My turn in the witness box was irrelevant. How could I be convicted of a charge resulting from a raid by an expert police team that didn't exist? But I enjoyed rubbing their noses in it.

The sergeant police prosecutor tried to get me to answer yes or no to his questions. I turned to the magistrate, who by this stage was enjoying hearing a little about an Australian Special Forces operator's life. My comment to him was, 'Your Honour, as no one in this room has served as a Special Forces operator, I would like the opportunity to explain my answers.'

The police prosecutor immediately started arguing points of law against this situation. I had briefed my barrister on what to say, and that was simply that the following evidence I was to give came under the *Official Secrets Act* of Australia.

'My client would like the court cleared by those who haven't signed the *Secrets Act*.'

The magistrate pondered the request in silence for a short time. His comment was to the police prosecutor.

'I have found the police witnesses to not be credible and to have lied in my court.'

The cops were sitting in a group up the back, obviously to intimidate me. The magistrate continued, 'Your army witness didn't prove to have enough knowledge of explosives to testify against the defendant.'

The police audience didn't hear what the magistrate said to the police prosecutor. His comment was, 'I adhere to the defendant's request.'

The police prosecutor threw his hands up in the air. The magistrate ordered that the courtroom be cleared. The prick who had threatened me in the waiting area approached the police prosecutor. They had a short interchange. The cop stated to the magistrate, 'I have sworn to the *Official Secrets Act* of Australia. May I be permitted to sit through the proceedings?'

I was ready for this. I asked my barrister to approach me. I said, 'Ask the cop if he can produce the *Secrets Act* that he has signed. If not, he must be asked to leave due to the magistrate finding his evidence not credible.'

This was done.

The cop complained.

The magistrate said, 'Leave my courtroom now.'

Even the stenographer was asked to leave and just leave her tape recorder running.

Over the next few hours I defended myself against the lies the police had told in court.

There was still the issue of the police using excessive force and carrying Uzi submachine guns that night. I didn't care if nobody believed me. It was protection for myself.

I started to give my evidence in an Australian court, stating that they did have Uzis with them that night. The reason I believed this was fact was that not only did I see them, but I was trained to never assume, always to assess. Be sure of what you report.

The magistrate accepted this as true evidence and admitted that the police used excessive force that night. So now if I got hit or if a mysterious accident befell me, there was evidence to this fact that the police couldn't destroy.

I was acquitted for the simple charge of goods in custody. I was awarded costs of $9500. It took two and half years to complete the trial and it cost me $13 500 and the death of Liz.

So much for justice.

A well-dressed man with a large-barrelled frame and a bald head, who looked familiar, entered through a side door and walked up the stairs directly towards the magistrate. The magistrate saw my body shift as my instinctual protection urge sent adrenalin to the necessary motor nerves in my body, telling me to cut the distance between the stranger and the official I was programmed to protect. The man smiled at the conditioning that he had been somewhat responsible for instilling in me some years ago.

The magistrate held his hand in a stop gesture, and the bald man smiled at me. I recognised him: it was Kojak, the man who I first meet as my senior instructor on the SAS selection course.

The magistrate hooked his finger and gestured for me to follow him. All three of us filed towards his room. He stopped at the door and allowed us to enter his room while he remained outside. Kojak's large frame obscured any visual appreciation of the room. He looked intently into my eyes.

'We need you as a covert operator for your country, soldier. Yes or no is the answer.'

I looked back hard at him. From where and why was this offer suddenly appearing? Did they want me back in the fold so they could keep an eye on me? If I said yes, would the Perth fiasco disappear? If Liz was alive, I would tell him to fuck off!

'Yes sir.'

Those two words rolled out of my mouth as if this destiny was the only choice I had. He reached past me and opened the door and whispered into my ear. 'You're dead.'

I smiled. This wasn't a threat; this was a lifestyle. A name would be chosen from one of the thirty thousand Australians that go missing every year. I had no idea what was going to be asked of me. I just knew that the back of my neck pressed against the back of my suit coat as I walked through the side door with my head high and my eyes to the front, and left the magistrate with a look of pride shining across his face and the legal team's jaws opened, completely bewildered as to what had transpired in less than a minute.

The New South Wales Ombudsman was brought in to do an inquiry. The result was that the conspiracy against me started the Royal Commission into corruption within the New South Wales Police Force. The then-commissioner was given the usual six-month resignation period and a wealthy handshake.

The new Commissioner of Police for New South Wales was brought in from London. The corruption was so entrenched in the New South Wales Police Force that they couldn't find anyone honest enough to do the job.

A Police Internal Affairs Inquiry found that the search warrant was not exercised properly. I was wrongfully arrested but no excessive force was used, meaning that there were no Uzis present that night. The denial continued, but they were all sweating, for now they were to be investigated.

I read the ombudsman's report and looked at the photocopies of the logbooks where the New South Wales TRG squad were required to sign for their weapons. Any idiot could show you how these logs were doctored to give false information.

I did stand up to these corrupt cops. A lot of them were charged with associated crimes. Many officers resigned before they could be charged, but the jewel was the upstart commissioner who should have pulled his head in and dropped the charges before I went to the media.

I know for a fact that if I was ever accused of any crime in this country, I would never go to court.

I returned to the spot in the bush where Liz's memories assisted me back to reality.

'Hey Liz, we won,' I spoke out loud.

The soft wind returned to nuzzle at my ear. I smiled.

'Just one more injustice to set right.'

Chapter Twenty-Two

Rectify an injustice

I was aware of being cold and cramped in the roof of the Veterans' Affairs building in Brisbane, totally committed to the task ahead. My mind was ceasing the rapid imagery I had been experiencing of the past events that had led to the decision to carry out this siege.

I was steaming at the evidence I had, totally proving the truth of my conspiracy theory. My mind ran through the incidents that I had experienced and suffered, or those of other operators that I knew.

I summarised my own near-death during my interrogation cycle, and the mental and physical torment I had endured; the responsible deniability situation I found myself in on the West Australian coast; the set-up in Perth; the bullshit that the New South Wales Police Force put me through; the years of surveillance and invasions of privacy that led to the death of Liz; the paranoia, the stress, the depression, and the panic attacks, all symptoms I now lived with; the labels they affixed to my name to discredit me. All of this because no one switched me off!

The hours had disappeared as I concentrated on slowing my mind down. I looked at my watch; it read 0830 hours, almost time.

The door to the commissioner's office opened. I waited while holding my breath, and then I heard it shut. By peeling back the tape, I could see a cup of coffee or tea had been left behind. I was pleased to see this, as I didn't want his receptionist as a hostage. However, once the commissioner sat at his desk, everyone who entered his office was going to become my hostage.

About twenty minutes passed and his door opened. I felt a rush of adrenalin flow through me as I said to myself, this is it!

He had just sat in his chair. With balaclava on and the replica Browning semi-automatic 9 mm pistol in hand, I placed one hand on the cross-beam to ensure I would be upright on landing. I punched through the ceiling feet first, bursting through the butcher's paper, landing on top of him in a sitting position, straddling his legs and shoving the replica pistol under his jaw.

I took a length of gaffer tape off my overalls. I now had approximately twenty pieces stuck to me, all of various lengths, already prepared thanks to my lengthy stay in the roof. This one was a small one and I placed it securely over his mouth.

Looking into his eyes for the first time, I saw that unmistakable stare of dreaded fear was present. I raised my mouth to his ear and softly whispered, 'Put your fucking hands together.'

He immediately complied. Quickly taping his hands together, I smelt a stench emitting from his body. This aroma also belonged to fear; however, it was mixed with another identifiable aroma: urine. I was expecting him to piss his pants, due to the sudden covert entry I had achieved. After all, this wasn't the movies.

I quickly rose out of the sitting position I was in and swung his chair, so the high back hid the fact that he was bagged and under my control. I sat in front of him, completely out of view of anybody entering the office. With my replica pistol shoved into his groin, I waited for him to compose himself. It took about five minutes for the physical shaking to stop.

When he finally stopped shaking I pulled out two plastic ties, making a loop with one and interweaving the second with the first tie. Instantly I had a pair of homemade handcuffs. I pulled them tight and now he was secure.

I wrote on my notepad, 'I don't want to hurt you, but you will do what I say.' He nodded in agreement.

Good, I thought. Always allow your hostage to believe that they are going to get out of the situation safely. They are always more willing to comply with your demands.

I wrote again, 'I want you to order your deputy commissioner, claims manager and payroll manager to your office.'

He hesitated, so I shoved the replica pistol into his groin, causing immense pain. He finally nodded his head.

I wrote again, 'Say only four words: come into my office.' He nodded his head once more.

I reached up to his mouth and held my notepad up to his eyes with another command.

'I want you to repeat these words over and over again, nice and softly: come to my office.' He nodded his head.

I sat back on top of him, ignoring his wet pants, which forced his hands into his groin. I then slowly pulled the tape from his mouth. His voice was shaky at first, but after repeating my command roughly twenty times, it sounded like a normal person summoning his troops to an informal meeting.

I picked up his intercom system and held it up to his mouth, whispering, 'Don't fuck up.'

He followed my command and there were three quick replies. 'Yes sir.'

Assured that my operation was going to plan, I smiled at him and he breathed a sigh of relief.

I quickly scrawled, 'Tell them to sit down when they enter. Call a fire drill immediately,' to which he softly whispered, 'Yes.'

He was starting to realise who was in charge. The three bureaucrats arrived at his door together, a blessing for me. With the commissioner's back to them and my replica pistol, which he was totally convinced was real, pointing straight to his heart, he spoke to them. 'Take a seat.'

He pressed the button on his intercom with me holding it in his lap, and his voice boomed through the speaker system.

'All personnel, this is a fire drill.'

A commotion started outside the door as his staff began moving towards the nearest fire exit.

I moved like lightning, taking the intercom with me, the cord ripping from the junction box. I snapped a front kick into the sternum of the male sitting down, buckling him over and causing him to fall to his knees. The two females had surprised looks on their faces, as I pointed the replica towards them, softly ordering them, 'Lie face down with your hands behind your backs.' I then kept repeating, 'Move, move, move, move,' until they complied.

Stepping over them and pulling gaffer tape off my overalls, I bound their hands and gagged their mouths. I then proceeded to do the same thing to the male who had just received my solid kick; he was still quite incapacitated from the strike.

With all the hostages bound and gagged, and the commissioner removed from his chair, once again gagged and lying next to his coworkers, I sat in his chair to collect my thoughts.

The clock said 0930 hours. I moved around to my hostages, pulled out the plastic ties from my backpack and made another three pairs of improvised handcuffs. I then pulled them tight onto my hostages.

I pulled out the ex-SAS files and spread them out in front of their eyes.

I had to create time, so I moved to the only door offering entry or exit to the office. I removed my lock-picking set, found the correct tool for this type of door lock, placed it in the lock and broke it off. With the door closed behind me, I said to myself, 'No one's coming in here now.'

With what I had done to the door, only a locksmith could regain entry. Now back to my hostages to complete Phase One: rectify an injustice.

Addressing them I said, 'Have you worked out what we are here to do?

'Today you people are going to do your jobs the right way for the first time. As you can see, I have discovered the conspiracy you people operate within. We are all going to agree to finalise those claims in front of you.

'All monies owed for back pay will go into the individuals' accounts this morning. If we all agree, you can go home to your families tonight.'

The commissioner nodded his head first and the rest followed.

'Good.'

I moved to the commissioner and removed his gag and asked him, 'How?'

He replied, 'I can do it alone at my computer.'

Again I responded with only one word. 'Good.'

I replaced his gag and removed his cuffs. 'Don't fuck up,' I commanded and continued, 'As for the rest of you people, you are going to stay, as punishment for personally fucking operators around for years.'

I addressed the commissioner. 'Right, get to your chair and start punching keys.'

I picked up the files and placed them on his desk. He began, and I watched him hit the keys of his computer. Within about ten minutes he closed the first file and reached for the next file.

'You mean to tell me that you fucked around ex-Special Forces Operators for years to avoid ten minutes of work!'

I picked up the phone and rang a number.

'Kojak, guess what? I have taken over Veterans' Affairs in Brisbane.'

'What?' he screamed back into the phone.

'There's a major conspiracy going on against ex-SAS operators. Here's a list of names.'

I called off the names of the files belonging to our mates.

'I want you to contact them all and tell them to empty their accounts so these pricks can't freeze their just entitlements. Tell them to wait three hours. I'm making the commissioner fulfil his duties right now.'

Kojak asked me if I was armed and I replied shortly, without emotion.

'Yes.'

'They're going to kill you!'

I was speaking to my Covert Control, who by now was ringing Special Forces command and the prime minister all at the same time. Special Forces command would be activating the Counter Terrorist Assault Team, and the prime minister would be signing my death warrant. I wasn't sure if Kojak would ring or get someone to ring the boys; I thought he might, as he was once one of us.

The power of this man: he managed to get everybody to believe I was dead; he in all probability covered my exit from Western Australia after the drug cartel debacle; he was probably the power that assisted in my acquittal against the New South Wales Police Force; and he helped me adjust and dry out after Liz's death by posting me to hot spots so I couldn't dwell on what I couldn't change. This protection was done all without my knowledge. I knew he didn't believe that they wanted me killed because I was threatening a simple Veterans' Affairs commissioner; he wanted me dead because I had gone rogue.

Chapter Twenty-Three

The siege

The phone call had started Phase Two of my operation involving the Assault Troop Counter Terrorist Team, SASR.

With the speed at which the commissioner was finalising the claims, Phase One would be completed in less than three hours and Phase Two would be swinging into gear.

The prime minister would have to authorise the SAS involvement, which he would do without hesitation given I was an ex-SAS with six years' operational experience and covert experience that he wouldn't be privy to or wouldn't want to know. Kojak would advise the prime minister not to send under-trained nine-to-five cops up against someone who was trained as well as I. It would be certain suicide for cops to go up against me, especially now they believed I was armed. Also, these were bureaucrats who worked for the federal government. The federal government would also be very concerned about the evidence I had discovered. A responsible deniability situation would be enforced; civilians, even cops, are not trusted on that level.

Another certainty was that my brother Digby would not be allowed into the assault team. Being a Counter Terrorist Team leader, he would be given a protection role and it would not be explained why he was withdrawn from the assault. One of the conditions I'd insisted on before becoming a 'dead man' was that I knew of his progress, and I was quite proud of how professional he had become. I knew that Kojak would not let two siblings face-off against each other. The outcome would be too unpredictable, especially when one of the brothers believes the other one is dead.

I remembered the front door, disconnecting the phone and taking it with me. I left my hostages. A group of staff was waiting at the door that I had previously made inaccessible. They saw me approach dressed in black and waving my replica pistol around. They quickly moved towards the fire exit, and then they were gone.

Quickly I headed back to the commissioner's office. The commissioner had not stopped finalising the claims. He was onto his fourth one, as ordered. My other three hostages were still where I had left them.

I positioned myself in the corner of the room and reconnected the phone. I lay on the carpet with the phone next to me. I waited for the police to contact me to begin negotiations.

An hour and a half passed and the commissioner had finished thirteen files. I quickly removed my soiled overalls, keeping my pistol pointing at him. With my back to them, I threw my soiled overalls and balaclava in the direction of the commissioner and ordered him to get dressed. I quickly got dressed into my spare overalls and fresh balaclava, placed my backpack on my back and secured my SAS gasmask down the front of the fresh overalls.

The commissioner sitting at his desk in black overalls and with the balaclava on looked a daunting sight. He almost looked scary.

At 1215 hours the commissioner looked up at me and told me he was finished.

'Good,' I said.

My next move was delightful; I had practised it for hours. I reached into my pocket to grip a 9 mm round. With the commissioner looking at me, I unlocked the magazine within the weapon. It slid neatly into my hand and I gripped it with my lower palm, wrapping my little finger around it to keep it secure.

I reached up with my left hand and cocked the weapon, simultaneously flicking the 9 mm round into the air as though it had been chambered all the time. My left hand shot into space and caught the 9 mm round without me even removing my gaze from the commissioner. It was beautiful.

I crawled towards his desk. With gaffer tape I secured the weapon to his hands. As he was raising himself from his chair, my survival instinct kicked in. I dived to the left and felt the breeze of a sniper's round finding its mark. The commissioner's head had a neat hole in the back of it, and skull fragments splintered all over the wall and onto my hostages. He landed on top of the other hostages as I found myself hugging the left wall.

Another round went into the wall in front of me; I kept rolling to distance myself from the hostages. 'Fuck, how did the boys get here so fast?' I wondered.

If it was the SAS, the sniper shots meant that they were at the front door and they needed to distract me.

The lights would go out next. The power was cut and I stated out loud, 'One for one. One for Liz!'

Chapter Twenty-Four

The assault

I heaved myself into roof cavity and stepped on a beam as I watched the events unfold below. This was not a clever idea, maybe, but I wanted to see the skills of the lads who were carrying out the assault.

The windows exploded in, the commissioner's door was kicked in and loud explosions went off around me as flash-bang grenades were thrown in. Torch beams went flashing around the room. Looking down, I could see that there were now four operators in the room. Two had entered on ropes through the windows and the other two were entering through the commissioner's disintegrated doorway. I froze. Silence followed as their torch beams travelled the room. Not a sound was heard as these professionals assessed their own safety.

I needed a distraction so I could make a quick move to the light fitting I had used to enter the roof space. The silence was broken; no immediate threat to the assault team was assessed. A man with a familiar stance spoke into his radio.

'One dead terrorist, black overalls, black balaclava. Three hostages, cuffed, plastic ties, gagged, gaffer tape. Wait.'

It wouldn't be long before one of these professionals noticed the hole in the roof and a quick death would be a certainty. I knew the man below talking into his radio; he was one of the survivors from the chopper crash. Troy, look at the desk, I pleaded in silence.

He bent down and was about to roll the commissioner's body when fortune favoured my miserable life. Another operator now had his boot on the desk of the man who had thought it was safe to stuff around men who were prepared to die for their country, denying them their opportunity to be switched off. As he ripped the velcro strap off his leg bag that had carried the rope during his entry through the window, a file caught his attention. He raised his gasmask.

'Troy, look at this and these.' He was now holding up the collection of files in his hands. 'These lads' names, they're all ex-SAS.'

Was this my moment? Was this the distraction I needed? I had to move soon as another operator was just about to remove the commissioner's assistant's gag. He would definitely give me up. I could see the defiance in his eyes as I eyeballed him from my beam.

There was a flurry of movement, a flash of energy. Whatever it was, it was quick. Troy now had his foot on the assistant's chest and was shoving his submachine gun barrel into and through the gaffer tape of the man's gagged mouth. Panic rose in his eyes. I looked at his helplessness, and smiled and offered a courteous nod to the individual. If he escaped the boys' wrath alive he would definitely be posted out of Veterans' Affairs.

Wait, wait, wait till someone talks. Almost there, I told myself.

'Arrrrgh!' The women screamed in unison; their gags must have been removed simultaneously. Once on their feet, they ran, taking long strides to escape the madness of this terrorist siege situation, where now their supposed rescuers were damaging their workmate far more than the terrorist had.

I moved, silently and stealthily, and reached the opposite side of the roof. I waited to drop out of the cavity that was my original entry point. It would be soon. An officer was on the way to determine that the site was secure and that it could be handed over to the police. Once the assault team was distracted, I would be dropping out of the roof wearing the same gear as them and hopefully mixing in until I reached the other cordon.

'Just wait.' My timing had to be impeccable, I told myself.

I could hear Troy ranting and raving at the hostage. I assumed files were being thrown through the air directed at the ex-Veterans' Affairs employee as the flutter of papers filled the air and a whimper escaped the man's mouth past the barrel of a submachine gun.

'What is this sort of conspiracy against SAS lads? Don't pay their entitlements and fuck them around until they give up? Are you people insane? Don't you know how dangerous it is to stuff around people like us? Listen, we are switched on to kill. Doesn't that scare you just a little bit?'

'Troy, get that weapon out of that man's mouth.'

That was the assault team's boss. Shit, I had been listening so intently that I didn't notice him and his lackey pass underneath me.

'Who's the fuck is that?' I heard the boss ask.

'That's the commissioner. Your fucked-up SAS buddy set him up to die,' the assistant commissioner answered.

Time to go. I dropped out of the roof and quietly slipped into the same fire-escape I had entered the night before. I quickly jogged down the steps and knew that there wouldn't be any operators between me and the alley that I had chosen during my reconnaissance. The sun partially blinded me as I opened the heavy door, pressing my shoulder against it. This movement left me unaware of what was behind the door and also what was at the end of the alley, a monumental oversight on my part. If I had known then, I could have chosen to re-enter and consolidate my next move.

At the far end of the alley was an operator who was diligently providing protection and not letting anybody slip in behind the operators already engaged in the siege. There was one way out of this precarious situation: offer up my identity. The code of behaviour dictated that I raise my gasmask with five metres or I would be shot. Being unarmed, I had no alternative. I needed some space, for as I raised my mask the other operator would also raise his. I would wait to see if I could identify the other lad and maybe, if we had worked together, he might let me slip by.

Five metres. His hand went to his mask and I raised mine to my mask. The only difference in body movements was that he had his submachine gun poised to drill two holes into my head. His face was clear but then partially obscured as the bottom of my mask covered my eyes. He looked familiar but my thought processes jumped to another sphere.

He must be concerned about me not carrying any weapons. You must identify him, I told myself. My eyes were adjusting to the sun as I faced its direction; it wasn't his face that gave me his identity, it was his voice.

'Paul, Paul is that you? I thought you were de—'

He didn't get to finish his sentence, because I stepped into his personal space and drove into his face with my fist. It stung like hell. It always did hurt to hit his boof head, even as kids. For the man crumpled at my feet was my brother Digby. I hoped he would wake thinking he had seen a ghost or that there must be some logical explanation as to why he thought he had seen his dead brother.

I was almost there. I just needed to make it to the industrial bin to strip off my black gear and walk off towards the river in civilian clothing that might be a bit smelly, but would still be suitable to the task. I looked up the alley and Digby was starting to rise. I quickly slipped behind the side of the bin out of view of the siege sight.

'Goodbye brother, you owe me one,' I said, without looking towards him.

The job was done. I slowly walked the path towards the river, my route chosen to ensure that I criss-crossed between buildings and against the flow of pedestrians who poured through the area. I didn't look out of place because some of my escape route, although away from the siege site, gave me the opportunity to follow the crowd and listen to the comments being made, and no one seemed to notice me.

'They reckon the terrorist is ex-SAS.'

'If he is, he's dead.'

'It happened at some government building down that way.'

Keep your mouth shut and don't get cocky, I told myself.

There it was: the path that would take me to my next destination. I was just about to cross over the road as I felt the rush that kept me alive. I was too cocky.

Two men outside a pub enjoying a beer had me bundled into the back of a black SUV before the crash of their glasses could be heard. A second later I was sitting next to the man I had deeply respected but now despised. Kojak had his favourite Gnock 9 mm pistol stuck deep into my ribs. Well, I supposed I would be doing three lifetimes, in solitary, with the key thrown away. I sat looking out the tinted window of the door with no handles, waiting for Kojak to speak.

'Paul, a bit over the top, don't you think?'

'What happens now?' I answered his question with a question.

'Off to jail or back to work. What is it going to be? You are some find. You just managed to get a target hit and escape under the noses of one of the best anti-terrorist units in the world. What's it to be, jail or covert ops?'

Kojak liked the sound of his own voice, I thought.

'You said I was going to get help.' I would never trust this man again.

'Paul, you know and have always known that there are some men who just can't be switched off. You will always be one of them.'

A lone plastic bottle moved with the current in the middle of the city river. I thought to myself: that's me, alone and swept away on a path that has an unknown destiny.